4x   5/10 ✓ 5/10
4x 5/10 ✓ 4/11
6x 6/11 ✓ 3/12
10x 2/16 2/17
11 x. 4/18. 4/20

THE POWER OF ONE

Recent titles by Jane A. Adams from Severn House

The Naomi Blake Mysteries

MOURNING THE LITTLE DEAD
TOUCHING THE DARK
HEATWAVE
KILLING A STRANGER
LEGACY OF LIES

The Rina Martin Mysteries

A REASON TO KILL
FRAGILE LIVES
THE POWER OF ONE

THE POWER OF ONE

A Rina Martin Mystery

Jane A. Adams

severn
House

This first world edition published 2009
in Great Britain and in the USA by
SEVERN HOUSE PUBLISHERS LTD of
9–15 High Street, Sutton, Surrey, England, SM1 1DF

British Library Cataloguing in Publication Data

Adams, Jane, 1960–
    The power of one
    1. Martin, Rina (Fictitious character) – Fiction
    2. McGregor, Sebastian (Fictitious character) – Fiction
    3. Women private investigators – Fiction 4. Computer games
    industry – Employees – Crimes against – Fiction 5. Murder –
    Investigation – Fiction 6. Detective and mystery stories
    I. Title
    823.9'14[F]

ISBN–13: 978–0–7278–6762–9 (cased)

All Severn House titles are printed on acid-free paper.

Typeset by Palimpsest Book Production Ltd.,
Grangemouth, Stirlingshire, Scotland.
Printed and bound in Great Britain by
MPG Books Ltd., Bodmin, Cornwall.

ONE

Frantham baked in the August heat. The sea, flat calm and an almost unnatural blue, was dotted with bathers in bright suits and the promenade thronged with families, clattering their buckets and spades and hauling their picnic baskets and plastic coolers down on to an already overcrowded beach.

The season had started slow, bad weather – and a bit of a crime wave – keeping the tourists away until early July. Then the sun had come out and so had the holidaymakers. The B&Bs in Rina's street, the owners of which had despaired of survival at the start of the season, were now turning visitors away or cramming them into so-called 'family rooms'; a couple of single beds forced in beside the double so that the little children could share with mum and dad. Even Rina's precious Peverill Lodge had been inundated by would-be guests hammering on the door in the hope that the 'No Vacancies' sign outside was an oversight and she might be concealing a couple of secret apartments. Rina, as a rule, hung no sign outside of her guest house advertising vacancies or the lack thereof; her guests were family and there until . . . well until they shuffled off, but this summer, in self-defence, she had been forced to have a little sign made and a second stuck in her window just in case anyone missed the point. It hadn't worked, Rina reflected as she paced slowly along the promenade. She was still turning away two or three callers a day.

To be truthful, she preferred Frantham in the off season though she was not so churlish as to begrudge any of the fast-reddening crowd their week or two in the sun. She understood that for many folk this was their one proper break. She did wish though, that they'd learn to wear suncream.

Rina paused to look out to sea, puzzled by something she had spotted half an hour before when she'd been out shopping and which had now drawn her back on to the promenade. The boat was still out there. Still turning circles, though she fancied it had come closer into shore than when it first caught her notice. A second boat had joined it now, the coastguard launch. So something *was* wrong then? The coastguard stood off from the other boat as though those on board were trying to figure out what to do and, as Rina watched, the inshore lifeboat joined them, the orange inflatable drawing up alongside the circling vessel. Rina found twenty pence in her purse and fed it into one of the pay-to-view telescopes dotted at intervals along the promenade. She trained it on the activity in the bay. A motor yacht, rather a nice one from what she could make out, was turning increasingly flabby circles and listing slightly. She could see the wheelhouse, but no one steering. The lifeboat crew were trying to get a line attached and the motion of the yacht dragged the little boat with it. Rina wondered how on earth they were going to get a man on board and what had happened to the crew?

Her time ran out and she didn't have another twenty pence. Frustrated, she shaded her eyes with a broad hand and tried to make out what was going on. No one on the beach seemed to have noticed anything untoward. Children shrieked and squabbled and parents chided and tried to delay the moment when they'd be forced to accompany their offspring into the still-cold sea, even the hottest of August days being insufficient to warm such a stubbornly chill stretch of ocean.

'Best go and see what's happening,' she said to no one in particular. There was a good chance that the coastguard would tow the boat into the newly built marina just beyond the old town. She might just head out there, get herself a nice cool drink and sit under one of those pink stripy umbrellas on the clubhouse terrace and wait to see what came ashore.

Rina had quite a long wait, but she didn't mind. Sitting in the shade with her sunglasses on and her sandals off, she observed the action in company with a dozen more who had also noticed it and were exchanging enthusiastic speculation. Rina listened. The crowd at the marina was an interesting mix of locals and regular visitors; boat people who ran charters, or fished, or practically lived aboard floating homes that ranged in fit up from ramshackle wooden vessels to luxury surpassing the average upmarket semi. Unlike some marinas further along the coast and dedicated to the pleasures of the summer crowd, Frantham's boat club was not a particularly snobbish affair and she knew, at least by sight, all of those who presently shared her vantage point.

'Heart attack. I betcha,' someone said. 'Owner went out on his own and popped his clogs.'

'Steering problem? I know it doesn't seem likely. Boat of that class shouldn't go wrong but . . .'

'Got a man aboard. Finally!'

Rina sipped her drink and nodded thoughtfully. A heart attack seemed like a possible explanation, she thought, or at least a partial one. It didn't explain why the boat was sailing in circles. Well she was quite comfortable here and had nothing pressing this afternoon, so she would just have to wait and see. She borrowed a pair of binoculars and took a closer look at the activity on board. A second man had joined the first and the boat, no longer under power, bobbed gently in the calm water and Rina could get a good view of men gesticulating, one coming back to the rail to shout something to the coastguard.

Something very wrong, Rina thought. Something very wrong indeed.

She handed the binoculars back to their owner with a word of thanks.

'Bit of excitement on a summer afternoon,' the man said with a smile.

'Certainly is,' Rina agreed and settled more comfortably in her chair to enjoy the rest of the show.

'You look cool and relaxed.'

Rina smiled at the familiar voice. 'Oh I am,' she said. 'Pull up a seat and I'll order you a drink.'

Mac laughed and sat down. He was in his shirtsleeves this afternoon, his jacket dangling from one finger. A new jacket, Rina noted. Linen and rather expensive-looking. She guessed Miriam must have chosen it for him and nodded approval. Miriam had been very good for DI McGregor and he was taking much more care of himself, remembering to shave most days and actually visiting the barber on a regular basis instead of making do with a pair of nail scissors and the bathroom mirror. He looked less exhausted too, the blue-grey eyes no longer so deeply shadowed. Rina was very gratified, knowing that while Miriam had worked her magic, his recovery from the effects of grief, followed by massive consumption of alcohol, was also due to Rina and her mad little household and the very real affection in which Mac was held and which, in full measure, he returned.

A waiter appeared magically at her shoulder and she ordered Mac a Pimms and a second for herself.

Mac raised an eyebrow. 'I am on duty, you know.'

Rina waved airily. 'Pimms has too much fruit in it to count as alcoholic,' she said. 'Anyway, it's not as if you've got to drive anywhere. Nowhere in Frantham is more than a ten-minute walk.'

He laughed. 'Too true,' he agreed, 'and if I do have to follow the body back to the mortuary, Andy can drive me, he should be here in a minute or so.'

Rina sat bolt upright. 'Ah,' she said. 'From the boat?'

'From the boat,' Mac agreed. He smiled at her. 'I might have known you'd be here. I don't think anything can happen in Frantham without Rina Martin knowing about it first.'

Mockingly, she tapped the side of her nose. 'I like to keep my hand in,' she agreed, then said more seriously, 'Do they know what happened?'

Mac shook his head. 'I've no more details yet, Rina.' He accepted the drink that had just arrived and then squinted out across the water. 'Looks like they've got her under tow,' he added. He sat back, made himself comfortable and sipped appreciatively. 'This is nice, the drink, the umbrellas, the company. Pity it's likely to end badly. Death on a beautiful summer day like this doesn't seem quite right.'

'Chances are it was just a heart attack or something,' Rina suggested. 'You'll get off early.'

Mac laughed at the seemingly innocent supposition. 'Come on Rina, if the coastguard thought that then they'd have simply called an ambulance and yours truly would have continued with his quiet afternoon catching up on paperwork.'

'So . . .?'

Mac leaned forward to deposit his glass back on the table. 'The coastguard seem to think there's been a shooting,' he said quietly. 'And they don't seem to figure it for suicide.'

TWO

It was close on another hour before the yacht was brought into the marina. Andy Nevins, the young probationary officer based at Frantham, had arrived by then. His bright-red hair flamed in the afternoon sun and his freckled skin displayed signs of disliking such exposure. He waved away Rina's offer of suncream with an attempt at dignity. 'I'll be fine, thank you, Mrs Martin. I don't think I can really stand here in uniform smearing meself with goo, can I?'

She saw Mac stifle a smile and tucked the tube of 'goo' back into her capacious summer bag, a welcome present from her young friend, Ursula, a thirteen-year-old with a very distinctive sense of style. Fuchsia-pink candy stripes were not really Rina's usual choice, but she had to admit that the bag brightened up her usual pastel outfits and did make her question the received wisdom that older women should stick to lilacs, creams and lavenders. The long skirt she was wearing today was a further result of Ursula's influence and Rina had to admit that she loved the indigo linen and the way the bias cut encouraged it to swish around her ankles. It made her feel positively girlish, though for Rina it was more than fifty years since she had matched Ursula's age.

'Looks like this is us,' Mac said. 'Andy, you hang on here for a while, if I need you, I'll shout.'

'Right you are, boss.'

The police medic had arrived and Rina and Andy watched as he and Mac were taken aboard and the coastguard directed them aft. Andy took the seat Mac had just vacated.

'Who has jurisdiction here?' Rina mused. Usually at a crime scene the first uniformed officer on scene became, by default, the crime scene manager and secured the scene, kept it pristine until the CSI had done their thing and only then were the detectives allowed free rein.

'Coastguard,' Andy said. 'Then they'll sign off to uniform. I guess they just want to get the doc to confirm death and get the boss down there just to tell them what to do next.'

Rina nodded, then frowned. A vague feeling of familiarity had been growing as she had seen the yacht brought
in. She knew this boat. At first she had just assumed that
the familiarity stemmed from long pleasurable hours spent
watching the comings and goings in the marina, but now
as she caught sight of the name painted on the bow the
vague feeling solidified into certainty.

She grabbed Andy's arm, much to the young man's discom-
fiture. 'You OK, Mrs Martin?'

She nodded. 'Andy, I know whose boat this is. It's *The
Greek Girl*, it's Paul's boat. Paul de Freitas' boat.'

'What, as in the people who bought the airfield? Those de
Freitas's?'

Rina nodded. She released her hold on his arm and patted
him instead. 'Tell Mac,' she instructed. 'I'd better be going,
Andy. I won't be the only one who recognises that boat.'

Andy stared at her, open-mouthed, then he glanced back
towards the vessel, looking to see if Mac was returning yet.
By the time it occurred to him that maybe the police should
be the ones to deliver the news of possible murder and not
the redoubtable Mrs Martin, Rina was long gone.

THREE

'Registered owner is Mr Paul de Freitas,' the coastguard told Mac. 'We found him down in the aft cabin. The other man isn't known to us and we've not checked for identification. No one wanted to move the body until CSI had been down.'

'And you're sure it's de Freitas?'

The coastguard nodded. 'I know the man,' he said. 'Or rather, I knew him. Practically lived aboard his boat. Mind you, if I owned something like this, so would I.'

Mac glanced around. They were standing in the main cabin. Well-upholstered seats surrounded a cherry wood table on which was a scatter of marine-related magazines. A small, but well-equipped galley kitchen could be glimpsed through a half-open sliding door. It was not the most luxurious yacht that Mac had ever seen, but it looked comfortable and, from the variety of personal items carefully stowed on shelves and racks, obviously well loved and well used. Other doors hinted at berths and heads and, although *The Greek Girl* was not new, Mac could see that the finish and quality had been high when she was and had stood the test of time.

'Very pleasant,' he agreed. Or would have been. He studied the body of the unknown man lying face down just below the steps leading down into the cabin. Through the open door, Mac glimpsed the second body in the aft cabin. He had not gone in. The coastguard had confirmed death – the large bullet wound in de Freitas' head making that an easy task; the second, similar wound in the stranger's body also easy to identify. Once he had realized this was a crime scene, the coastguard had then backtracked on to the deck, taking care to mark his route, improvising with a pack of tissues he happened to have had in his pocket.

Miriam would be proud, Mac thought. She had recently conducted a seminar for the coastguard and lifeboat crews about the handling of crime scenes. Familiar voices drifting down from the deck told him that the local doctor who served on the police rota and who had now confirmed the coast-guard's judgement of death was chatting to the SOCO team. He listened, but did not hear Miriam's voice, just that of the crime scene manager, Philip Olds, and Kieran Bates, one of his newer recruits. Mac waited for them to come down.

'I like the tissues,' Philip commented with a laugh. 'Nice bit of lateral thinking. Kieran, lay the plates on top, will you. Afternoon, Mac, how are you today?'

'I'm good, thanks. I'll leave you to it, then. Not a lot more I can do here so I'd best get on and see the family.'

Philip nodded. 'You've got an ID, then?'

Mac pointed. 'The man in there is Paul de Freitas. As yet, we don't have a clue about his friend.'

'Whoever he was, he's a big bugger,' the coastguard said. 'You'll have your work cut out getting him back up on deck.'

Mac left them discussing the most effective way of extrication and took the designated route back on to the deck. He thanked the doctor and then started back on to the shore. He could see Andy was upset about something, practically jumping up and down in his agitation. Of Rina, there was no sign.

'OK. Where's she gone?'

'She said she knew who the boat belonged to,' Andy explained. 'I'm sorry, boss, I looked away for just a second, like, and she was gone. Going to see the de Freitas's she said. She reckons it's their boat.' He looked anxiously at Mac, wondering if he'd get the blame for Rina's sudden departure.

Mac sighed. 'Well you'd better drive me over there, then,' he said. 'I sometimes think it might just be easier for me to retire and let Rina get on and do my job.'

FOUR

The house owned by the brother and sister-in-law of Paul de Freitas was about a mile outside of Frantham and set back between the coast road and the cliff top. The views were magnificent, Mac thought, as they pulled into the drive and took in the scene of Frantham Bay and, just beyond the headland, a glimpse of the larger and more impressive Lyme Bay. Mature trees provided a windbreak for a large and well-planted garden that wrapped right around the house. The trees were older than the house, Mac noted. Vaguely, he remembered Rina telling him that the original had burned down and been replaced with this very seventies, very angular, picture-windowed block of pale brick and dark slate.

It was not, Mac thought, the most attractive place in the world, but as the anxious-looking woman in the dark-green dress, who introduced herself as Mrs Simms, the housekeeper, led them through into the massive rear lounge, Mac conceded that even seventies architecture could have its moments. The rear of the house was given over to the largest windows Mac had ever seen outside of a department store. A half-dozen steps led down into the room.

'Wow,' Andy Nevins whispered, far too loudly as he followed him in.

Wow indeed, Mac thought. The room dropped down some two or three feet from the level of the hall and the architect had devised the windows so that, somehow, from that lower point, you lost all sight of the lawned garden. The view through the massive windows was of sea, blending today into the bluest of sky. Sea and sky and nothing but sea and sky.

The effect was giddying, oddly disorientating, but Mac would have bought this ugly, angular house for that view alone. He guessed this was what had swung things for the de Freitas's.

'Inspector, what has happened to my brother?'

Mac turned to face the man. He knew Paul de Freitas by sight and would have taken this man for close kin even had he not known him to be. The same rather ascetic good looks, deep-brown eyes, dark curls, though Edward's were cut closely to his head as though he tried to tame the unruly mop his brother had possessed.

His face was grey beneath its light tan and the hair looked, to Mac, to be the only thing over which he currently had any control.

Edward de Freitas shook himself. 'I'm sorry,' he said, extending a trembling hand and coming over to greet his visitors properly. 'I'm forgetting my manners. I'm forgetting everything. Rina here arrived just after we'd had a phone call from the marina, something about *The Greek Girl* being towed into the marina and police swarming all over. I was just about to go and see for myself when Rina arrived. She says . . .'

'She says Paul is dead?' The woman standing by the picture window sounded disbelieving.

Mac turned his attention to her. Tall, slim, blonde, dressed in faded jeans and an expensive-looking white shirt that was cut to emphasise a very slim waist and a surprising degree of curve for a figure so slender. 'I'm sorry . . . Mrs de Freitas? We don't have all the facts yet, but your . . . brother-in-law?'

She nodded.

'I'm afraid you were told right. He's dead. I'm truly sorry for your loss.'

He glanced over at Rina, seated in a large armchair set close by the window and nursing a china cup and saucer. 'I'm also sorry that other people got to you before I did,' he said quietly. 'You really should have been properly informed.'

'Oh, rubbish,' Edward told him briskly. 'I'm so glad Rina *did* come to see us. I could have gone down there, not knowing anything, been completely out of my depth. No, no, I don't blame you, Inspector, of course I don't, but I've already learnt that news travels faster round here by word of mouth than it does by the average internet connection. But what happened? Was there an accident? Rina seemed to think . . .'

Edward de Freitas sat down and his wife came over to him. She stood behind the easy chair with her hands tightly clasping the back, fingers digging in to the upholstery and the knuckles white with tension.

'Rina seems to think that someone killed him,' she said. 'Is that what happened?'

She was daring him to confirm it. Waiting for him to tell her that there'd been a mistake and it was either not her brother-in-law or that at the very worst, he'd had an accident, died of natural causes, anything but . . .

'I'm so sorry,' Mac said again. 'But he was shot and so was his friend. We know nothing more at present, but the CSI are there and in an hour or so, I may be able to tell you more.'

'Oh my God,' Edward whispered.

'Shot?' Lydia de Freitas stared at him. 'Shot by whom? He was on board his bloody boat! How could anyone have shot him?'

'We don't know,' Mac said. 'I'm so sorry not to be able to tell you any more.'

'You said there was someone with him?' Edward seemed only just to have registered that fact. 'Who? Could this other man have shot Paul?'

Mac shook his head. Both men had been shot from behind. Murder followed by suicide seemed, on the face of it, very unlikely. 'It was someone else,' Mac said. 'A third person.'

'But who was with him?' Lydia was clearly baffled. 'Paul hardly ever took anyone on board. He liked to be alone out there. That was why he *bought* the bloody boat. He liked to think things through, to work on his designs without anyone bothering him. Why would he have taken someone out there with him?'

She seemed, Mac thought, almost more upset by the fact that he'd let someone into his private space than she was at his death. He logged the thought for later analysis. 'We don't know who the second man was,' Mac said. 'When I left the marina they'd found nothing on the boat that identified him. Nothing on the . . . nothing on the body. He's a big man, six two, six three. Very broad?' He paused, hoping for a moment of revelation from the de Freitas's.

Lydia shrugged, her face blank. 'That's all you can tell us?'

'I'm sorry, yes.'

'Hair? Eye colour? What did he look like?' Lydia de Freitas hadn't quite got it yet; just why Mac could give so little description.

Her husband was quicker. 'You couldn't tell those things,' he said. 'You couldn't see. He was shot in the head?'

'From behind, yes,' Mac confirmed. From behind, at close

range and, Mac and the coastguard had speculated, from a
slight angle, as though his killer had been above him on the
steps. There was now a large and messy exit wound where
most of his features had once been. Mac guessed that even
dental records would be problematic.

Lydia found a straw to grasp and held on to it like it was
a life preserver. 'So, how do you know it's Paul, then? If you
can't tell much about the other man, how come you're so sure
about Paul?'

'Because the coastguard knew him,' Mac said. 'Well enough
to be sure. Paul was shot . . . differently.' It was still possible
to see his face. The track of the bullet seemed to have been
from the base of the skull and upwards, so far as Mac could
tell from the swift look he had taken. He preferred not to
speculate further, especially in the current context. The top of
Paul de Freitas' head had been missing, but his face was still
there, more or less. Enough to identify.

Edward closed his eyes. 'When can I see him?'

'Not yet,' Mac said gently. 'Not for a little while.'

Half an hour later, Rina left with Mac and Andy Nevins,
having been promised a lift home. The de Freitas's had declined
the use of a family liaison officer, but had gratefully accepted
Mac's assurance that he would arrange to have someone keep
the inevitable press presence under control. The property was
screened from the road by a low wall, topped by a wrought-
iron fence and sealed with a pair of electric gates, but it would
be easy enough to take the cliff path and gain access via the
hedge to the rear. This had been cut low enough so as not to
obstruct the view but it also made access to the rear of the
property pretty straightforward. Mac guessed that only the
locals would realise that and they wouldn't be about to share
their knowledge with incomers. That might buy the de Freitas's
a little extension on their peace, but it wouldn't be long before
a double murder brought media interest back to Frantham and
Mac had suggested they might go away for a few days. So
far, they seemed reluctant even to give that a thought.

'I want to be on hand,' Edward de Freitas said. 'To be close
by, in case I'm needed, you know.'

Mac had left it at that, nothing more he could do.

Rina settled herself in the rear seat and Andy drove. Waiting for the electric gates to open, Mac turned round to look at her. 'So,' he said, 'what aren't they telling me?'

'Whatever it is, they didn't tell me either,'

She sounded slightly miffed about that, Mac thought. 'The fact that he wasn't alone, I felt that shook them both. Especially Mrs de Freitas.'

'Maybe she fancied him,' Andy suggested, driving through the now half-open gates. 'Maybe she was ticked off because *she* didn't get an invite on to her brother-in-law's yacht.'

'Oh, you do have an elegant turn of phrase, Andy,' Rina told him. 'But he might have a point, Mac. She did react oddly.'

Mac nodded. 'I thought so too. But I really don't think either of them had a clue about the identity of our mystery man. I wonder how close they actually were as a family. And if Mrs de Freitas was involved with Paul, how well she *didn't* really know him in spite of that?' He sighed. 'Something tells me this is going to get messy. How come you know them, Rina?'

'Mrs Martin knows everyone,' Andy said.

'True,' Mac laughed, 'but aside from that.'

'Oh, I went to a meeting they had when they first bought the airfield. They wanted to get a steering committee together, local people mainly. Edward wants to reopen the airfield to light commercial traffic, but he wants to employ as many locals as he can, there and in that new factory they've been building behind the tin sheds. And he wanted to know what else he could involve the community in. Open days, that sort of thing. It's going to make a big difference to the job market in Frantham.'

'And you volunteered for this committee?'

'I did, yes. And we became friendly after that.'

'Friendly, but not friends?'

Rina laughed at him. 'There is a difference, you know. I think in time,' she mused, 'that friendly might turn into friendship but it's a little early in our acquaintance to be sure of that.'

Mac smiled, grateful that it had taken almost no time at all for Rina and her eccentric household to decide that he was definitely 'friend' material.

'But I didn't know Paul even *that* well,' she added. 'I liked

what I'd seen of him, but he was a quiet man, rather private,
I'd have said.'

Mac thought about the new build the de Freitas's had
constructed behind what the locals called the Tin Sheds, an
odd amalgam of old buildings left over from a wartime airbase,
and an additional concretion of Portakabins and small units
which housed a surprising variety of small business ventures.
Car repairs, a tiny and very specialised tool-maker, a man and
his son who restored boats and did repairs down at the marina.
Mac wasn't sure what else was there.

'What do they do?' he asked.

'Computers,' Andy said. 'Games mostly.'

'Software development,' Rina said grandly. 'And I think
they design special chips or something, there's a small R&D
department. Paul ran that, I think.'

Mac nodded but did not pursue the enquiry, guessing he'd
get more from Andy later than he could glean from Rina. She
was an internet addict, but had little interest in anything else
in the world of IT. Andy, on the other hand, was an avid
player of all things fantasy.

'Why base it here? Frantham isn't exactly the English
equivalent of silicon valley.'

'Oh, sentiment, I think,' Rina said. 'Apparently the de
Freitas' father or grandfather or something lived here. I don't
know more than that. Edward mentioned spending childhood
holidays close by. And I suppose it makes a kind of economic
sense, having the airfield and, I think, buying everything relatively cheaply. Who knows?'

She was irritated, Mac thought, that she hadn't probed
further into de Freitas family history. He guessed it was an
absence of information she'd soon be filling in.

They pulled up in front of Peverill Lodge. 'Well,' Rina said,
as Mac helped her out of the car. 'I dare say I'll see you soon.
Give Miriam my love, won't you?'

'Will do,' Mac said. He watched her go inside then ducked
his head into the car. 'Go and park up, Andy. I'll walk back
via the coffee shop.'

Andy greeted the idea with a grin of approval. The police
station was at the far end of the promenade, a strictly pedes-
trian zone, so the parking of the police vehicles – and Mac's
car, involved a bit of a loop round by the back roads. Since

Mac had taken over the reins of power from his predecessor, DCI Eden, now retired, police patronage of the little Italian coffee shop on the promenade had risen dramatically. In Eden's time, the coffee at the station came dangerously strong and frequently adulterated with single malt. It was not a tradition Mac had continued, preferring vanilla or almond in his. He had converted Andy and was working on the wearing down of Sergeant Baker's resolve.

'*Tonino's*' was also an excellent place to take the temperature of community feeling and collect the local gossip. Whatever was being speculated upon with regard to the de Freitas murder, Mac would have collated by the time he arrived back at the police station.

FIVE

Lydia de Freitas was practically incendiary. 'You should have told him. Everything, Edward. Paul's dead. Are you going to wait for one of us to be next?'

Edward shook his head. He poured whisky into a tumbler with a hand that shook so much the ice rattled when he lifted it. 'You don't know this was related, Lydia. We don't know anything, that's the trouble. Paul didn't exactly confide in me.'

'Well he certainly didn't confide in *me*, if that's what you're suggesting.'

'I'm not a fool, Lydia.'

She came over, cupped her hand around his, holding the glass steady. 'That's just it,' she said softly. 'You are a major, massive, big-time fool. I loved Paul, yes. Once upon a time; but I married you and, Edward, *I've* never regretted that. You're the one with the doubts, not me. Not Paul.'

She laid her head against his shoulder and, almost absently, he stroked the soft blonde hair, and inhaled her fragrance. Edward closed his eyes. 'I'm scared,' he admitted. 'I don't know what to do to be right, Lydia.'

'You should have told him. That policeman.'

Edward pulled away impatiently. 'Look, I don't doubt the man's good intentions, but he's a country bobby, probably never encountered anything more major than a stolen boat. He couldn't handle this.'

'Then we need someone who can,' Lydia told him. 'And fast, Edward. They killed Paul, just like they threatened. They aren't going to stop.'

Mrs Simms padded quietly across the hall of the de Freitas' house. At least they weren't shouting any more, she thought, and this last month they'd seemed to do nothing but. What she'd taken for a happy marriage when she'd accepted the job was proving to be anything but if all the arguments were anything to go by. So different from when they'd first come. She wondered if it was the countryside that wasn't suiting them. After all, townies didn't always settle, did they, but today topped everything. A murder!

She paused before knocking on the door to the Big Room as she always called it. Stuck her head around the door. 'I'll be off then?'

'Oh, God, is it that time already?' Edward and Lydia stood so close together as to almost be touching but Margaret Simms could feel the gulf breeze blowing between them even from across the room. She opened the door wider and stepped inside, genuinely sorry for her employers.

'I'm really sorry to hear . . . you know. I mean, if there's anything I can do? Folk round here tend to rally round in a crisis.'

Lydia managed a smile. Edward looked as though he was about to choke.

'Thanks, Margaret. We really appreciate that, but we don't know what's going on at the moment. We just know that Paul is . . .' She looked away, unable to continue.

'Dead,' her husband said. 'Paul is dead.' He sounded so utterly desolate that Margaret Simms felt her own throat tighten and her eyes prick with tears.

Quietly, she closed the door on their grief and let herself out, crossing the rear lawn and taking the cliff path home as she did on fine days when the walk was nice. Once out of sight of the house, she dug in her bag and found her mobile phone. Her sister, Chrissie, was on speed dial. 'You'll never guess,' she began. 'Oh, you've heard? No, I had it switched off at the house, didn't seem right, gossiping about it when I was there. Shot, they said. Blood everywhere. Yes, a shoot-out, on *his* boat in our little bay. Oh, in bits they are.' She glanced back towards the house and paused, frowning, certain just for a moment that she'd seen someone, a tall man, standing close to the rear gate, then, when she looked again, the man was gone.

'Oh, you're back. Everybody, Rina's back.' Bethany greeted Rina with such effusiveness she might have been away for weeks and not just a few hours.

'Matthew's cooking lamb for dinner.'

'Smell's good,' Rina approved. 'What do you have there, Tim?'

The dark-haired man looked up from the papers and miscellaneous pieces of wood and glass spread across the kitchen table.

'It's a new illusion,' Bethany announced, clasping her hands joyfully together. 'It arrived by special delivery about an hour ago.'

Rina glanced at the title on the typewritten sheet. 'Pepper's Ghost. Oh, if I remember right, that's quite an old illusion, isn't it, Tim?'

'First performed by Mr J. H. Pepper on Christmas Eve in 1862. I got dad to make up a model so I could demonstrate the effect to Blake. They're keen to make it happen, but I don't think Blake and Lilly quite get how it works.'

Rina examined the little model. Tim's father was an artist and set designer and the model was based on measurements and photographs Tim had sent him of the newly restored art deco stage at the Palisades Hotel. Tim, magician and mentalist extraordinaire, worked there four nights a week and the new owners, Blake and Lilly, were keen to spread the reputation of the recently reopened hotel. Their clientele was rather more upmarket than was typically catered for in Rina's street.

'Isn't it lovely,' Bethany cooed. 'Eliza and I think we should find a permanent display for it when Tim's done. We thought we could put it on the piano, so we can see it and enjoy it whenever we play.'

'Good idea,' Rina approved. 'Tim, your father did a wonderful job.'

'He did, didn't he, and the stage at the Palisades is just crying out to be used like this.' Tim was grinning from ear to ear in his enthusiasm. Sometimes, Rina reflected, he was more like a boy than a man who would not see thirty again, though that impression was, perhaps, enhanced by the fact that everyone else in her household was at least twice his age.

Rina smiled affectionately. Tim and his father were anomalies in a family that, to a man – and woman – had made their careers in the military. Army, air force, even the odd sailor. Most had then sidestepped on retirement into something equally official, like Tim's uncle who had joined the Diplomatic Protection Group or his other uncle who'd become some sort of Home Office advisor.

Tim's father, on the other hand, had gone to art school and Tim made a rather precarious living as a performer.

'Matthew, Stephen, is there anything you need me to do?'

Matthew was bending to remove a tray from the oven, from which rose a wonderful scent of roast lamb and rosemary.

'It's all under control, Rina dear. Stephen is just about to see to the gravy and I'll let the meat rest while he's doing that. Then I think we're there, if the ladies would like to lay the table?'

Eliza and Bethany skittered off to do his bidding and Rina took two large glass pitchers from the wall cupboard and filled them with water, setting them on the kitchen table beside the assorted glassware that displayed the varied preferences held by the members of her disparate household.

She watched as Matthew lifted the meat on to the serving plate, and then stepped aside to allow Stephen access to the stove. Apart from breakfast, which Rina always took care of, most of the meals at Peverill Lodge were taken care of by the Montmorency twins; Matthew, tall and elegant and hound-like with his mane of silver hair swept back from a thin face and Stephen, short and a little rotund about the waist. Getting very thin on top – though only a very foolish or thoughtless soul would draw attention to the fact.

The Montmorencys had performed as a double act since both were children and Rina supposed that, once upon a time, their physical differences would have been a source of humour. Over the years though, they had seemed to forget that they were not even blood relatives, never mind being twins. Twindom had become reality for them and Rina had to brief new acquaintances very carefully to ensure the tacit illusion was maintained.

Mac had, she remembered, been very quick on the uptake.

The Peters sisters scuttled back in and took the pitchers. Rina followed with the glassware. Eliza and Bethany were actual sisters, another double act whose career spanned that of magician's assistants to song and dance duo. They were by nature and inclination true vaudevillians, though even at the start of their professional lives, the golden days of variety had, in Rina's opinion, already passed and she mourned that passing.

She and her dear husband, Frank, had themselves pounded

the boards in little theatres and pier reviews, though after his
death just five years after their marriage, Rina had turned to
more serious roles, finding small roles with travelling companies and then finally leads. Her big break had come relatively
late in her career, the title role on the long-running series
'Lydia Marchant Investigates'. The television work had
brought with it a little more security and had, in the end,
allowed her to buy Peverill Lodge.

The Peters sisters, then the Montmorencys and finally Tim
Brandon had made their home with her and while it could be
argued, by less generous minds, that her 'lodgers' paid so little
rent it probably only just covered the food bill, Rina had no
complaint.

This was her family. Oddball and truculent it could sometimes be but, so long as she had the means, they'd be safe
here at Peverill Lodge.

SIX

I t was almost eight by the time Mac reached home. Miriam was cooking. She hadn't quite moved in, but she did spend several nights at the little boathouse each week. Mac acknowledged that neither of them was quite ready to give up their own space, but it was truly wonderful to have someone to share his for a good deal of the time.

The boathouse had been Rina's find, at a time when Mac had almost given up on finding somewhere to live and was seriously considering the possibility of camping out at the police station. The friend of Rina's that he rented from still stored his boat downstairs, but the upper floor had been converted into a surprisingly comfortable space, open-plan but with a separate bedroom with an en suite shower room. It was a surprisingly light and airy space, broad windows had been let into one wall and velux skylights in the bedroom. Scrubbed wooden boards and whitewashed walls reflected light and did not detract from the sense of what the loft space had once been. There was an odd, surprisingly large, porthole-style window at one gable end and, if you sat on the fireside chair Mac had placed there, it gave a magnificent view of the changing seascape across the bay.

Mac had loved the place on sight and the fact that Miriam happened to be there on the day he came to view had seemed like an excellent omen.

She had heard him coming up the stairs and turned with a smile as he emerged through what had once been the trapdoor leading from the boathouse proper. 'I hear you've had an exciting day.'

He went over, kissed her, then slipped his arms around her waist, standing behind her as she stirred, enjoying the movement of her body against his.

'Some kinds of excitement I can do without. Let me guess, Stephen Montmorency's recipe for tomato sauce?'

She laughed. 'Yes, but à la Miriam Hastings. I've added a twist or so of my own.' She paused to unlock his hands. 'Lay the table,' she said. 'It's almost ready. Andy called to say you were on your way, so I put the pasta on.'

Mac laughed. Friends and work colleagues seemed to be conspiring. 'They've managed to squeeze the post-mortems in for first thing tomorrow.'

'Yeah, I heard. Any ID on the second man yet?'

Mac shook his head. 'No. Exeter are sending reinforcements over in the morning. I'm teaming up with our friend, Dave Kendal,'

'Who'll be SIO?' Miriam asked.

'Oh, we'll fight over which of us will be in charge when he gets here.' Mac laughed. 'I'm guessing that the title of Senior Investigating Officer will be mine by default; Kendal isn't a Frantham fan. Of course, it depends how serious it all gets, We might both have to move aside if the powers that be decide this is too much for us country coppers.'

'Well, there has been quite a crime wave since you arrived.'

Mac set bowls and glasses on the table and opened some wine. 'It has been mentioned,' he said wryly. He paused. 'Can't you just put the sauce on the pasta and just shove it in the oven on a low heat?'

'Hmm.' She turned, smiling. 'Pasta al forno. I suppose we could always eat later.' She put down the spoon, grabbed the front of his shirt, and sniffed critically.

'Shower,' she ordered. 'I'll do the thing with the oven and then . . . well then we'll see.'

SEVEN

Bright and early the next morning Rina and Tim were at the airfield, examining the latest stage in reconstruction. This had become a regular walk for them lately, the footpath running along the perimeter giving a good view of the ongoing work and then leading up on to the cliff path.

'Was that postcard from George?' Tim asked. 'I just spotted it when Matthew collected the mail.'

'Jointly from George and Ursula. She added a postscript. They should be moving back next month when the repairs to Hill House are finished.'

Tim grinned sheepishly; he'd been rather responsible for the damage to the front of the house which meant that the childrens' home had to be relocated for a few months. There'd been talk of moving out for good but no one seemed to want to buy the place and the council had been unable to find other premises so it looked as though George and Ursula would be moving back there after all. Currently, they were both in temporary foster care in Dorchester though for the past two weeks they'd been away on some sort of outward bound scheme in 'wettest Wales' as George described it.

'He says that he hasn't been dry since they got there,' Rina said. 'They've either been rained on or participating in "river things". I get the feeling he isn't keen.'

'And Ursula?'

'Says he's just exaggerating. I must say, though, I'll be glad to have them back. I had a letter from Stan too.'

'Oh.' Criminal turned hero in Tim's eyes, Stan was currently awaiting trial for what Tim and Rina both viewed as a very justifiable homicide. 'He's well and hopeful. His legal team seem to think they have a real argument to bring to the CPS.'

'Well with the Duggans throwing money at the problem, I think he's got a good chance. Rina, what do you reckon happened on Paul's boat?'

She shrugged sturdy shoulders. 'I'm most intrigued by the identity of the second man,' she said. 'Something very odd is going on, Tim. The old antenna is twitching. Paul was keeping secrets from everyone, including his family, which makes me think one of two things. Either he was deliberately deceiving them or he was trying to protect them from something.'

'And your money is on?'

'The second. Paul didn't strike me as a deceitful man. I'd have said that his job probably instilled a degree of caution. From what I understand, this whole hi-tech business attracts industrial spies, but I wouldn't have said he was a dishonest man. His sister-in-law certainly didn't seem to think so, at least, that was the impression I gleaned from the way she reacted yesterday. She was surprised. No, shocked at the idea that there was something she didn't know about.'

'Unless Paul was a very practised liar,' Tim suggested. 'And the brother?'

Rina frowned. 'Something odd going on there too. I think he was worried about their relationship. His wife and brother, I mean. But added to that he's a man with something important on his mind; something he doesn't know how to deal with.' She flicked her walking stick impatiently at a clump of nettles. 'The annoying thing is, I have no idea what.'

Tim hid his smile as Rina's stick whipped out again, this time taking the head off an errant thistle. She didn't need the stick for walking, it was more potential weapon or fashion accessory than utilitarian but it could be a dangerous accessory. 'I've no doubt you'll figure it out,' he said.

'Oh, of course I will, but it is aggravating, Tim, not to be in possession of all the facts. There are questions I should have asked earlier; things I should have discovered.'

'You had no reason to want to know things then,' Tim argued.

'Which just goes to show, Tim. One should always gather intelligence anyway. One never can tell.'

Mac and Collins, the coastguard who had attended the scene the previous day, met in the morgue. The post-mortems had already begun when they arrived, Mason, the pathologist, having come in very early in order to slip the two dead men into his schedule.

Mason confirmed what they had observed but had some interesting additions. 'Mr de Freitas died from the effects of a bullet wound to the back of the head, but the angle seems odd, look. The bullet entered here, close to the base of the skull, and exited almost through the top of the head.'

'He was kneeling with his head bowed?' Mac tried to figure it out.

'That's one possibility. The other, I suppose, is that he was diving for cover. His companion was coming down the steps when he was shot, at least that's what I'd surmise. The angle of the shot is slightly from above and exits through the face. The shot was fired at close range. Like de Freitas, the shot was through and through and the bullet has been recovered. It was lodged in the planking of the cabin floor. Our mystery man was shot, fell forward and his assailant doesn't seem to have bothered with him after that, but we can now be pretty sure that he was armed.'

'Armed!' Collins, the coastguard, was startled. 'There was no sign of a gun.'

'Gunshot residue on his right hand and a 9mm bullet found in the bulkhead of the wheelhouse. Neither de Freitas nor our second victim was killed with a 9mm. There's also blood on the handrail close by and drips on the floor of the cabin near de Freitas' body. Our killer paused, dripped blood, then left the way he'd come. It doesn't belong to either of our victims. Wrong blood group.'

'So, our mystery man fired at least one shot, presumably at the killer, then ran down the steps into the cabin,' Mac confirmed.

'Tried to, yes. He was shot, and from the position of the body probably when he was only part way down the steps. He dropped, the gunman went on and shot de Freitas. Then, we've got to assume, he picked up the spare gun and left.'

'Do we know if anything was taken?' the coastguard asked.

'De Freitas' wallet was still in his trouser pocket. Our unknown male just had some loose change and a couple of keys in his pockets. Nothing to identify him unless you can find what the keys fit.' Mason shrugged. 'I can show you what they had for breakfast, if you like, but apart from that, I'm probably done, for now.'

Deciding that they would pass on that offer, Collins and Mac retreated to the outer office where Miriam was waiting for them. She smiled at Mac, a light flush rising to her cheeks.

'Coffee?' she offered. 'Don't worry, Mason didn't make it. He makes truly dreadful coffee.'

'So,' Mac said. 'What have you got for me?'

Miriam laughed and Collins looked from one to the other, understanding dawning.

'Hmm, right. Well.' She set a plastic box on the table and began to sort through the evidence bags inside. 'Paul de Freitas' wallet, with credit cards and thirty-five pounds in cash. Assorted pocket change, car keys – they were in the bedside cabinet. There was a PDA cradle set up in the wheelhouse but we found no sign of the computer. It's possible the gunman took it. His mobile phone seems to be missing too and if our unknown man had one, well that's gone too. No wallet. But we did find this.' She laid a neat, subnotebook computer on the tabletop. 'It belonged to Paul de Freitas, according to his brother. I'm about to send it across to the geek squad.'

'Do we know what's on it?' Collins asked.

She shrugged. 'Password protected. But it's where the CSI found it that's weird.'

'Weird, how?'

'Tucked in the bed, shoved down under the covers.'

'Bunk,' Collins said absently. 'Why?'

Mac visualised the scene he had glimpsed through the doorway of the inner cabin. 'De Freitas was shot next to the bunk,' he said. 'What if he tried to hide it in a hurry? If he heard the first shot, or the other man shouted a warning, there might have just been time to do that, shove it into the bunk.'

'You're assuming our gunman was too thick to think of that?' Collins objected.

'I'm assuming he didn't know what he was after. Maybe he thought he had it when he took the PDA. Maybe de Freitas even told him that before he died. And we know he'd been shot, we just don't know how badly. It might have been enough to put him off his stride.'

Collins nodded. 'I can see how it might be distracting. You know,' he went on, 'we examined his charts. Paul de Freitas had either got a long trip planned or he'd just been on one.'

'Trip? To where?'

'Well that's the funny thing. His heading would have taken him out into the middle of nowhere. Just Atlantic Ocean.'

'Could he have planned a rendezvous with someone?'

'That's what we wondered. But he'd almost no supplies on board. Trip like that, a full two days out and two back, you plan for emergencies. He was an experienced sailor, thought the world of his boat . . . Mac, de Freitas would have planned, he never struck me as one to take chances.'

'Meeting who? And, when?' Mac frowned.

'And there's another thing. The wheel was tied off like the helmsman had to leave it for a few minutes. Ordinarily, he'd have set the heading, tied the wheel.

'But, well, my guess is that whoever tied it wanted the boat to keep heading out to sea. If he'd done it properly it might have taken days before anyone found it, but he either didn't know what he was doing or maybe getting shot was a real distraction. Either way, he was no sailor. Only a landsman would use a mess of a knot like that one. It had slipped, let the wheel turn and then lock.'

'Hence the ever-decreasing circles. Interesting.'

'There was blood on the rope,' Miriam told them.

Collins stood up. 'I'd best be off, let me know when you've got anything definite.'

Mac was thoughtful after he'd gone.

'Penny for them?'

'I'm thinking about that second man,' he said. 'I've got all sorts of possibilities running through my mind but they all sound like they've come from some second-rate spy film.' He smiled up at her as she started to pack away the evidence bags. 'So, I won't be seeing you tonight.'

'Fraid not. You'll survive.'

'I'll try.'

She bent and kissed him quickly on the mouth. 'Now go and catch criminals and let me get some work done.'

EIGHT

Mac had found Edward and Lydia de Freitas in the Big Room at the rear of the house. Lydia stood framed by the massive window and Edward still sat in the winged chair. It was, Mac thought, almost as though they had been frozen in position since he went away, an illusion broken only by the change of clothes. Lydia still wore faded blue jeans, but a soft grey sweater replaced the white shirt of the previous day. Despite the density of the cable knit, she still looked cold.

Behind her the seascape shifted, cloud shadowed and sun lit, and that strange vertiginous quality instilled by the absence of land viewed from the picture window for an instant almost convinced Mac that they were floating.

Mrs Simms brought coffee, setting it down on a low table close by Edward's chair.

'Do you need anything else?' She cast Mac a speculative look, clearly wondering if he had news and if so, was he going to be able to share it.

Lydia shook her head. 'Thanks, Margaret. We'll be fine now.' She sounded tired, Mac thought, and dark circles, not helped by the drab colour of her sweater, underlined the pale-blue eyes.

'Who benefits from your brother's death?' Mac asked when they had settled with their coffee. 'I'm sorry to ask, but . . .'

'You have to look at all angles,' Edward said. If Lydia looked tired then he seemed to be on the verge of exhaustion.

Lydia shrugged. 'We don't have family,' she said. 'So unless there's some mistress or abandoned cat charity we don't know about, I assume we will.'

She sounded bitter, flippantly angry. Mac wondered what was going through her mind.

'We didn't really talk about it,' Edward said. 'I can call our solicitor, tell him to co-operate, of course, but so far as I know everything will come back to us.'

Come back to us. An odd turn of phrase in the circumstances. 'Did he have much to leave?'

'Well, there's the boat, of course and he had a flat in Dorchester. Not that he was ever there. Half the time he'd just sleep here when he wasn't on *The Greek Girl*.'

'Here?'

'Yes, we kept a bedroom for him,' Edward said, just a touch defensively, Mac thought. 'The house has five bedrooms. Too much space for the two of us really.'

'May I see his room?'

'Of course. Margaret will show you.' Edward's coffee sat untouched on the tray. He didn't seem to have the strength to move.

'She'll be in the kitchen,' Lydia added. 'Across the hall and down the little corridor. On the right.' She turned away, seeming unconsciously to dismiss him as she stared out at the shifting scene of sea and sky. Sun streamed in through the window, illuminating and heating the entire room but she hugged herself as though she could still not get warm.

Mac went to find Margaret Simms.

'This is his room, nice view over the garden and the water. Three of the rooms look out to sea, Mr & Mrs F, they have the big room at the front. Good view of the garden from there and the hills, you know. And that has the biggest en suite so . . .' She paused, realising that she was chattering nervously just because he was a policeman. 'They're a lovely couple, you know,' she said. 'And he was ever such a pleasant man. What on earth was he doing to get himself shot like that?' She opened the bedroom door and stood back, waiting for Mac to enter. 'Will you need me to stop with you?'

'I'll be fine,' Mac said. 'If I need to take anything away, I'll give you a list. I don't want to disturb the de Freitas's again.'

She nodded. 'No news then?'

'Not yet. Did he stay here regularly?'

'Once a week, maybe. Sometimes more. He'd bed down here if he was working late and didn't want the drive home. Or if they'd got an early meeting and sometimes if he and Edward were off to London or wherever. They'd drive up together and Paul kept his good suit here.'

'His good suit?' Mac was amused.

'Oh, he had a couple but that was all. Wasn't a suit man.

Paul wore jeans and old jumpers when he could get away
with it. He just dressed up when his brother told him he had
to. Paul called it "putting on the uniform".' She smiled rather
sadly. 'He knew his brother was the business brains, always
did what was best; what Edward told him was for the best.'

'Would you say they had a close relationship?'

She thought about it and then nodded. 'They were like chalk
and cheese, but yes, they were close. It wasn't like they wanted
to change each other, it was like they both knew they had a
different role to play and the business worked best with both
sides, if you see what I mean.'

'And Mrs de Freitas? Did Paul get along with her?'

This time there was an almost imperceptible hesitation
before she told him, 'Oh yes, no doubt about that,' cutting in
just a little too quickly and a little too emphatically. Mac
waited but she said nothing more.

'I'd better go now,' she said. 'I've got some work to do.'

Mac scanned the room. Comfortably, even immaculately
furnished, it was still essentially a guest room. Two small
watercolours in broad mounts adorned the wall on either
side of the door, but Mac would have put money on the
pretty landscapes being Lydia's choice. Heavy brocade
curtains would have been more at home in an upmarket
hotel, as would the matching comforter draped across the
divan bed.

Mac opened the cupboard of the bedside cabinet and
found it empty. The drawer contained a paperback thriller,
well thumbed, and a handful of loose change and a pack
of painkillers, local supermarket brand. The light-oak
wardrobe was empty but for a dark suit, with a blue silk tie
wrapped around the hanger and a couple of smart, button-
down shirts. Polished shoes on the wardrobe floor, next to
a worn pair of deck shoes and a suit bag folded and sitting
on the corner. Mac looked underneath and inside but found
nothing but a dry-cleaning tag from two months before.
Nothing either on the wardrobe shelf. A search through
the chest of drawers revealed a couple of pairs of jeans,
three T-shirts and an old sweater that matched Mrs Simms'
description.

No photographs, none of the normal debris that gets left
behind when someone truly occupies a space for even a brief

time. Mac had seen more individuality in an empty hotel room and it was in direct contrast to the normal human clutter he had observed on the boat.

The window, as Mrs Simms had told him, gave a view out across the bay and echoed that of the Big Room which must, Mac judged, be directly below. This window, this room though, was on a more human scale; the view, though of itself still wonderful was somehow predictable and of more manageable proportions.

Back downstairs he remembered that there was one more thing to ask and he'd have to disturb the de Freitas's after all. He tapped gently on the door of the Big Room.

Lydia was absent but Edward still sat with his now cold coffee.

'Did you find anything?' he asked, but seemed disinterested in the response as though expecting the answer to be no.

'Did Paul say anything about planning a lengthy trip on his boat?'

For a second, Edward looked startled, then the mask of exhaustion returned. 'No,' he said. 'He had no plans. We were due to launch a new game next week, Paul was to be involved. We had publicity and press . . .' He broke off. 'I'll have to do it alone now.'

'Won't Mrs de Freitas help out?'

Edward looked at him directly for the first time since Mac had re-entered the room. 'Of course she will,' he said with sudden impatience, 'but she isn't Paul, is she? Lydia knows nothing about . . . about any of this. Promoting our products was one of the areas where Paul excelled. People *liked* him. He *liked* people. Not like me.'

'And was that what Paul did in the business? He promoted your products?'

Edward shook his head. 'No, that was just a part of it. Paul designed . . . Paul's strengths were on the technical side. He was utterly brilliant, Inspector. A mind that could see solutions where most people didn't even perceive there was a problem . . .' He broke off as Lydia came back into the room, those moments of animation that had restored the sparkle to his eyes and the colour to his face departing as suddenly as they had appeared.

'Sorry, Inspector. I thought you'd gone.'

'I'm just about to.' He asked Lydia about the trip too, but she claimed ignorance. Paul had said nothing.

Mac left, still wondering what it was the pair of them were holding back.

NINE

D inner at Rina's was always a pleasant affair if a somewhat chaotic one, given the company. Tim had already
left and Mac, though pleased his friend had now gained
meaningful employment, found that he missed him sorely.
Tim had added a darker, more solid note to the often rather
frilly and frivolous tone of the rest of the household – Rina
excluded, of course. Rina was the drumbeat that kept the rest
of her world in time.

The Montmorencys had taken over in the kitchen as
usual, and Mac arrived in time to help Rina lay the table.
The first time he had dined with Rina's family, he had been
surprised to find that none of the crockery or glassware
matched. Each member of the family had their own pref-
erence and Mac now knew them all well enough to have
identified their personal belongings even if he hadn't previously been told.

The Peters sisters had china plates, Shelley, apparently.
Chintz pattern, Rina told him. Bethany preferred yellow and
Eliza the pink. The Montmorencys liked blue and white and
even Mac could recognise the willow pattern on Matthew's
plates.

'How is Tim getting along?'

'Oh, very well. The management have given him another
night a week and he's building quite a local reputation. He's
there from Wednesday through to Saturday and from a
fifteen-minute slot to three of the same length per night,
mostly table to table. They've gone for an old-fashioned
cabaret feel to the entertainment, you know. A house band
and rather glamorous singers and Tim, of course. It's all
rather classy.'

'Glad to hear it.'

'Any progress with the murder?'

He shook his head. 'Nothing as yet. The coastguard think
Paul was preparing for a long trip. That's what his charts seem
to indicate, but his brother-and sister-in-law say they know

nothing about that and we've nothing yet on our second man. You know, Rina, I can't get away from the feeling that Edward de Freitas is scared of something. He's not just knocked sideways by his brother's death, he seems . . . I don't know, completely and utterly floored. He mentioned that his brother was a designer and that he also did a lot to promote the work. Andy reckons they've made some of the top-selling RPGs around. They're . . .'

'Role Playing Games. Yes I know. I googled them. I do so love the internet, don't you. But the R&D department they've got set up in that new build behind the Sheds, that's not games, apparently. The website was a bit vague, but they're manufacturing specialist chip sets and there, Mac, my knowledge base is distinctly lacking. But as everything you care to look at these days seems to have computer in it, I imagine it's a pretty lucrative business to be in.'

'And Paul seems to have been key to that side of things.' Mac wondered how usual it was for software designers to suddenly begin to design hardware. Or maybe that had been Paul's speciality all along. 'They don't look like games designers,' he announced.

'Oh and what do games designers look like?'

'I don't know. Younger, I suppose. Less . . . conventional?'

'We were all younger once,' Rina reminded him. 'De Freitas Productions started *Iconograph* twenty years ago.'

Mac laughed, and considered himself reprimanded.

'I did find one thing out though,' Rina continued. 'Paul wasn't in it at the start. He joined the company five years ago. From what little I managed to glean, Paul had a business of his own, but it went under half a dozen years since. I found a couple of newspaper articles online. One suggested that while he might be a brilliant designer, he wasn't much of a businessman.'

'So older brother gave him a job.' That made sense of a lot of the things Mac had heard that day, not least the comment about Paul's possessions 'coming back' to them.

The Peters sisters floated in, announcing that food was ready and the serious conversation came to an end. But Mac was left speculating. Edward had taken his brother on, given him money for his boat and flat, maybe even set up the new arm of his company just to accommodate his brother's skills.

But Edward was the businessman. Paul, the technician and Paul also the face of the company perhaps?

Mac could see how that would work. He wondered again how Lydia fitted into this.

TEN

Andy had waited in the car while Mac visited the solicitor the following morning. They got there just as his offices opened and Mac was relieved to find that Edward had been true to his word and asked for his solicitor's cooperation.

Mr Geoffrey Bliss was Mac's vision of a proper solicitor. Dark suit, rimless, half-moon spectacles perched on a hook nose. Despite his appropriate appearance, he was able to tell Mac very little.

'Everything of significance was left to his brother,' Mac was told. 'There are a few small bequests, mostly personal items, books and the like, left to friends, but let's just say, it's a very simple will.'

'Nothing to the sister-in-law?'

'Yes.' Geoffrey Bliss laughed. 'A first edition of A.A. Milne's *When We Were Very Young*. It seems like an odd little bequest, but presumably she will understand.'

Presumably she would, Mac thought.

Next stop, Paul's flat.

Paul de Freitas had sunk just about all his disposable income into his boat. His flat was modest; a top floor of an Edwardian house not far from the local secondary school.

Andy pulled up outside the house. He was staring into the rear-view mirror.

'Something wrong?'

Andy shook his head. 'I don't know. The car that just parked up behind us, it's been with us since you went to the solicitor's office.'

Mac glanced over his shoulder; nothing remarkable about the dark-green Rover with the two male passengers. 'Are you sure?'

'I'm sure.'

Mac got out of the car, Andy trailing after, and headed towards the house. He was somehow unsurprised when the two men followed him. Only slightly less surprised to find that the police seal on Paul de Freitas' door had been broken and someone was already inside. He could sense Andy's unease.

The man sitting in Paul de Freitas' favourite leather, wing-backed chair rose as they entered and held out his hand. 'You must be Inspector McGregor.'

Mac shook the hand, eyeing its owner carefully. Expensive suit, a plain white button-down shirt that was oddly like those in Paul's wardrobe. The man was, Mac guessed, in his late fifties. Greying hair, light tan to the skin. Manicured fingernails that made Mac immediately self-conscious of his own. Not that he bit them or anything, but the odd attack of clippers and nail file didn't exactly do a lot to improve their appearance.

'And you are?' He glanced at the two men who had followed up the stairs. 'You are aware that this is a crime scene?'

'I am, yes. The late Paul de Freitas did some work for us. You'll understand that we needed to be sure he hadn't left anything here that shouldn't be.'

'Work for you? And who exactly are you?'

The grey-haired man produced his ID. Mac studied it. 'And I should believe that?'

He was aware of Andy craning round him trying to see and of the young man saying, 'Cool,' as he read the legend MI5.

Grey hair smiled. 'My name, as you can see, is William Hale. Your superintendent will be in touch once you get back to your HQ, but feel free to call him if you like. He'll confirm my identity, but in the meantime there are a few things of which you should be aware.'

'The second victim was one of your people,' Mac guessed.

'He was. Yes.'

'And am I to know why Paul de Freitas needed a minder?'

'I'm afraid not. No.'

'And if that information is pertinent to his death? I remind you that I am conducting a murder investigation.'

'And we are aware of that. Our interests no doubt run parallel, Inspector.'

Mac frowned. 'Andy.' He pointed to a door behind William Hale. 'We'll start through there, I think. Any objections, Mr Hale?'

'As you will.' He stood back, let Mac and Andy go past into what turned out to be Paul's bedroom.

Mac closed the door.

'Won't they have already searched the place?' Andy whispered.

'Of course they will, but we may find something they judged unimportant and, besides, I'm not letting some jumped-up pseudo official tell me I can't investigate my own murder.'

Andy grinned at him. 'Pseudo official?'

Mac didn't reply. He knew there was something off here. Hale might well be MI5, might be from another department acting under their auspices. May be something else again but he just hadn't figured it out yet. He directed Andy towards a low chest of drawers that stood in the bay by the window and Mac took the bedside cabinet.

'We looking for anything in particular?'

'Personal papers, anything relating to *The Greek Girl*. I don't know, Andy, but we're not leaving here empty-handed.'

For a while they worked in silence, moving methodically through the room and then going back into the main living room with a handful of papers and photographs in plastic evidence bags, Mac viciously aware that the place had already been ransacked. Oh, not in an untidy way, or so the casual observer or even someone who knew the place reasonably well would notice, but the search had taken place all right and it had been thorough.

Hale was back in the winged chair close to the fireplace. No fire in the hearth now, of course, the August weather behaving for once, but Mac could imagine that in winter this would be a friendly, comforting position in which to sit and read. His two attendants seemed to have departed; obviously, Mac thought, they didn't expect him or Andy to cause any trouble. He felt a little put-out at such a slight.

A check of the kitchen and bathroom revealed little and they returned to the living room. Hale had not moved.

A small portable television sat on a table with barley twist legs that Mac recognised as a Victorian aspidistra stand. Old bookshelves lined the whole of one wall and a roll-top desk stood beside the window, a modern office chair the only jarring element. Dark floorboards were covered in one large and a couple of smaller rugs, and instead of curtains the window was dressed with wooden, slatted blinds. Mac, watched by Hale, took time to check each book, flicking the pages and looking behind. Paul had possessed eclectic tastes and cheap, well-thumbed paperback thrillers rubbed shoulders with poetry and classics. He had a small collection of first editions, including the A.A. Milne the solicitor had mentioned.

He'd had a habit, Mac noted, of tearing scraps of paper from the margins of magazines or newspapers with which to mark his pages. Some of the paperbacks still had their improvised markers stuck between the pages, their position telling Mac that they'd been replaced at random and with some degree of impatience. Still more of these lay on the shelf between two volumes of poetry, together with three or four 'real' bookmarks advertising local bookshops or an online dealer Mac had also used on occasions. A couple more such markers lay between the pages of the 1919 first edition of W.B.Yeats' *The Wild Swans at Coole*, and an ageing gazetteer of the south-west.

Mac moved on to examine the stack of papers on the bottom shelf but found them to be paid bills and bank statements, all mixed in with printouts of directions and leaflets from the local takeaways. He bagged them anyway, reflecting that if the state of Paul's personal filing system reflected that of his business papers, it was no wonder Edward did not rate him as a businessman.

Andy focussed on the roll-top desk, flicking through notebooks and photographs and the assorted detritus that gets pushed into the cubbyholes of desks and is then forgotten. Once or twice he called Mac's attention to something and Mac, erring on the side of caution, told him to bring it all; they'd sift through it later. Hale had made no comment. He sat with his fingers steepled, elbows resting on the arms of the leather chair, his face a noncommittal blank. Mac, feeling increasingly foolish, stuck to his firkling and ferreting, Hale's pale eyes burning into the back of his neck.

'Andy?' Mac straightened up.

'About finished.'

'Good.' Hale rose to his feet. 'Then we can all be off. I'm sure you both have better things to do.'

Mac made no comment. Pride caused him to re-seal the door once they had all left.

'What now?' Andy said as they got back in to the car.

'We make a call on the de Freitas's, then Frantham,' Mac said. 'You park up, I'll get the coffee.'

Andy turned to look at him, eyes narrowed in expectation. 'You went and found something, didn't you?'

'I might have done,' Mac admitted. He dug out his phone and made a few calls. Was unsurprised, but chagrined to find that Hale was to 'be given every cooperation'. Then he put in a call to forensics.

'You're getting the CSIs in?'

'Hale wasn't wearing gloves. Either he's confident he won't show up in the system or he thinks I'll be too impressed by his credentials to bother.'

'Superintendent Aims won't like you doing that. Not if he's already been briefed.'

'Well, Andy, we definitely *haven't* been briefed, have we? We don't know those men from Adam.'

Andy laughed but he sounded a trifle nervous. 'What did you find then?'

'Maybe nothing, but there was a prescription packet in the medicine cabinet, and it wasn't Paul's. Then there was a scrap of paper, wedged in one of the books. It looks as though Paul de Freitas folded it up and used it as a bookmark, which is probably why no one took any notice of it, and there might be nothing to take notice of but . . .'

'But you think . . .'

Mac sighed, suddenly deflated. 'I think I'm rather desperate for them to have missed something,' he said, but, offhand, he couldn't think of any good reason why an obvious book lover would mark a first edition with a scrap of folded newspaper. And added to that anomaly was the fact that the book was *When We Were Very Young* by A. A. Milne, the one the solicitor had told him was promised to Lydia in Paul's will.

ELEVEN

They had driven halfway to Frantham when Mac's phone rang. It was Miriam and she had disturbing news. Someone had taken Paul's laptop.

'An official someone?'

'Hell no, Johnny got in this morning and it was gone. He checked the evidence locker and with other colleagues, thinking they might have already started on it, but it is most definitely gone.'

'Nothing else taken?'

'Yes, a PDA, but it was totally unrelated to our case. In fact, it belonged to one of the techs. He is not a happy bunny. Of course, we have the last laugh on them. Whoever it was doesn't know how we work.'

'What do you mean?'

'Well you never work on the original hard drive. You make an image first, and work from that. They might have taken the laptop, but we've still got the information.'

'Miriam, is there any chance . . .'

'Already done. On the QT of course. I had Johnny make a copy of his copy. Of course, anything we find is inadmissible and, frankly, I don't know what on earth you think we can do that Johnny can't but . . . Anyway, he says you owe him dinner at the Palisades. He wants to see Tim's act.'

'Dinner it is then.'

Andy had been listening in. 'This is too unreal!'

'You're enjoying this?'

'Too right. It's like being in a James Bond film.'

'I hope not. In the average Bond film half the locations get blown up and most of the cast die well before the final credits.'

'Yeah,' Andy agreed reluctantly, 'but that's fiction, ain't it. This is for real.'

TWELVE

Rina had been about bright and early and walked along the cliff path to the de Freitas' house. She found Lydia alone.

'Do you mind if we go through to the kitchen?' Lydia asked. 'It's Margaret's day off and I was just making some tea.'

'Is Edward not here?' Rina asked.

Lydia shrugged. 'I think he went out.' She led the way to the sunny kitchen and Rina sat down at the scrubbed wooden table, as like the one in her own kitchen as to be its twin. This kitchen was definitely more modern than her own though, melamine and faux granite instead of old pine. It was, Rina thought, strangely at odds too with the rest of the house which had been furnished with an eye to quality and luxury. This was off-the-shelf utilitarian and a little tatty and tired at that.

Lydia must have noticed her appraisal. 'This will be the last room to be done,' she said. She opened a drawer and then dropped some sample books on the table. 'I'm trying to decide whether to go for country kitchen or seventies retro. Margaret wants a proper hob and split-level cooker and a better dishwasher, and I suppose seeing as she's the one that uses it most, she really should have her way but I'm kind of drawn to . . .' She sat down suddenly, and looked at Rina with a stricken expression on her pretty face. 'Oh, God, Rina, what does it matter? Really, what the hell does any of it matter?'

Rina reached out across the table and took Lydia's hands. It was evident that the younger woman was bursting to tell someone whatever it was that *did* matter, but Rina knew she mustn't rush things.

'It's been an awful shock,' she said gently. 'Such violence. It really isn't what you'd expect in a place like Frantham.'

Not, she thought ruefully, that Frantham had exactly been free of such violence this last year, though Rina preferred to think of this as a statistical blip rather than a growing trend.

'You must be devastated,' she went on. 'To lose someone like that . . . and of course, the man who was on board with Paul; from what I've heard they still don't know who he was. Just imagine what his family must be going through. They don't even know yet.'

Lydia stared at her and Rina knew she was on the verge of revelation.

'Imagine,' she went on. 'Someone goes missing and you don't know where to start looking and then you find out that they've been murdered. Shot dead.'

Lydia's eyes had filled with tears.

'Do you know who he was?' Rina said.

Lydia shook her head. 'I already told that policeman I don't know his name.'

'So you did,' Rina agreed. She thought for a moment, weighing the woman's reply. 'But, Lydia, you may not have known his name, but do you know *what* he was?'

'Oh God.' She buried her face in her hands and wept noisily. Rina got up and switched the kettle back on. Tissues were nowhere in evidence but she found a kitchen roll and tore off several sheets, handed them to Lydia and, with surprising gentleness, stroked the younger woman's shoulders and back.

'I know, I know how hard it is to lose someone. Here, wipe your eyes and I'll make some tea and you can tell me what's going on here and we can start to work out what we can do about it.'

'There's nothing to be done,' Lydia told her tearfully. 'They killed Paul and now we're just sitting here, like we're waiting for our turn. Edward won't see . . . he just won't see.'

Rina tried to stay calm, not push too hard. 'Who killed him, Lydia? Who is threatening you?'

Lydia shook her head. 'I can't tell you. I can't tell anyone.'

'You have to confide in someone,' Rina objected gently.

'I can't, Rina. I really can't,' Lydia said, but her expression said something very different. *Persuade me*, it said. *Make me tell you, and then I won't feel to blame.*

Rina opened her mouth to speak but then, echoing through

the house with a piercing jangle, the doorbell rang. 'Bugger,' Rina thought. She got up with a placatory smile. 'Probably someone trying to sell you something.'

Lydia sniffed and wiped her eyes, the moment lost. Rina knew she'd have to work hard to get it back. 'We've had journalists calling all morning. I put the answerphone on. It might be . . .'

'I'll get rid of whoever it is,' Rina told her. 'You stay there. You don't need to talk to anyone.'

Irritated, now, she marched back into the hall. The front door was partly glazed and it became obvious before she got there that she'd be unable to keep her promise.

'Mac, you do have the most lousy sense of timing. Can't you just go away and come back later?'

Andy, standing just behind his superior officer, sniggered at the sight of him being told off by the redoubtable Mrs Martin. Mac scowled.

'No, Rina, I can't. What are you doing here anyway?'

'Well, I was on the point of making a breakthrough, that's what. Fat chance of that now.'

'Making a . . . Rina, this is a murder investigation.'

'I know that! Look, Lydia says she doesn't know the name of the man on the boat but I'm pretty sure she knows why he was there and I'm equally sure now that he was some sort of bodyguard. Not that he did much good.' She lifted her chin, daring Mac to argue about her conclusions. Revealingly, to Rina, he did not.

'Rina, please. Go home, leave this to the police.'

'She's in the kitchen,' Rina said. Still irritated, she led the way.

Lydia's eyes were reddened by the tears she had shed, but she'd had time to compose herself again and she stood, leaning against one of the counters, the kitchen towel Rina had given her screwed tightly in her hand.

'Inspector McGregor,' she said. 'Do you have any news?'

'Very little, I'm afraid. Mrs Martin, I really don't want to delay you. I'm sure Mrs de Freitas will understand if you have to go.'

Rina glared at him, her eyes shooting daggers. Andy, catching only the backwash of her anger, nevertheless took a quick step back. Rina gathered up her bag.

'Lydia, if you need me, you know where I am,' she said. She swept out of the back door, and strode across the lawn to the cliff path.

Mac watched her go with very mixed feelings, knowing that, for her own good he had to make her back off but aware also that he'd offended a friend.

THIRTEEN

D I Dave Kendal was waiting for him when they returned
to Frantham. Pre-warned, Mac had brought him coffee
from the cafe on the promenade. Andy had arrived
first and Mac could hear him regaling Kendal with descrip-
tions of Hale and his associates and his speculations that they
were caught up in some sort of spy ring.

Kendal looked up with a smile as Mac deposited his coffee
on the desk. Sergeant Baker came through from the front
office, pulled up a chair and claimed his coffee and Andy took
up a position by the door so he could keep an eye on the
outside world while being included in the briefing.

Mac brought everyone up to speed. Hale and the papers
they had taken from the flat; the fact that Hale had claimed
the second man on the boat as one of his own and that Lydia
de Freitas had clammed up ever tighter than before.

'You should have let Mrs Martin wear her down,' Sergeant
Baker decided. 'I don't know of many people who can resist
that woman. Maybe you should give her details to that Hale
bloke. Chief interrogator to Her Majesty's Forces.'

Mac laughed but he was aware too that Baker was probably right. Had he not interrupted, Rina would probably have
the whole story by now, but that was hardly the point, was
it? Rina was a civilian. She should learn when to leave well
alone, shouldn't she?

'From what I've seen of Mrs Martin, I'm inclined to agree,'
Kendal said. 'Though I suppose we really shouldn't even be
thinking about it. This Hale, Mac. Did he give a rank?'

Mac shook his head. 'No, I don't believe he did. He was
adamant that Superintendent Aims knew all about him and so
it seemed, when I called in to ask.'

'Well, Aims has certainly been briefed,' Kendal confirmed.
'Being his usual officious self, he's keeping us plebs in the
dark as to what that briefing told him.' Ostentatiously, Kendal
tapped the side of his nose. 'Need to know and all that and
apparently all we need to know is that we'll have an officer

from the MOD assisting us in our enquiries. He should be joining us later today.'

'Do we have a name?'

Kendal consulted his notebook. 'Jackson,' he said. 'Abe Jackson. Sounds American. Do we have Americans working with the MOD? Who knows? Anyway, I'm told he's a military man, a redcap originally, now on secondment. I did ask what the military police had to do with a civilian operation. I mean, you wouldn't find them bending over backwards to assist us if we were on their turf. However, Superintendent Aims seemed to think that was *need to know* as well.'

'Which,' Mac commented acidly, 'probably means that no one thought he needed to know either.'

'Very likely. Mac, just what is going on here? We've got a man shot aboard his yacht, together with another man who may or may not be MOD but is almost certainly a minder of some kind and now various government departments running interference on our investigation.'

'Not to mention two people too afraid to confide in anyone,' Mac added. 'Though one of the big questions in my mind now is what Lydia was about to tell Rina.'

'You've got more than one?' Sergeant Baker queried. 'And here's those experts saying we men can't multitask.'

Mac chuckled. 'Andy, where's all the stuff from Paul de Freitas' flat?'

'In the corner, back of DI Kendal.'

'Ah.' Mac got up and rummaged in the box. All of this would have to be gone over later, see what needed to be shipped out to documents for further analysis. 'Two more things actually.' He dropped a couple of evidence bags on to the table, slid the contents of one out and, after donning a pair of gloves, unfolded it carefully. 'This was slipped, like a bookmark, in to one of Paul's books. He seemed to have a habit of using torn paper from magazines and the like.'

'Lots of people do that,' Sergeant Baker commented.

'True, but this was in a first edition. Would you really want to risk marking a collectible book with newsprint?'

'Maybe Hale's lot just put it back in the wrong place,' Andy suggested. 'We know they searched the place.'

'Maybe, but I happen to know that the book was mentioned

in Paul's will. It was left to Lydia de Freitas. His sister-in-law. I just find that interesting.'

'So, what's on it?'

Mac sighed, turned the paper over, and shook his head. 'Probably not a thing and Andy's right.'

'Something from the classified ads by the look of it,' Kendal said. 'What's on the other side?'

'Half of an announcement in the personal ads,' Mac said. 'Looks like a funeral announcement, but there isn't enough to tell.'

'Imagination running away with you?' Kendal suggested.

'Oh, probably. You know, I think I was just so eager to get one over on Hale, I'd convinced myself . . . anyway, these are maybe more interesting. What woman leaves her contraceptive pills in a man's bathroom?'

'One who expects to be there to take them,' Baker said. 'You sure that's what they are.'

'I'm sure,' Mac said, earning himself a guffaw and raised eyebrow from his Sergeant.

'Lydia de Freitas?' Kendal suggested.

Mac shrugged. 'I asked. She said no. Then she got annoyed with me and asked me to leave. After which she said she hoped I'd be sensitive enough not to ask her husband about them.'

'Which implies . . .'

'Which *may* imply that she was having an affair with her brother-in-law, but that would also imply she spent sufficient time at the flat to be able to take half a pack of pills without missing one. I think her husband or the housekeeper might have noticed that and while he might not have said anything I'm betting Margaret Simms might.'

'So, he had a girlfriend,' Kendal shrugged. 'Is that so unusual? Though I agree, it might be useful to know who and where she is now.'

'Well she missed the last four days of her pill,' Andy commented, looking at the pack. 'See. The days of the week are marked and she stopped taking them four days ago.'

'That's two days before Paul de Freitas was shot.' Significant?

'That's if it's not an old pack that just got left behind months back,' Kendal objected. 'Have them dusted for prints, you never know, we may get lucky.' He rose to leave, pushing back the chair and scraping it across the red lino that Mac kept meaning to get replaced. 'I'd best be going, I'm supposed to be meeting this Abe Jackson.'

'And when do I have the pleasure?' Mac asked.

'If you're a very good boy, I'll bring him over tomorrow. Oh, you can join me today, if you like, but I'm warning you, Superintendent Aims has set up the meeting and he's insisting he has to be there, oversee us lower orders.'

'In which case, I'll pass,' Mac told him with a wry grin.

'Lucky you. It all makes you wonder though, if Andy's pleasant flights of fancy really are so wide of the mark.'

FOURTEEN

Tim, an expert reader of Rina's moods, had realised immediately that she was upset about something. He had swiftly but gently deflected the Peters sisters and ushered Rina into the small sitting room at the front of the house that everyone knew as Rina's Den.

'So,' he said. 'What went wrong?'

'Is it that obvious?'

'Oh yes. It most certainly is. Who upset Rina's master plan?'

She flopped down into one of the fireside chairs, wishing that it was cold enough to have the fire to go with it. There was something comforting about a fire; something that salved bruised feelings. 'Mac,' she said. 'With his impeccable sense of bad timing and then he had the affront to suggest I leave!'

Tim hid a smile. He threw himself into the other chair. 'So tell,' he said. 'Then I'll go and fetch some of Matthew's cake and the coffee Steven is making for us and we'll discuss what to do about it.'

By the time Matthew handed over coffee and cake – chocolate, on account that it was apparently good for the nerves; Tim knew better than to debate that – Rina had finished ranting and was in a calm, considered mood.

'Do I call Mac and tell him an apology and a white flag are required,' Tim wanted to know, 'or are we talking chocolates and flowers here?'

Rina sectioned her cake with delicate actions of her fork and Tim winced as she stabbed a selected piece, wondering which part of Mac's anatomy she was visualising. Then she sighed, her shoulders relaxing for the first time since she'd come home. Tim wondered if Matthew could be right about chocolate cake.

'He was only doing his job,' she said. 'I think an apology will do in the circumstances.' She stabbed the second morsel of cake more thoughtfully and Tim, relieved, saw that she was recovering her usual good humour.

'So what did you think she might have been about to tell?'

'That's the thing, Tim. I'm really not sure. I really *don't* think she knew who was aboard with Paul, at least, not the man's name but I'm pretty sure he was there to look after him in some capacity or other.'

'Well, on that score, I don't think he'll get a reference,' Tim said. 'So, some sort of minder then. Presumably the de Freitas's didn't employ him so . . . Do you think Paul hired him?'

'Possibly, but again, surely his family would know all about that . . . mind you, Paul wasn't confiding in them, I don't think. I got the distinct feeling the day he was shot that they knew something was going on but were in the dark as to precisely what and I also got the very strong feeling that Lydia wasn't used to that. She expected to be in Paul's confidence. She was most put-out to realise that wasn't the case.'

'Well, Rina, sorry to say this, but unless she comes and tells you what's going on, I'm not sure there's much more you can do.'

Reluctantly, she nodded her head. 'You're right, I'm afraid. Timing is everything, Tim, and mine was off today. I missed my moment and now all I can do is leave the door open and hope she decides to walk through.'

FIFTEEN

Seven when she looked at the clock. When she looked again it was only a quarter past. Rina tried to concentrate on the game but Bridge didn't hold her attention at all tonight. Steven and Matthew partnered one another as usual and played with the same eccentric intensity they brought to everything they did. The Peters sisters – in tandem – were paired with Rina and they were losing badly tonight. Rina's turn to call. 'Three clubs,' she said, then realised that she'd be lucky if she got two. Relieved, she realised that Steven had called a higher bid and she wouldn't have to back it up.

'Are you all right, Rina dear?' Bethany asked. She and her sister perched on a two-seat music stool. Rina had never known either of them to play as an individual at Bridge or at the piano come to that. Like the Montmorencys, they seemed to have spent such a long lifetime as a double act that they found it almost impossible to think or act one without the other. There were times when Rina truly worried what would become of the one left behind once the inevitable happened.

'I'm all right, dear,' Rina told her. 'I suppose I just have a lot on my mind.'

'Rina had a spat with our pet policeman,' Matthew said.

'Oh, Matthew, I did not.'

'You did, Rina darling. We all know that.' Bethany was indignant. 'Why else would Tim get all protective and big brotherish and hustle you away like that?'

Rina was both amused and exasperated. 'And how do you know it was Mac I'd argued with?'

'Oh, Rina.' Eliza laughed coquettishly. 'Outside of the people in this room, oh and apart from Tim, of course, there's only one person you'd get upset over and that's our policeman. We aren't entirely blind, you know.'

'Or lacking in empathy,' Matthew finished. He laid down his hand of cards. 'So why don't we give up on this pretence of a game and I'll pour us all some nice G&Ts and you can tell us what's stopping you from enjoying our family evening.'

Relieved but also reluctant, Rina laid down her cards and allowed Steven to administer alcoholic balm. Bethany's notion of Tim being big brotherish amused her; though, she admitted, sometimes he seemed like one of the elders.

'It was nothing really,' she said. 'Mac was trying to do his job and I suppose I was overstepping the mark a little.'

'Oh, but you always do that,' Bethany exclaimed. 'He doesn't usually mind.'

'And you know he'll come and say sorry just as soon as he's able to,' Eliza added. 'And eat cake and get back to plotting with you and Tim and everything will be fine again.'

'Of course he will,' Matthew reassured. 'And if he doesn't realise he's upset you, Tim will tell him your feelings were hurt and he'll come round at once. Sebastian would never let a little police formality come between you.'

Sebastian, Rina thought. Matthew was the only person who ever called Mac by his given name and it was a mark of regard, she knew, that Mac merely winced.

'Right, so now we have that settled,' Steven said, 'I believe there's a Hitchcock film on one of the cable channels. Shall we?'

Lydia stood in the Big Room staring at the dark as it crept landward across the stretch of steel-grey ocean. Pale streaks of sky broke up the inky blue and the last echoes of the day's sun touched pink at the very tips of the cloud. It would rain, she thought. Later tonight or in the early morning, drenching the garden. The thought relieved her; she knew that Edward's beloved roses needed watering and the bedding plants were crisping in the summer heat but the thought of leaving the house, even for the relative shelter of her own green space, terrified her just now. Inside, she didn't exactly feel safe, but at least less threatened and in this room, with its vertiginous view of sea and sky she could imagine, almost, that she floated above the world and its troubles.

More practically, she couldn't see the wilting flowers.

The door opened and Edward came slowly down the steps into the sunken room. He crossed to where she stood and laid his hands hesitantly on her shoulders.

'It's like being on the prow of a ship, this room,' Lydia said. 'I used to imagine that's what Paul liked so much.

That feeling of floating above and beyond it all. Nothing to see but open water and that big sky.' She sighed, suddenly sick of the sight that had fascinated her only seconds before. 'Can't we move, Edward. I can't stand this place now. It didn't save him, did it. Getting away from everything. I thought, being aboard *The Greek Girl* he should have been safe. He should have been . . .'

'I know. I know.' He hugged her, awkwardly, as though he'd almost forgotten how. 'Lydia, we knew he was in trouble. We should have forced him to tell us what was going on.'

'It isn't just him, though, is it? Those phone calls, those threats. Edward, if I knew what they wanted, they could have it but I don't. I'm scared enough to give them just about anything they want, but how can we when Paul never told us . . .'

Edward couldn't think what to say. She leaned against him, hands tight on his arms as though unable to stand unless he held her.

'We have to tell someone,' he said. 'Lydia, this is all too much for us.'

'I know. But who? Paul said there was no one he could trust and he was right, wasn't he? He tried to protect himself and they still found him.'

'Whoever *they* are. Lydia, I don't know what to do, but we have to do something. I can't stand this nothingness. This limbo land. If there's something we have to face, I'd rather do it head on, take my chances with it.'

She nodded but he could tell she was unconvinced. He couldn't tell whether that was because she was not convinced that this was the right course of action or that he truly meant what he said.

It was late. Miriam slept and for a while Mac had watched her sleeping, cherishing the sight of her long hair tumbled across his pillow and the soft rise and fall of her breasts as she slept more peacefully than Mac ever could.

In his hand he held a photocopy of the scrap of newspaper he had found at Paul's flat. He knew now that this was not some random act, some meaningless selection. Beyond that, he was still mystified.

Miriam had brought the copy of the hard drive her colleague

had taken from Paul's computer. Most of it was irrelevant stuff, so far as Mac could tell. Letters and stored emails, music downloads and the odd video from an internet site that specialised in short films. Mac had been curious enough to look at the Screening Room and found that it was mainly dedicated to showcasing new film makers, and random information gleaned from the computer disk confirmed that cinema in all its forms was another passion of Paul de Freitas.

There were also many files containing pictures by artists that Mac recognised and many more that he did not, and folders of ideas and visuals that looked to Mac as though they were rough workings for new games.

Almost everything on the drive was in the clear. He didn't even have a password on the start-up screen. But there were two folders that were protected, and it had taken Johnny the Geek, as Miriam fondly called him, quite some time to find a way in to them – even to find; hidden as they were in a partition that looked at first sight to be something the manufacturer had set up simply for BIOS files.

Mac, frankly, couldn't make head or tail of them and Miriam told him that they were in two separate programmers' languages. Unhelpfully, she couldn't read them either. Old-fashioned, she said. No one does this any more. A phone call to Johnny had confirmed that one was binary and one machine code.

'The man knew his stuff,' Johnny said. 'He talked directly to the machine.'

It would take time and probably more skill than even Johnny the Geek had to unravel that mystery but it was the title that Paul had given to one of his files that told Mac he held in his hand a photocopy of a genuine clue.

On one side of the sheet was an advert for a riding stables but on the other was a funeral announcement for a man called Payne. His first name was missing, the tear passing between the first and second name and Mac only had fragments of information about his funeral; single words and half a date, the number twenty-three. But the name of one of the hidden files Johnny had found, the programme he was told was written in binary code, was entitled *The Power of One*. The other was *Payne 23*.

Unable to sleep, even with Miriam, Mac dressed and walked slowly through the darkened streets of Frantham Old Town, the original harbour village in which his boathouse home was situated. Narrow streets, a fierce determination of the local people to keep it local and a definite lack of vehicular access meant that this little settlement possessed a distinctly different atmosphere from the Victorian town of Frantham-on-Sea, for all that it was only a ten-minute walk. At one time there had been a solid path round the headland and linking these two halves, but winter storms some twenty years before had finally washed it out and the link now was a wooden boardwalk, raised high on the cliff face, beneath which the sea surged and struggled. Mac had yet to walk it in full winter; he had a feeling that by then he might have to resort to the longer road, but often unable to sleep, he had frequently passed this way in the dark. Troubled dreams disturbed him, the death of a child he had been unable to prevent. A killer still loose because of his own, very human reaction which meant he had run to the dying child and not pursued the man who had just cut her throat.

It had taken a long time for Mac to learn to function once more in the waking world. Time, new friends, a fresh start. And now Miriam. But the nights were still bad.

Mac paused as the walkway rounded the headland and gazed out to sea. Chill air rose up from beneath his feet and he shivered, despite the fact that he'd had the foresight to don a fleece and long-sleeved shirt. Nights could be cold here even at the height of summer. Out on the horizon the sky lightened as though anticipating a dawn that was still hours away. Mac had noticed this phenomenon before but still didn't understand how it worked. He had lived by the sea for most of his life and usually the horizon darkened as it touched water.

Moving on, his feet in canvas deck shoes feeling the cold now, he rounded the headland and trotted down the steps onto the Victorian promenade. He realised that, subconsciously, he must have expected to see the woman on the beach.

She looked up as his feet crunched on shingle and then fell more softly on the sand closer to the waterline. 'Can't sleep?'

'No, too much to think about. You?'

Rina nodded, she slipped her arm through his. 'I never grow tired of looking at this,' she said. 'Fred loved the sea, you know. We always planned to settle down at the seaside, raise a family.'

Mac smiled. It was rare for Rina to talk about her beloved husband. They had been married only five years when he died and she had never, to his knowledge, settled on anyone else. 'Well, you have a family,' he said. 'Perhaps not the kind you planned.'

'But I think he would have approved.'

They stood for several minutes in companionable silence and then Rina said, 'So, what particular puzzle brought you out here? I know it wasn't bad dreams tonight, so it must have been something else.'

'And how do you know it wasn't the dreams?'

'Because you've left Miriam in bed and you don't get the dreams when she's with you. Or at least, not so terribly that you have to walk them away.'

'How?'

'Oh, Mac. I can smell her perfume on your skin.' She hugged his arm. 'Women notice these things, you know. So what's the puzzle? Two heads and all that.'

'I should be telling you it's police business.'

'And then we'd have to fall out again and neither of us want that.'

Mac told her, about the computer files and the scrap of paper folded as a bookmark and then he fished into his pocket and gave the photocopy to her, knowing for certain now that he'd hoped to see Rina tonight. Why else would he be carrying it around?

'Go home to bed,' Rina told him. 'I'll take a look in the morning, get Tim involved. I'll tell him you came waving the white flag, no flowers and chocolates required.'

A few miles away a little hatchback, dark green, pulled up outside of the house where Paul de Freitas had lived. A dark-haired woman got out and crossed the road. She had a key to the house door, let herself inside, and softly climbed the three flights of stairs to Paul's flat. The police seal caused her a moment's pause, then she broke the tape and slipped her key into the door.

She spent only a minute or so inside, going straight to the

bookshelf and using the light slanting through the window to find the volume she sought.

Then she left, tiptoeing back down the stairs, silent as she had come.

SIXTEEN

Early the next morning, Mac drove over to see DI Kendal. Abe Jackson, the MOD liaison, was not quite what Mac had expected. Recalling Kendal's joke about his sounding American, he was amused to find that Abe's father had, in fact, been born in the US. He was a cheerful soul, on the surface at least, round faced and smiling, with a shock of sandy hair growing at odd angles and a complexion that belonged to an outdoorsman, tanned and slightly reddened. He asked a lot of questions, rummaged through the evidence bags that Mac had brought from Paul's flat and then asked, frankly, what Mac and Kendal thought was going on.

Mac sensed something odd behind the question. He glanced at Kendal looking for a clue as to what.

'Abe here has never heard of anyone called Hale,' he said.

Mac absorbed that. 'So who the hell is he?' he asked.

Abe shrugged. 'Beats me,' he said. 'Complex business you seem to have gotten into. All I do know is, your Superintendent Aims believed his credentials and gave him full access.'

That sounded like Aims, Mac thought. Not that the man was stupid; just a little too ready to be overwhelmed by title for Mac's taste. 'Did anyone think to check him out?'

'Not as easy as it might sound,' Kendal pointed out. 'Apparently Aims called the Home Office but the wheels of enquiry turn slowly. It's not like you can phone someone and say, look, we have one of your spooks here, can you tell me if he's the real deal or some Walter Mitty wannabe.'

'And I'm afraid when I got involved, it seemed to just confirm this Hale's story. Aims just assumed we were part of the same team.'

Mac sat down and pulled his coffee mug towards him, then, finding it empty, pushed it hopefully in Kendal's direction. 'And I suppose you're for real,' he said.

'I can give you a number, you can check me out.'

'No, what I can do is call someone who says of course this

man is one of ours. They could be anyone; you could be anyone. You see my problem.'

'I see your problem.'

'And this Hale, no chance he could just be from another department? Some other branch of your secret society. Different set of handshakes?'

'It's possible, of course, but no. Hale is a phoney. A well-informed, well-prepared phoney but still not the real thing.'

'He's a man with resources though,' Mac said. 'And that's worrying.'

'No hits on his fingerprints?' Kendal asked hopefully.

Mac shook his head. 'CSI dusted everything that didn't move. Nothing but Paul's prints and those of his brother-and sister-in-law and a couple of unknowns. One partial on the pill packet that CSI think matches others found in the flat and so is probably the girlfriend, but they noted that they only found a half-dozen in total attributable. I have to think that the relationship was over and Paul had cleaned since she left. Unknown prints on the leather chair, that almost certainly belong to Hale, but that gets us no further.'

Kendal had taken the hint and refilled his mug. Mac sipped gratefully, lack of sleep the night before making him feel slug-gish and irritable. 'It would help, of course, if we knew why your people were involved with Paul de Freitas?'

Abe Jackson laughed. 'Perhaps it would,' he said. 'Perhaps not. But that leads me neatly on to my next point. Despite Hale's attempts to claim him, we lost a man too on that boat, so you can expect my company, Mac. On the upside, you can also expect use of our resources.'

'And on the downside?'

'You mean, other than having me around?' Abe laughed at his own joke. 'On the downside, while we would never presume to tell you what not to investigate and while, obviously, it would look really bad on the publicity front if you didn't throw all you could in terms of manpower into investigating this murder, be warned. There are boundaries here which you will not cross.'

'Boundaries?' Kendal was irritated.

'Two men are dead, Inspector Kendal, and we have reason to believe that they are dead because of work Paul was doing for us. Work which, shall we say, other parties would like to

have got their hands on. By all means, investigate. Be seen
to be doing all you'd usually be doing, but be aware, and in
this your superiors will back me all the way, this is our game
and you will play it by our rules. If I say back off, you don't
argue, you just ask me how far.'

SEVENTEEN

Lydia had left the answerphone on since the day of Paul's death. There had been calls to offer condolence, some of which she had returned and many of which she had left in the capable – nay, eager – hands of Margaret Simms. Calls from business associates, shocked by the news or reluctantly posing practical problems, Edward had dealt with and then set someone from the factory on to the task of fielding such enquiries. Then there were calls from journalists, which she had ignored, and from the police which she had reluctantly responded to only if they were repeated often enough to become insistent.

They had kept the gates closed and visitors who knew them well had either used the cliff path or parked at the next-door farm and walked back across the field and then through the small gate at the rear, kept locked unless they phoned in advance. Lydia was relieved that so far no one had thought to come across the lawn from the cliff but she figured it was just a matter of time.

She wanted to leave, now before things got worse. 'How worse?' Edward had queried and she wasn't sure what to say. 'What if the journalists find the back way in? What if *they* come?' That mysterious 'they' that had taken Paul's life. She was sure she had seen someone watching the house.

Most frightening though, were the phone calls that left no message. She wasn't sure why these disturbed her so much more than those which had previously threatened; perhaps the length of time the caller waited before hanging up. The utter silence. The feeling that they were waiting for her to lose her nerve and grab the phone, yell at whoever was on the other end, and in doing so demonstrate that they were in control and not Lydia, not Edward.

Twice she had disconnected it altogether arguing that anyone they actually wanted to talk to could reach them by mobile. Twice, she had found the line plugged back in, though both Edward and Margaret denied having done so.

Lydia wondered if she was going slowly mad.

The phone rang again as she was passing through the hall. A journalist this time, though she had missed the start of the message and did not know where from. He expressed condolence and the wish for an interview or comments. He rang off just as she started up the stairs.

The phone rang again and Lydia glared at it, in half a mind to just flip it off the hook and leave it there. The answerphone delivered its usual denial that anyone was home and then Lydia froze. The voice leaving the message was Paul's. Unmistakeably Paul's.

Lydia screamed and didn't stop screaming until Edward had half carried her into the Big Room and thrust a glass of brandy into her shaking hands.

'Drink,' he said. 'Lydia, what the hell?'

She turned on him, fierce now. 'Listen to the message. Just go and listen to the damned message.'

Reluctantly, Edward returned to the hall. He paused in the doorway, looking back at his wife and she rose, came to join him, took his hand. He keyed the machine to play.

'Oh my God.'

Paul's voice, tinny and unclear, as though this was a re-recording of a poor recording, but unmistakeable. Equally unmistakeable was that he was terrified.

'Ian?' Paul called out. 'What the hell is going on?' Then the voice was drowned out by an explosion of sound that even Lydia could recognise was a gunshot. 'What? Oh no, no!' A second shot and then silence, then the sound of a man breathing hard, gasping as though in pain. Lydia lashed out, sending the machine spinning from the telephone table and across the parquet floor of the hall.

'We've got to get out of here. Now. Edward, we've got to go.' Her voice cracked, verging on hysteria. Her husband didn't argue. Moments later, in a locked car, willing the gates to open faster than they were ever designed to do, they were fleeing their home.

EIGHTEEN

'Rina, I'm so sorry. I didn't know where else to go. We just drove here.'

It had taken a while to coax from the de Freitas's exactly what had terrified them so much and longer spent trying to convince them that they should call the police; Mac in particular.

'We can't.' Edward was as adamant as his wife. 'Rina, one of the last things Paul said was that he no longer knew who to trust. That even the authorities were unreliable. He said he was worried, that he felt he was in danger and he was right, wasn't he?'

'Did he say why he felt so threatened?'

Edward shook his head. 'He'd taken on some outside work, some special project, that's all I know. It was something he did from time to time, development work for other companies. It increased our turnover and more important, added to our reputation.'

'But always before, he'd told us what he was doing,' Lydia objected. 'Rina, I'm so scared. Before Paul died we were getting these phone calls, threatening calls, saying Paul was going to die if he didn't deliver. Deliver what, I don't know and he wouldn't tell us. Then afterward, just silence. The phone would ring and then there was nothing. Then this!' She got up, suddenly. 'We shouldn't have come here. What if they come after us here? Oh Rina I'm so . . .'

'Sit down,' Rina said firmly. 'Drink your tea. We've dealt with worse, believe me. Now. What we need to do is find you a safe place to lie low for a while and I think I know just the spot.'

'We came away with nothing,' Edward said. 'We can't go to a hotel. We can't . . .'

'That can be sorted,' Rina told him stoutly. 'Tim and I will go and fetch you some things and bring them back here. Then we'll need some camping equipment and spare blankets and the like. I'm not sure the power is connected at the place I have in mind, but I believe it has its own water supply and . . .'

'I know where we can borrow a generator,' Tim added. 'You're thinking about the farm, aren't you, Rina?'

She nodded. 'Middle of nowhere, I'm afraid, but all the better for that,' she told the de Freitas's. 'And the next thing is to organise some security. If we're not trusting the regular authorities then we must fall back on our own resources.'

'Fitch?' Tim said.

'Fitch,' Rina agreed.

They left Lydia and Edward to the tender ministrations of the rest of the family. The Montmorency twins could be relied upon to keep up the supplies of tea and cake and the Peters sisters were already playing the piano by the time Rina and Tim left.

'You sure they'll be all right,' Tim asked doubtfully. 'Our lot can be a bit, well, full on.'

Rina nodded. 'But can you think of anything more likely to take their minds off current troubles,' she said. 'An afternoon being serenaded by Eliza and Bethany and force-fed tea and sympathy by Steven and Matthew will put everything back into perspective, won't it.'

Tim growled something about them being glad to escape at the end of it. 'We should tell Mac,' he added.

'And we will, but not yet. If Lydia and Edward think we've involved the police they might well do something silly. At the moment, we can control the situation. We will know where they are and that they're safe. Neither of them knows Mac like we do; they have absolutely no reason to trust him.'

It was a mark of their panic that the de Freitas's had not shut the gate after leaving. Neither, Rina found, had they secured the door.

The gate she could just about understand, but as the door was fitted with a Yale lock, all they had to do was to slam it behind them. It seemed to Rina unlikely that they would neglect such a simple and automatic action.

'I don't think we're the first to get here, Tim. Keep your eyes open just in case.'

Tim glanced warily around. The house was silent and it felt empty and already abandoned.

'They said the message came through on the hall phone,' he queried. 'Rina, you've been here before. Where would that be?'

She pointed to a small table at the foot of the stairs. 'There,' she said. 'Next to the phone point. Lydia said she knocked it off, in which case I'd expect to see it on the floor, wouldn't you?'

'I think we might have noticed that,' Tim said. He knelt down and picked a sliver of plastic from the floor. 'A green phone, was it?'

'Yes, sort of olivy green. One of those digital answerphone things.'

Tim showed her the tiny splinter he had found. 'I suggest we get what we came for and leave,' he said. 'Just in case our visitors come back. And before you suggest it, no, I don't think it would be quicker if we split up. I've watched too many horror films to fall for that one.'

Rina chuckled but he could hear that she too was shaken. They found Lydia's bag on the kitchen table where she had said it would be. Rina glanced inside. Phone, purse, make-up. Assorted till receipts and tissues. If it had been searched Rina didn't think she would be able to tell. Upstairs they packed clothes enough to last about a week, hoping that by that time the situation would either have been resolved or would have been handed on to someone else. 'It feels strange, going through someone else's drawers,' Tim said. 'I'd hate to think of someone doing this for me.'

Rina cast him a sideways glance.

'And not just because mine are always such a mess,' he retorted. 'I have a lot more to store than Edward de Freitas and a lot less room in which to do it.'

'Yes, he is a little lacking in the magical props department,' Rina agreed. 'To say nothing of the odd collection of militaria and the vast library you manage to cram on to those poor shelves.'

Rina glanced around. 'I think we have everything,' she said. 'I'd quite like to leave now, Tim, if you don't mind.'

Tim held up a hand signalling quiet. Rina opened her mouth to speak and then thought better of it. 'Did you hear that?' he whispered. 'It sounded like a door opening.'

'Mrs Simms?' Rina wondered.

'Lydia said she wasn't in today.'

Hefting the bags and hoping they wouldn't have to run with them, they crept to the top of the stairs and Tim risked a quick glance down. He saw nothing but the sound of someone walking across the parquet flooring of the hall was unmistakeable. Tim wished he'd had the foresight to park the car elsewhere. Wished even harder as he heard the footsteps pause and, risking another quick glance down the stairs, saw a shadow cast on the polished floor and knew that the intruder would have seen it on the drive.

He looked back at Rina, she had lifted the holdall into her arms, ready to make a run for it if that's what they had to do. Tim reached into his pocket and took out the keys to his car. Cursing softly, he heard the figure in the hall start to move again, more cautiously this time but coming towards the stairs.

Just hope he's on his own, Tim thought. He moved back to stand beside Rina, trying to keep as much of the stairway in his sight as he could without being seen. Hoped Rina would be as good at catching on and taking his lead as Tim was in picking up hers. He waited, ears straining, breathing through his mouth to extend his hearing even by the smallest degree, lifted the suitcase to waist height and, as the figure of a man came into view, threw it with all the force he could muster directly at him. With a muffled cry the figure tumbled back down the stairs and Tim followed, Rina on his heels.

Encumbered by the holdall she took action, dropped the bag down over the banister and into the entrance hall. It landed with a dull splat upon the wooden floor. Then she hurtled after Tim.

The man had begun to rise as Tim leapt from the last steps. He seized the only weapon that came to hand; the little table that had once supported the phone. Tim grabbed it by the legs and as the man began to rise, Tim swung it with full force at his head. As the man went down for a second time they heard a shout from the back of the house.

Tim swore, grabbed the suitcase and followed Rina who had retrieved the holdall and was now storming through the door.

Pressing the key fob, Tim unlocked the car and Rina bundled the holdall inside, throwing herself after it and down on to the back seat. Tim threw the case into the car and then himself, locked the doors and shoved the key into the ignition. He swung the car about in a swirl of gravel, praying that the men in the house had no means of closing the gates before he could reach them.

'Are you all right?'

'Will be if you keep your foot down,' Rina urged from the back seat.

'Shit! Keep your head low, Rina.' Tim, glancing in the mirror, could see the gun aimed directly at his rear screen. He swerved wildly, jinking as well as it is possible to jink in an ageing estate car, heard the shot but not the expected shattering of glass. Clipping the wing mirror as he practically threw the vehicle through the gate he turned sharp right, away from the house. Away from Frantham.

He was laughing by the time Rina sat up, straightened herself out and sedately fastened her seatbelt.

'Funny is it?'

'Oh, don't mind me. Just a hissy fit. I'm getting used to facing down men with guns. It seems to have happened quite a bit this year. And me, the only member of my blessed family that refused to go in the army!'

'Where are we going?' Rina asked.

'I thought I'd take a bit of a detour. Get back on to the Honiton Road as fast as I can and take the back way back home. I'm hoping they didn't get too good a look at our license plate.'

'Did you get a good look at *them*?'

Tim shuddered. 'At the gun, yes. At the man holding it, I'm not too sure. I'll be in need of Matthew's tender ministrations I think before I can get it clear in my head.' He sobered, the full realisation of the situation coming home to him as the adrenaline receded. 'This is serious, Rina,' Tim said. 'Much more than we can handle on our own.'

NINETEEN

B y the time they reached Frantham, Tim had called in reinforcements. It would take their friend, Fitch, a few hours to get to them from Manchester, but he sounded happy to be summoned. Tim said they'd brief him properly when he arrived.

'Good to have willing friends,' he said. The Duggans had sent their love, and Joy announced her intention to visit once the crisis was over, which had cheered Tim up no end. Joy Duggan, now just turned twenty years old, had come into their lives rather precipitously earlier that year when her brother had been murdered and she had been kidnapped. Tim, while horribly aware that she was twelve years his junior, really had quite a thing for her, as Bethany would have said, and, from what Rina had seen, the feelings were reciprocated. And, after all, Rina thought as she watched Tim's expression soften at the thought of Joy, the one thing stopping them from taking things further was easily fixed by waiting a year or two.

Fitch, originally an employee of Joy's father, was, as a result of what had happened that Spring, now more a member of the family and Rina knew the Duggans felt they owed herself and Tim a great debt. She was profoundly glad to be able to call on that now.

'We shouldn't tell Lydia and Edward,' Rina said. 'That we've been shot at, I mean.'

'Lucky he missed then,' Tim said. 'But Rina, as soon as our guests are safe, we have to tell Mac what happened at the house. Someone else might get in their way and not be so lucky. As it is, I think you'll be the one waving the white flag this time. And I think you should have those flowers and chocolates ready in reserve.'

An hour later and with basic equipment quickly gathered, the de Freitas's were ready to leave. Rina had revised her earlier plans and they would now be taken to the old farm she had thought of, just until Fitch could get to them. He would collect them from there and take them North, the Duggans having far more resources of the security kind at their disposal than Rina could possible muster. And, Rina figured, given the late Jimmy Duggan's various criminal contacts and connections – many of which, Rina admitted, she'd still rather not know about – it was likely that they might be able to get a handle on what was going on.

'Can't we just stay here?' Lydia had asked, nervous of moving from a place of safety.

Rina exchanged a glance with Tim. 'We think someone was watching when we left the house,' she said, resorting to a half-truth. 'Just in case they trace the car, I'd like to get you away from here.'

Lydia stared at her, then nodded. 'I'm scared, Rina. I thought I could handle just about anything. I've always been the strong one, the organised one. Kept things anchored while Edward did his thing, you know? But I can't handle this.'

'You can,' Rina told her. 'You are. Our friend will come and get you and take you somewhere safe and we'll sort things out at this end.'

'But what if they come after you? Rina, I just can't believe I've been so thoughtless as to involve you and the rest of them. What if . . .'

Rina patted her arm. 'We'll be fine,' she said. 'Let's just get you away, shall we?'

They took the de Freitas's out the back way, into a narrow street where Tim regularly parked the car. It was a dead end, used mainly by local residents, so strange cars stood out as did anyone hanging about. Matthew did a quick reconnaissance, walking round the block and coming back in the front door, while Steven watched from the upstairs window. Their bags already in the vehicle, it remained only for Lydia and Edward to join them. A last check and Tim hustled them inside. They ducked down in the back, plaid blankets Tim kept in the car pulled over their heads.

'I'll have to go straight on to work,' Tim told Rina. 'I'll give you a call about eight thirty, after my first set. Meantime, you get on to Mac, OK?'

Rina nodded. 'Now go, and Tim, take care.'

TWENTY

R ina waited half an hour before she called Mac. Half an hour of pacing and fretting and looking anxiously out of the window for cars that might suddenly have moved or strangers that showed too much interest in Peverill Lodge.

Mac wasn't there, and Sergeant Baker, curious as to what the redoubtable Mrs Martin wanted, didn't know when he'd be back.

'No, thank you,' Rina told him. 'I don't think you can help. Will you just ask him to give me a ring?'

She stood in the hall, undecided. Then tried Mac's mobile only to be diverted on to his voicemail.

'Oh, for goodness sake.' She gave up and instead marched into the kitchen and, for want of anything else to do, filled the kettle and set it on the range.

'You won't help anything by storming around like some unhappy rhino, Rina dear,' Bethany told her from the doorway. 'Not that you are anything like a rhino, of course, you're far too slim and elegant for that.'

'But they do talk about a crash of rhino, don't they?' Eliza attempted to come to her sister's rescue. 'And you are crashing rather.'

Rina turned, exasperated, harsh words rising to her lips. She swallowed them down; the sight of the Peters sisters, pretty, still artfully blonde, still, Rina thought, children despite their now advancing years, doused her anger.

'I've always thought of Rina more as a secretary bird,' Matthew said, wandering in. 'All elegance and jaunty feathers and long neck but with a sharp beak at the ready to impale her prey.'

Rina, who in turn had always thought of Matthew as a man-sized saluki, couldn't help but laugh. 'I'm not sure I like your version of me any better,' she said. 'But you're right, this really won't help anyone. Better to be doing.'

She patted Matthew affectionately on the arm and sailed out of the kitchen, thinking about the photocopy Mac had

given her. That was a puzzle to solve and, hopefully, something to take her mind off the worry. She knew Tim had been
as shaken as she had by the gunshot and was as concerned
as Rina that the gunman would have found out who and where
they were. He'd be alert and careful.

Perhaps she should have confided in Sergeant Baker.

Shaking her head and forcibly pushing her anxiety aside,
Rina went into her little room and closed the door.

'What is this place?' Lydia asked as they got out of the car
in front of the old farmhouse. The drive was even more over-
grown than Tim remembered it, nettles and brambles reaching
out across the gap, hawthorn scraping the sides of the car.
The privet hedge that surrounded the farmyard itself was a
good foot higher, twined through with bindweed and
belladonna. Birds sang, but beyond that there was utter silence.

Two of the farmhouse windows had been boarded up since
Tim had last been there and the front door had gained a
padlock; Tim supposed the police had affixed that when the
house was still considered a crime scene.

'Who owns this place?'

'I actually have no idea,' Tim said. 'But no one's lived here
in years. You won't be here for long and you saw how long
the drive was. We can't be seen from the road.'

'It still looks . . . I don't know. Creepy. How did you know
about this place?'

Tim was rummaging in the boot of the car, sorting through
his tool kit, trying to find something to break the padlock off
the door. He wondered what to tell Lydia in response to her
question. He'd been puzzling about this since they left Peverill
Lodge and now decided something close to the truth would
have to do. A large screwdriver found to attack the door, he
emerged from behind the car. 'Just before you came to live
in Frantham, there was a kidnapping, just a few miles away.
Two little girls. They were held here for a while. Our friend
Fitch helped to find them.'

'Oh, my God,' Lydia said. 'I read about that in the newspaper. Wasn't there a siege or something?'

Tim nodded. He slid the blade of the screwdriver behind
the door and pulled, wrenching the screws out of the door
frame with a splintering crack.

He held the door open. 'Shall we? Don't worry, it's only for a few hours. Fitch has somewhere far more comfortable in mind.'

Reluctantly, they followed Tim in. 'Kitchen on the left, living room on the right. There's a toilet through the back there and I can soon get the water back on.' He stood, uncertain, at the foot of the stairs, 'Look. I know it's kind of, well, primitive . . .'

'Do we have to stay here?'

Edward took his wife's hand. 'Think of it as camping out,' he said. 'We've not done that since before we got married.'

Looking at him, Tim was surprised to find that Edward actually looked better than he had since he'd arrived at Peverill Lodge. Some of the colour had returned to his cheeks and he had a look of purposefulness in his eyes.

'Camping out?' Lydia stared at him in disbelief, then to Tim's relief she laughed out loud. 'Oh, lord; you are such an idiot sometimes.' She kissed him gently on the cheek and Tim retreated to fetch their gear from the car. Something about that little kiss was so tender and so intimate he could not have felt more like a voyeur if he'd surprised them making love. He took his time taking the suitcases and the supplies from the car. As Edward came out to help, Tim's phone rang. It was Fitch, with an ETA. Tim handed the phone to Edward so that he could speak with their incipient rescuer and by the time he gave the mobile back to Tim, he was looking happier and more confident.

'I'm going to have to be off soon,' Tim said as they carried bags and supplies back into the house. 'I've got to get to work and I want to take the long way round.'

'We'll be fine,' Lydia told him. 'Don't worry. And we really are grateful, you know.' She smiled, wryly. 'It's all a bit surreal, isn't it? Paul would have used this as a scenario for a game.'

She glanced anxiously at her husband, suddenly aware that she might have said the wrong thing. Edward slipped an arm around her shoulder.

'Well,' he said softly. 'I think we shall have to do it for him, won't we?'

Rina was trying to work out where the clipping might have come from. Not having the actual article was a nuisance;

The Frantham Gazette, a little pamphlet of a thing imparting
parish news had quite a distinctive pinkish look and the *Echo*,
the local free paper, purveyor of coastal news and advertising
for local business had a buff hue, like most of the bigger
locals, for whom that was a little offshoot.

She dragged out various examples from the recycling bin,
collecting a mug of tea on the way through the kitchen and
then began the task of comparing typefaces. Her worry was
this advert came from one of the national papers and therefore might be much more difficult to place but a quick flick
through of the personal ads, and more precisely the funeral
announcements, convinced her that she was looking at a torn
up bit of the *Echo*. Same typeface, same typical layout, so far
as she could tell, the real giveaway being the double black
line that surrounded all funerary announcements.

Returning to the kitchen with her discards and helping
herself to more tea, Rina rummaged in the recycling for any
other copies of the *Echo*; came up with three.

'Births, marriages and deaths,' she said as she passed a
mystified Steven in the hall.

She was familiar with the layout of these columns in the
Echo, but she had only ever scanned them before, not analysed
the layout in any depth. Death announcements, as was usual,
were in the later columns, with funeral information always on
the right hand page and in the column closest to the edge.
They all had this double black line, though they varied in size
and some had other emblems of death and mourning. Ivy leaves
and funeral urns seemed popular, she noted. She wondered, in
a spirit of mischief, if she could arrange to have dancing skele-
tons on hers and then abandoned the idea on the grounds that
she wouldn't be there to share the joke.

The announcement for *Payne 23* seemed to have come from
the top of the column, the margins still running along the
right-hand edge and the top corner still intact. She compared
it to the way others were laid out.

'So your last name was Payne. Obvious enough and the line
below must have been your year of birth and death.' Stopped
in her tracks by the obvious nonsense of that, Rina looked
again at the columns. 'But no, that definitely can't be right,
can it. If you'd been born in 1923 then that would be the date
left on the page when this piece was torn off. The left-hand

date, not the right hand . . . and as we haven't got to 2023 yet, well . . . now that really doesn't make sense.

'And if it had been a funeral date, say, September the twenty-third, well, no. That doesn't work either, does it?'

She scanned the pages for clues, but found nothing at first. A second newspaper made her wonder if this was part of a phone number. Beneath the name of one Betsy Marriot, for example, was the invitation for her friends and relatives to phone should they need further information and the number was given. But, surely, you wouldn't just put a number without an advisory message and it was clear from the placement of the number 23, immediately beneath the PA of Payne, that no additional message had been present.

What was going on?

Rina scanned the other copies of the *Frantham Echo* for any further clue and found it, tucked at the bottom of a column from three weeks before.

'Arthur Payne,' she read, 'b. June 1923. To give all friends and family the chance to attend, the funeral of Uncle Arthur has been delayed. Please call Paul for further details.'

The hall phone rang and Rina heard Bethany answer it. 'Hello, Peverill Lodge. Oh Rina, dear, it's for you.'

Mac, Rina thought. She took the receiver from Bethany and retreated once more to her room. 'Yes, Mac, something is very wrong and I need to speak with you properly. Now. And I've solved the puzzle, or rather I've found another piece of it. *Payne 23*. I've found another death announcement for the poor man.'

Fitch had called them to say he was five minutes away. To be ready to leave. Lydia and Edward stood in the hallway, conscious of the dark stairs behind them, of the dramatic events that had taken place here and which now seemed to poison the atmosphere of the place, despite its peaceful, tranquil surroundings.

They would be glad to leave.

The car headlights coming up the drive caused a feeling of panic which Lydia fought to control. What if this wasn't the man Rina had sent for them? What if it was . . . *them*?

Lights were doused. The bulky man who eased himself from the driver's seat matched the description they had been given. The surprise was the smaller, slighter figure that slipped from the passenger side.

'Hello,' the girl said, fair hair gleaming in the headlights. 'I'm Joy Duggan. Mum thought we ought to balance things up a bit, you know, all this macho stuff going on? This is Fitch. Fitch, say hello to the nice people.'

Fitch came forward, hand extended. 'Don't mind her,' he said. 'She has one little adventure and thinks she's Lara Croft or something.' He shook Edward's hand and then Lydia's. 'I suggest we get a move on,' he said. 'Rina doesn't think we should hang around down south longer than we have to.'

He put their suitcases in the car, assured them that it was fine to leave everything else behind. Tim would take care of that later. Got Lydia and Edward settled in the back of the Range Rover. It wasn't easy to turn the large vehicle in the small space in front of the house, but Fitch made it look casually simple. Within minutes of their arrival, they were heading back down the long drive, brambles and hawthorn scraping at the windows and the paintwork and then back out on to the little road and heading for the motorway.

'We thought the four-by-four would be best,' Fitch told them. 'The rear windows are smoked glass, gives you a bit more privacy. Bridie, Mrs Duggan, she's getting one of the guest rooms ready and you'll be welcome for as long as you need.'

'This is really kind,' Lydia said.

'Oh, Mum will love having you. She's been wanting to do something to say thanks to Rina for ages. Rina isn't the easiest person to pay back favours to, you know.'

'You've known her for long?'

'Only since spring. My brother was murdered. Rina helped out.' She hesitated for a moment and then asked, 'Is Tim all right. Did he, um, say anything?'

'What she wants to know,' Fitch said, 'is did Tim give you any message for her. I mean any additional messages to the ones he texts to her three or four times a day or what they manage to fit in on those hour-long phone calls. Not to mention the emails and . . .'

Joy giggled, embarrassed but pleased.

'He didn't know you were coming, remember,' Fitch said. 'So he's not likely to have left you a love note is he? Mind if I put some music on? And if it's all right with everyone, we'll stop for coffee once were safely on the M5, I thought the services just the other side of Bristol. Then we'll do the rest in one if that's all right. Sooner we get home, the better I will feel.'

'We should let Rina know we're all right,' Lydia said.

'Yes, do that,' Fitch agreed.

'Use your phone,' Edward told her. 'My battery's about flat.'

Lydia rummaged in her bag, found her mobile, and switched it on for the first time since Rina had fetched her bag from the house. She dialled Rina's number to tell her they were safe with Fitch and on their way, not realising that the satnav transmitter in her phone, activated the moment she switched it on, now made them anything but.

Mac, unable to reply to Rina's summons immediately, had arrived some twenty minutes after Lydia called. He took one look at her face and demanded to know what she'd been up to.

'You are not going to be pleased with me,' she said. 'But, please, Mac, take a deep breath and keep your mouth shut until I tell you everything.'

Mac seethed as she filled him in. Telling him about the de Freitas's suddenly turning up on her doorstep, that she and Tim had gone to collect their things and the events at the house.

'Someone shot at you? Rina, why the hell didn't you call me? Dial nine, nine, nine? For God's sake, woman, if there are people wandering around the countryside with guns . . .'

'There are,' Rina told him coldly. 'Regularly people wandering around the countryside carrying weapons. We usually call them farmers. But no, I suppose you're right and I'm sorry, but if Lydia and Edward thought we were involving the authorities, they'd have run further than Peverill Lodge and who knows what would have happened to them.'

'Instead of which they are?'

'With Fitch, on their way to Manchester to stay with the Duggans.'

She watched as Mac absorbed this, understanding that he may not be quite as impressed as Rina had hoped. The Duggan family were, of course, not quite on his side of the law and order divide. 'Bridie Duggan will look after them. I can't see many people trying to get into their place; she's got it done up like Fort Knox.'

'I still need to talk to them,' Mac said sternly.

'And I'm sure she'll make an exception in your case and let you in. Mac, I didn't know what else to do and I still think it was the best course of action.'

Mac relented. 'I suppose it's not a bad option,' he conceded. 'But, Rina, we could have protected them, you know. That is kind of what the police are for.'

'And Lydia was convinced that even the police couldn't be trusted, Mac. She doesn't know you so how can she be sure you aren't part of what Paul warned them about?'

'And what did Paul warn them about?'

'Well,' she admitted. 'I'm not really sure. But Paul told them no one could be trusted. No one in authority. He was sure he was in danger and, well, he was, wasn't he? Mac, I don't know what was going on any more than you do and I don't think Lydia and Edward have a clue either. They just know he was threatened, that he's dead, that they are terrified.'

Mac considered. 'And the phone was gone when you got there?'

'Yes. Tim found a fragment of plastic on the floor. Lydia said she knocked it off the table and it skidded across the floor, but it was definitely gone. It was one of those digital things, no tape to take out, so I suppose they'd have to have taken the whole thing.'

'So we've no evidence that the message was left.'

'Why would they lie? Mac, I've seen scared people before and Lydia was terrified. Edward not much better. They said it was Paul's voice. That they heard him call out to someone called Ian and that there were two shots. They are both convinced that the second shot killed Paul.'

'Why would anyone tape a killing?'

'Evidence?' Rina suggested. 'Proof that they'd done the job?'

Mac shook his head. 'If they needed proof then a photograph would have worked better I'd have thought.' He frowned. 'Most mobile phones have cameras these days. Most can record sound as well. I suppose . . .'

'Mac, even if the tape was made up afterwards and created just to scare the pants off Paul's family, well, you can say it did the job.'

'Which was? Oh, yes, put the fear of god into them, certainly, but to what purpose? To get them out of the house?' Mac frowned. 'I don't think Lydia has been out of the house since Paul was killed, but to be frank, Rina, I don't think that would have kept Paul's killers away. They attacked him on his boat, what's to stop them attacking the de Freitas's in the house? The closest farm is half a mile away. No one would have heard or seen anything.'

'Scare tactics then.'

'And what do most scared people do? What do most sensible people do when they need help? I mean, when they don't have a Rina Martin available.'

'Go to the police, I suppose,' Rina said. 'Confide their problems to the authorities.' She stared hard at Mac, the ramifications dawning. 'They would tell the authorities all they knew and ask for protection.'

'Exactly what Paul warned them not to do.'

'Which means,' Rina said slowly, 'that someone on the side of the angels definitely isn't. You have a mole, Mac. Someone who should be trusted, definitely cannot be.'

Mac thought about Hale and Abe Jackson and the way Aims had been taken in. By one, by both, so far as Mac was concerned, the jury was still out.

'Rina, I'm going to hate myself for this but . . .'

'You've got a job for me.'

'I'm going to have to go and organise a team to get up to the de Freitas's house. Rina, Tim has relatives with military connections, doesn't he?'

'Yes, and his Uncle Charles was part of the Diplomatic Protection Group until he retired. He's still got the contacts. Why?'

'I've got a couple of names I'd like him to check out. Rina, this is so unofficial as not to be happening, you know that, but there are things I need to know and I think I'm getting to be as paranoid as Paul de Freitas.'

'More so, I hope. Look what happened to him.'

He wrote down what scant details he had concerning the mysterious Hale and Abe Jackson. 'Write small, just in case

I have to eat the evidence,' Rina told him mischievously. 'Tim said he'd call in his break, so I'll ask him then. I think we should get moving on this as soon as possible.'

Mac nodded. 'Rina, lock the doors, let me know when Fitch and co. are safe. I'll get a patrol car to sweep by but I think that's probably the best I can arrange tonight.'

'Mac, we'll be fine,' she reassured him. 'Chances are, no one has connected us to the de Freitas's.'

'I hope you're right,' Mac said.

Tim watched from the wings of the small stage as the singer finished her set. Lucy had a great voice and the management recognised that they were lucky to have hung on to her this long. She was booked to the end of the season but then off to pastures new having acquired a significant supporting role in a West End musical. The Palisades was an art deco hotel that the new owners had restored with loving attention to detail. The small stage even had its own orchestra pit though at present it was occupied only by the grand piano that was used to accompany Lucy's first set. Later in the evening the action became more intimate, shifting to the raised platform at the other end of the grand dining room on which the five-piece band set up. Tim's own act was divided into two elements. The first set stage based and the second close-up magic performed table to table.

He loved the little stage with the miniature orchestra pit and heavy velvet curtains. There had been photographs taken of the original and Lilly, the wife of the new owner, had gone to great lengths to have everything put back just as it was. What Tim loved most was the new idea he had put forward for its use and which Lilly and husband Blake had embraced with an enthusiasm that had taken him by surprise. The stage set-up lent itself perfectly to the reconstructions of some poten-tially impressive illusions, Pepper's Ghost being just one. Mentally, Tim had already positioned the mirrors, lights and plate glass and was meeting with an engineer next week to look at the best ways of fixing everything from the point of view of modern health and safety regulations. If all went well, Christmas would see the launch of a Palisades extravaganza.

He kissed the pretty singer as she came off the stage and walked back with her to her dressing room, listening to her latest news. She'd just got the rehearsal schedule for her new role and couldn't wait for it all to start.

'How's the illusion going?'

Tim smiled, enthusiasm lighting his face. 'I got the model a couple of days ago,' he said. 'I meant to bring it up tonight but events kind of took over.'

'You were nearly late, we were getting worried.'

'I've got the set-up clear now. It's going to look amazing. I just need to meet with the engineer and get the final positions worked out. Then get someone to write a narrative so we can hang everything together.'

He glanced at his watch. Ten minutes until his next set. Leaving Lucy to change for her next performance, he slipped along to the office to use the phone.

'Got to be quick, Rina. Any news?'

'Lydia and Edward are with Fitch. Mac has been over and we've exchanged stories. And yes, he was mad, but not too angry, I don't think. And he wants you to do something for him.' She gave Tim the names and the message.

'Will do. Look, I'm likely to be a bit late back. Blake has some drawings to show me and we've a few things to discuss about the Christmas performance so don't worry. Better go.'

He glanced curiously at the names he had written down, then tucked them in a pocket he didn't use in his act and made his way back to the grand dining room, shifting focus from men with guns to diners eager to try and guess how his tricks were done.

TWENTY-ONE

I t was ten o'clock by the time Mac had a full team assembled at the de Freitas' house. He had tried to keep things as low key as possible, but knew that the lights would attract a lot of attention, the position of the house just back from the road and perched high on the cliff making it difficult to be discreet.

DI Kendal joined him just as the CSI team arrived. 'Who's getting charged the overtime on this?' Kendal wondered.

'Maybe we should send the bill to the MOD,' Mac suggested. 'After all, they are supposed to be giving us extra resources. Speaking of which, our friend Abe Jackson . . .'

'Didn't answer his phone. I left him a voicemail. What do you make of him, Mac?'

'Let's just say I'm reserving opinion on a lot of things,' Mac said. 'Jackson included.'

They stood in the doorway, watching the CSIs in white overalls move carefully across the hall. Mac could see the broken table which Tim had used to attack the man who had been blocking their way out. He could see the telephone point at the foot of the stairs, but definitely no phone.

'Let's go and sit in the car,' he suggested, 'and I'll fill you in. Then we can decide what we'll tell Jackson when he gets here.'

Kendal was curious. 'You mean our cooperation won't be full and frank?' he joked. 'My car, then. I took the time to make coffee and Fliss packed some sandwiches. I've a feeling we're going to be here for a while.'

'Fliss? Should I be congratulating you?'

'Unfortunately, no. Unlike certain people I could mention, I'm still, shall we say, between relationships. Fliss is my big sister. She and her kids come down for a few weeks most summers, take over my house, have themselves a cheap holiday.'

It struck Mac just how little he knew about his colleague. Kendal listened as Mac told him about the phone call the de

Freitas's had received, their subsequent flight and Rina's adventure. CSIs busied themselves near the gate, torches in hand, minutely examining the brickwork.

'And the phone has disappeared,' Kendal mused. 'That sort of implies that the message was purely for Edward and Lydia. Maybe there was something that Paul's killers didn't want anyone else to hear?'

'Then why risk it being recorded?'

'Seems they covered that risk pretty quickly. So our second man was called Ian.'

'Or Paul knew him as Ian.' Mac stretched uncomfortably. Tired now and, frankly, bored, wishing he could just leave the forensic team to do their work and get home to bed. Or that, at the minimum, Miriam was among them. A couple of nights before, she'd have been on call as it was, but tonight she'd gone out with her sister and Mac didn't yet know if she'd go home or come back to the boathouse.

A call from one of the white overalls fetched them out of the car and over to the gate. They had found the bullet, lodged in the brickwork at what would have been the top of Tim's car. Battered and distorted from the impact, Mac would not have liked to guess at the calibre, but the sight of it horrified him as it was suddenly brought home just how close his friends had come to disaster.

'We've got company,' Kendal said. 'Mr Jackson himself.'

'We just tell him there was a report of shots being fired,' Mac said. 'And the de Freitas's are gone, we don't know where.'

Kendal's eyes narrowed and for a moment Mac thought he was going to argue. He could not have blamed him if he was. 'Dave, I might not have told you any of this,' Mac said. 'Let's pretend I'm withholding information from you as well.'

Kendal seemed to make up his mind. He nodded. 'We'll keep it vague for now,' he agreed. 'Our old friend the anonymous caller?'

'Won't stand up to scrutiny but will do for now. You'll have to be the one that got it though. We close at six in Frantham. The anonymous caller would be wasting his breath.'

Kendal laughed, then nodded agreement. Abe Jackson, was out of his car now and headed their way.

TWENTY-TWO

As planned they had stopped at the services on the M5, close to Avonmouth. Fitch leaned against the Range Rover sipping his coffee and waiting for the others to come back from the toilets. Something nagged at the back of his brain, but he couldn't place what it was. It manifested as a feeling of vague unease, but he'd had this feeling before and it had never let him down. It was different from the anticipation and tension felt before combat. Different again from the kind of anxiety felt when you knew what the actual risks might be or the kind of stage fright or performance anxiety he had always experienced in his days working the door for Joy's father in one or other of his nightclubs; knowing he was on show, a prize exhibit, there to stop trouble before it started just by the force of his presence. And Fitch was a big man, a powerful man and right now a very twitchy man.

Relieved, he saw the three of them coming back, Joy chatting easily to Lydia, looking for all the world as though the two had been friends for years. Joy was like that, Fitch thought. She had a real talent for putting people at their ease and drawing them out of themselves. He was glad to see, though, that she was not so absorbed in the conversation to have forgotten to stay alert. Joy was more wary, these days. More conscious of potential danger and Fitch noted the way she walked, quickly and purposefully, keeping Lydia and Edward moving at pace between the cars instead of taking the clearer and quicker route via the road, her gaze shifting from side to side, even while she listened to Lydia.

She looked straight at Fitch as they came closer, inclined her head just slightly to the left. Fitch opened the doors, casually asking Edward if they'd found all they needed and were ready for the off.

His change of position allowed him to see what was bothering Joy. Two men in a red saloon, watching as they crossed the car park, their car paused but not parked close by the exit, as though they had halted, uncertain of where to go. He understood now why Joy had avoided the road.

Getting into the four-by-four, Fitch examined his options. The exit took them directly past the red car. A second lane, marked 'fuel', veered off towards the petrol pumps and then on to another slip road.

Fitch started the engine, drove slowly towards this second lane, keeping the red car in view for as long as he could. As he turned into the filling station, Joy took over the observation, flipping her sun visor down and checking her hair. Outside, it was getting dark, the deep-blue black of the sky mitigated by the yellow sodium lights.

'They're moving,' Joy said softly.

Fitch nodded.

He eased between the pumps, slowing as though preparing to stop, then, as though suddenly changing his mind, veered off towards the exit and accelerated away on to the slip road. The red car followed, also at speed. Not wanting to panic his passengers, Fitch accelerated steadily down the slip road, indicated, and prayed that whatever might be in his way would get out of it. Foot to the floor, he crossed on to the motorway, into the middle lane, past a line of lorries, finally settling down between a van and a family car. Three cars back he could see the red saloon.

Joy turned the radio on, and fiddled with the tuning. 'You think?'

'I think.'

'How?'

'They could have been waiting for us but . . . no. Too many possible services, too many possible routes. They're tracking us someway.'

He glanced once more in the rear-view. Not at the traffic this time, but at his passengers. Lydia had fallen asleep and Edward looked about to follow.

'Their phones,' Fitch said. 'Rina said that Lydia was in such a panic she even left her handbag behind. I'm betting her phone was in it.'

'What do we do?'

'For now? Nothing. Closer to home we call for reinforcements. For now, we don't stop again unless we have to get petrol, then we all keep together.'

Joy nodded, pale faced. Fitch knew she was remembering how her father had been killed. 'Should we try and get off the motorway?'

'I think we're safer on it than on some country road,' Fitch said. 'We keep traffic between us and them. I should have made you stay home,' he added, suddenly furious with himself.

'Hey, since when have you been able to make me do anything. Not even Mum can do that. Dad neither, when he was still here.'

She glanced behind to look at Lydia and Edward, who were now both asleep. The red car was now only two vehicles back.

TWENTY-THREE

It was after midnight by the time Tim started for home. The coast road, late at night, was usually deserted and, although it took a bit of concentration to drive it at any time, Tim knew it well enough to relax. He was halfway back to Frantham when he really became aware of the car that had been following. He'd noticed it a mile back, hoping it would dip its lights before it pulled behind him but thought little more about it. It was only as it began to close on him, and did not dip its lights, that Tim became at first irritated and then concerned. The headlights shone in his rear-view mirror, dazzling him whenever he tried to look behind. In the wing mirror he could see a dark car, glimpse the driver but the glare of the lights hid everything else. Tim was trying to figure out what was going on when the car suddenly pulled out from behind him and drew alongside. Just for a second, he relaxed. Better to have the idiot in front than tailgating, but the second of relief was all he got. The dark saloon swerved, broadsiding Tim.

Tim yelped. The dark car drew away, then clipped him again. Tim nearly lost control, the wheel torn from his grip by the sudden lurch.

When the car eased back for a third try, Tim acted. He accelerated away, surging out from between the car and the thick hedge that loomed beside him.

'Deep breaths, deep breaths. What would Rina do?' Rina didn't drive. Tim kept his foot down, taking bends at a speed he normally would not even contemplate, counting on the hope that he knew this road far better than his pursuers. It dawned on him that they didn't want him dead. To kill someone on this road would be an easy thing, especially in a car much larger and heavier than his own. Ramming him hard enough to send him spinning off the road, shooting out the tyres, shooting him for that matter. Any of the above and a good many alternatives would do the trick. No, they wanted him alive. Tim did not find that the least bit of a comforting thought.

'What to do? What to do? What the hell would Rina do?'
That was it! Rina didn't drive.

Tim travelled this road most days, in all weathers and at
all times. He knew it so well he could have done it blind-
folded. There had to be a place where he could bale out of
his car and hope to escape his pursuers. There were no lights
and the night was pitch black away from the town. Tim thought
hard. The other car was gaining on him, the road straightening out for a few hundred yards. Up ahead was a series of
bends and . . .

Tim accelerated, he took the first bend at sixty, the second
so hard he felt the back wheel lift. He undid his seat belt
and on the third bend he accelerated again, swung the wheel
and pulled as hard as he could on the handbrake. The car
skidded in the road, the spin slowed only when it hit the
hedge. Tim had the door open before it stopped, threw himself
sideways and rolled into the line of trees that he had remembered ran parallel to the road. He landed hard, stumbled to his
feet and ran, trusting that the engine noise would muffle
his crashing and tumbling through the undergrowth, then
threw himself to the ground and burrowed deep into a thicket
of hazel and thorn.

He lay still, listening to the sound of the car engine, then
the voices of the men, angry and frustrated. Beams of light
darted between the trees. Tim crouched lower, closing his
eyes and hiding his face in the dirt, blessing the fact that
he'd not taken time to change after his act and he still wore
the dark suit and black roll-neck that was his unassuming
uniform.

He just had to wait. Just had to lie still and not move and
wait until they went away.

He heard the car engine start up again. Lights flared and
he realised they had turned the headlights of the car on to the
little wood. Tim pressed even closer to the ground, wishing
that he dared to wriggle deeper under the thicket but he could
not, dare not move. He could hear his own heart pounding,
the ground magnifying the pulse until it seemed to echo so
loudly in his ears that he was sure the men would feel it,
never mind hear the sound. His breathing was ragged and
uneven; unsatisfying. He was light-headed, adrenaline pumping
so hard through his body that he felt almost dissociated from

it, as though his heart beat so hard it bounced him from the ground.

He could hear the men shouting, hear them crashing about in the undergrowth. Was aware of the light and shadows shifting as they crossed back and forth in the beam of the headlights. How long before they went away?

It seemed like forever. Tim tried to count, to focus on his breathing, to put himself somewhere else and not be there. Twice, their random search brought them within a few feet of where he lay. Twice, Tim was certain that he'd been discovered. He heard one of the men using his mobile phone, knew from his frustrated swearing that the signal was weak and kept dropping to nothing. They were asking advice, he guessed. No one had considered he might escape. Hearing the fury in the man's voice, Tim could only guess at the added beating he'd receive for having put them to such trouble. And that led to another thought, what the hell did they want to know. What did they think *he* knew and that in turn led to another worry. Rina. Whatever they might think he knew, chances were, they'd assume that she did too.

Finally, after what seemed like hours but was probably no more than twenty or so minutes, he heard them leaving the wood. Moments later two vehicles drove away. They had taken his car.

Tim lay still for a little longer, fearing that they might come back or that there might have been more than the two men; that they may have left someone else on watch. Then, slowly, he eased himself off the ground and looked back towards the road.

Nothing moved. He waited, then cautiously, keeping very low to the ground, he moved away and through the wood, into the fields beyond. Standing in the shadow of the trees he gazed down on to the shifting, grey-black water of the bay. He could see the narrow ribbon of the road, appearing here and there beyond the demarcation line of hedge and trees and the lights of the upper end of Frantham Old Town before it was swallowed by the cut between the fields and dropped down towards the inlet.

He checked again but nothing moved on the road.

Keeping close to the treeline he trotted towards the cliff edge, not sure what line the cliff path took at this point, reluctant to cross the open field. The hedge sheltered him on the field perimeter, but gave no access that he could see on to the path. He tried his phone, shielding the sudden brightness of the screen with his hand, panicking in case someone should see, the blue backlight seeming so unnaturally bright.

No signal. He checked again a little further on. To his relief the little bar across the top of the screen showed two slim points.

To his further relief, Mac replied on the second ring.

'Mac. I'm in trouble, Mac. I'm going to try and make it to the boathouse. Please, get to Rina, make sure the family are OK. Someone just tried to run me off the road.'

He listened to Mac's anxious response and demands for information.

'Please, Mac. I daren't talk. I'll get to the boathouse.'

He switched off his phone, terrified that Mac might call back and the ring be heard, knowing how well sound carried by night and unable, in his fear, to remember how to switch the phone to silent. Finding a gap in the hedge that he thought he could push through, he looked back for one last time and then forced the hedge aside, almost fell on to the cliff path, then ran, horribly aware of how narrow the path was, how loud the ocean sounded as it crashed upon the rocks below. Every moment he expected to see someone step out of the shadows in front of him, or to slip on the narrow path and fall over the edge. Tim, who hated heights and especially heights above water, looked straight ahead, watching for the lights of Frantham Old Town to come into view.

TWENTY-FOUR

F itch was considering his options. The red car had moved up the queue of traffic and was now directly behind. Joy had managed to take the number down and was straining to see the driver and the passenger.

Any moment, she expected the passenger to produce a gun, for the car to ram them from behind, to . . . she didn't know, but something. She figured that the fact they were in a four-wheel drive probably dissuaded the driver from ramming them. He'd be as likely to wedge himself as to do damage to their Range Rover and, she figured, if they shot Fitch, then having a vehicle go out of control directly in front of them in the middle lane might be as likely to take them out as the Range Rover. Rationalize it though she might, Joy was still very scared.

'Hold tight,' Fitch said. A line of lorries packed close in the slow lane. Fitch had spotted a gap between two just big enough for them to fit between. He swerved suddenly, a manoeuvre accompanied by a furious sounding of horns, then as abruptly took the slip road that Joy had not even realised was coming up.

Apparently, neither had the driver of the red car. Joy turned and stared back out of the rear window. The driver was desperately searching for the means to get from the middle lane and on to the slip, but Fitch had timed it to perfection.

'Yes! We lost them.' Joy was momentarily exultant and then the doubts crowded in. 'I thought you said we were safer on the motorway.'

'And so we are. They still asleep in the back? Good.' At the top of the slip road was a roundabout. Fitch slowed, waited for a gap. At this time of night traffic was light and he didn't even pull to a full stop. He took them part way round the island then, flicking on the hazard lights, pulled over on to the verge.

'You're letting them get ahead?'

'I'm letting them get ahead,' Fitch confirmed. He was

watching in his mirrors but there was no sign of anyone following them off the motorway. Amateurs then, or over-stretched, Fitch thought. He'd have had a second car, hanging back and unobtrusive, just to pick up the tail. He was troubled though, the way the two men had been so obvious that even Joy – and no offence to Joy; she was sharper than most people – had spotted them. It was almost as though they had been acting as a diversion, which made Fitch question, diversion from what? Or was he just being exceptionally paranoid and the men in the car just exceptionally stupid.

'Can you reach Lydia's phone?'

'It's in her bag. Yes.'

'I need Edward's too.'

'Edward's what?' a sleepy voice asked.

Joy leaned round her seat and put a finger on her lips. 'Hush, don't wake Lydia.'

'What's going on? Why have we stopped?'

'I'll explain as we go,' Fitch said. 'But I need your phone.'

'It's flat,' Edward said apologetically. 'I think Lydia's is . . .'

'No,' Fitch said. 'Edward, just trust me and give me your phone.'

Frowning, clearly dubious, Edward handed it over.

'Now what?' Joy said.

'Throw them out of the car,' Fitch instructed.

'What? You can't.' Edward protested, but Joy had already opened her window and dropped the phones to the ground. Fitch switched off the hazards, indicated and pulled away.

'What the hell do you think you're doing?' Edward was furious now.

'We were being followed,' Fitch said as he took the slip road back to the motorway. 'I think you'd been bugged.'

Miriam had arrived at the boathouse only minutes before Tim. Puzzled by why Mac should be knocking at his own door, she trotted down the boathouse stairs and put the door on the chain before opening it.

'Miriam, it's Tim. For god's sake let me in. Please.'

'Tim?' She closed the door, took off the chain and then opened it wide and he almost fell inside.

'Now lock the door. Has Mac called? He should be here.'

'He doesn't know I'd be coming tonight. I said I might stay

over at my sister's place but . . . well I changed my mind. Tim, you are covered in mud and leaves and . . . what the hell is going on? Come on upstairs, I'll give him a call.'

Tim followed her upstairs and then stood awkwardly in Mac's living room, shedding mud and leaves all over the bleached boards. Suddenly he was shaking. Fatigue and shock vying for domination.

'Sit,' Miriam ordered, pointing to one of the wooden dining chairs. 'Sit down before you fall down. And what on earth have you done to your arm?'

As though her noticing it allowed Tim to take notice, it started to hurt. Tim pulled up what was left of his sleeve and looked. Dimly, he recalled that when he'd thrown himself from the car he'd hit the ground on his right side, felt the sleeve tear and the burning sensation as he'd scraped the ground with his bare skin.

'Gravel rash, I guess,' he said, examining the mass of cuts and tears and painful grazes. 'I'm sorry, Miriam, I'm dripping blood all over the floor.'

She opened a drawer and grabbed a clean tea towel. 'Let me see. Here, wrap this round it. That must be Mac,' she added as the street door opened.

Tim felt himself tense. What if it wasn't? Two sets of footsteps coming up the stairs, then Mac appeared through the hole in the floor, followed by a man Tim vaguely recognised as DI Kendal.

'Before you ask, Rina is fine,' Mac said. 'Now, just what happened to you?'

Fitch had called ahead and the gates were opening as they arrived. Fitch watched them close behind as the Range Rover passed through, two of Bridie Duggan's men in attendance, scrutinizing the road outside.

Bridie was waiting at the front door. She came running out to meet them, a woman who looked like an older version of Joy, but with brighter lips and shorter hair. She hugged her daughter, then hugged Fitch, held out her hands to Lydia and Edward. 'Come along in. Fitch, are you sure you're all OK? We've been worried sick.'

'I'm not convinced we lost our tail,' Fitch said. 'Red car was on the hard shoulder a few miles further on. We figure they were waiting for us and someone else picked up where they left off. I didn't make anyone, but . . .'

'Well, you're here now,' Bridie said. 'That's what matters. Now, Lydia, Edward, how about I give you the grand tour. Show you our security system and then give you some supper and let you get some sleep. You must be exhausted.' She led the pair of them away and Fitch grinned at Joy.

'Your mother,' he said affectionately.

'My mother,' Joy agreed. 'I need a drink, Fitch, and I don't mean soft. Join me?'

He nodded. 'Sure you're all right?'

'I'm all right, but I don't mind admitting I was bloody terrified back there. You pour, I'll phone Rina, let them know it's all fine.'

'She'll probably be asleep,' Fitch pointed out.

'And if I don't call her she won't forgive me. I'll only disturb her beauty sleep for a minute.'

But when Joy called, Rina was wide awake and Joy soon found that they were not the only ones to have had a troubled night.

TWENTY-FIVE

Iconograph, the company owned by the de Freitas's, was not based in the most beautiful of buildings. Built on what had been wasteland between the Tin Huts and the old military base, it was a single story, prefabricated construct of steel and what Mac thought of as blue cladding. The entrance was all glass and chrome, leading into a surprisingly comfortable lobby with a surprisingly ancient desk set directly facing the door. The mix of the antique with the modern had been continued in the seating; comfortable, easy chairs that might, Mac thought, have looked more at home in a gentleman's club. Around the walls were pictures of people Mac vaguely recognised. Scientific pioneers and inventors, together with their technologies. Some, like Brunel, were familiar and much reproduced. Others, like the earnest-looking man standing proudly beside what looked to Mac like a steam-powered aeroplane, looked so absurd he wondered if they were from one of the games they developed rather than scientific history.

In fact, looking round, there was little here to do with software development or fantasy. He said so. Andy grinned at him.

'Oh, you should have come to the open day. Rina did,' he added. 'Um, Mrs Martin, I mean. This is just the R&D side, the software development that happens on site is in the old army base. They've started renovating some of the buildings and they've restored some of the others.'

'True,' Kendal confirmed. 'Unlike some locals, I did come to the open day.' He looked smug and Mac pretended to scowl back at him. 'Seriously, what they've achieved in just a few months is unbelievable. They've got temporary accommodation for some of their workers in what used to be the command centre.'

'Can't be very comfortable,' Mac commented.

'Oh, that's where you're wrong. You see, there was only really the shell of the place left. What they've done is gut out what was left and rebuild inside with these modular units they've shipped over from Scandinavia somewhere. Each little unit is insulated, high tech, very space age. And as most of the workforce they've brought with them is young and male and single, I guess it works out OK.'

'Not much for locals, then,' Mac said slightly huffily. 'The problem with most of these new enterprises is they don't provide decent local jobs.'

'Ah but that's where you're wrong Inspector McGregor.'

The woman's voice, amused and not the least bit insulted by his slights, surprised them all. Mac turned to see a dark-haired woman in her thirties walking towards them, hand extended and a bright smile on her round, plumply pretty face.

'Amelia Turner,' she introduced herself. 'I'm Edward's PA, he said I should give you any help I can. Mr Jackson is already here, by the way.'

'Of course he is,' Kendal muttered darkly.

Mac fell into step beside Amelia Turner. 'So far,' she said, 'we've employed thirty local people in a mix of part-time and full-time jobs and in a variety of roles from cleaners to technical supervisors. Edward is really keen to source as much of the workforce locally as he can. That was one of the conditions of the build and anyway, he feels strongly that this is where he and Lydia want to put down roots.' She frowned. 'Paul too,' she added. 'He loved it here.'

'You knew him well?'

She laughed. 'Only as a work colleague, but he was a good man to work with, we all liked him and he'd sometimes meet up with everyone for a drink after work. Edward isn't like that. He's a more formal soul.'

'I gathered that,' Mac said. 'Edward described his brother as, well I suppose as a people person. Would you agree with that?'

'Oh, yes, I really would. Paul enjoyed people; Edward wants to get along with everyone and, don't get me wrong, he's great to work for, but he doesn't have the same easy way with him as Paul did. You know though, I think it worked out. Paul was great at the meet and greet and the schmoozing. Edward was a bulldog when it came to getting the right deal.'

'So Paul softened them up and Edward went for the jugular,' Andy said.

Amused, she turned to look at him. 'I wouldn't have put it quite like that.'

'He's young,' Mac said. 'A bit lacking in the social graces.'

Amelia laughed. She had a nice laugh, warm and genuine. 'My office,' she said, indicating the next door. She held it open for them. 'And Edward's office off there,' she indicated a second door. 'And down that little corridor. That was Paul's domain.'

Abe Jackson had been sitting by the corner desk, one of two in the rather overcrowded little office. 'I waited for you before going in,' he said.

Mac caught Amelia's frown, and guessed she hadn't actually suggested he did otherwise. He could see that the door at the end of the short corridor had an alphanumeric lock and that Abe probably hadn't been given the option.

'Who else is in this office?'

'Lydia sometimes uses that desk,' Amelia said. 'She'll come in two, three times a week.'

Mac, who was still not clear what Lydia did in the company, was about to ask when Amelia added, 'It also acts as a hot desk for any of Paul's team who need outside access. Nothing in his inner office is networked. They've got their own proper office out that door we came in by and back down the corridor, but if all they want to do is send an email, it's easier to nip in here.'

'Nothing is networked? I don't understand.'

'It means that it's a closed system, doesn't it?' Andy contributed. 'You've probably got an airlock system. No one goes in and out without being checked for hidden . . .' He lost inspiration then. 'Stuff,' he finished rather lamely.

Amelia rewarded him with an ironic handclap. 'Very good,' she said. 'You see,' she went on, 'Paul's lab is right at the centre of the building. Tightest security. Anyone wanting to get in there has to know the codes, come through this office, get through the airlock system and be let in by whoever is in the lab.'

'What about fire?' Mac asked. The description made him feel claustrophobic even before he went in.

'It has its own fire control systems and a system override if anyone did have to get out in a hurry. There's a second airlock, but it's only opened up if you hit the panic button. Oh, don't worry, we had it all inspected.'

A light tap on the door preceded a young man with almost white blond hair, followed by a woman with dark-brown curls she had tried to tie back in a rather severe chignon. Piercing blue eyes were a surprise in a pale oval face. She should have been pretty, Mac thought, if she hadn't been so busy trying to look businesslike. He'd met this attitude before; woman in a perceived man's world. He had seen it in so many female police officers when he'd first joined the force. Now, most of the women officers he knew were decidedly, blatantly femin- ine and, he felt, all the better for it; Mac was a great believer in diversity bringing strength to any situation but a few years back the prevalent attitude had been very different.

'This is Ray Fowler,' Amelia said. 'And this is Lyndsey Barnes. They worked most closely with Paul. Edward thought they'd be the people you wanted to speak to.'

'Though we have already made statements,' Lyndsey said. 'I don't know what else you want to know.'

'Well, to start with, we'd like to inspect Paul's office and lab,' Abe Jackson said.

Mac frowned. 'And it would help to know exactly what he was working on.'

Lyndsey and Ray exchanged a look. 'Well, we'll tell you what we can,' Ray said. 'But the truth is, we don't know for sure. Paul was on one of his outside jobs and none of us were really allowed in his inner sanctum.'

'He'd call one of us in sometimes, if he needed an extra pair of hands or something, but that was about it. We had access to all the in-house stuff,' she added, trying to be helpful.

'But not whatever he was working on before he died. Do you know who he was working for?'

Again Paul's assistants exchanged that same look. 'We assumed it was MOD or something,' Ray admitted. 'We know he'd been involved in research for them before, but with all the anti-terrorist legislation that's been brought in, Paul was even more tight-lipped.'

'He took it all very seriously,' Lyndsey added rather earnestly. Rather enviously too, Mac thought.

'Well,' Kendal said cheerfully. 'I don't think I could recog- nise a secret device if I fell over it.'

'And we have authorisation to go into the lab,' Abe said quickly as though feeling left out of the conversation.

The two assistants looked doubtfully at Amelia. 'Edward did say full cooperation,' she said anxiously. 'And it is a murder investigation. Right. Follow me.'

She led the way down the short corridor and keyed a code into the door. 'How many people have that code, Amelia?' Mac asked.

'Well.' She stood back, and ushered them through the open door. 'There's me and Lyndsey and Ray. Paul, of course. That's all.'

'Not Edward or Lydia?'

'No, they had no need. Edward left this side of things to Paul and Lydia . . . well if she wanted to go in, Paul opened the lock from the inside, but that was almost never. She hates it in here, says it's so closed in. No windows or natural light.'

Mac was inclined to agree.

'This is Paul's office. His desk, his diary, his filing cabinet. Not that he ever filed anything.' She rolled her eyes.

'You did that?'

'Ordinary stuff, yes. Anything else, he kept in the inner sanctum.'

Mac leafed through his diary while Kendal inspected the filing cabinet. The diary was almost empty.

'I kept his appointments,' Amelia said. 'That diary is for any personal reminders.'

Mac bagged it. Abe Jackson was watching him. 'Anything relevant?'

'I don't know,' Mac shrugged. 'Kendal?'

'Mostly computer games, development ideas and drawings, I think.' Lyndsey came over and looked in the drawers. 'Mostly,' she said. 'He was a real magpie. See this news clipping.' She pulled out a full-page advert for women's shoes. 'He kept this because he thought the background colour was great. So far as I know he was still looking for a place to use it. And this, he just liked the way the dancers were moving. He wanted to emulate that in one of the cut scenes for something Edward was working on.'

'Cut scenes?'

'Oh,' Andy said. 'They're the filmic bits you get between sections of game play.'

'I thought I told you to wait in the office,' Mac said.

'Did you?'

'And through that door there?'

'Is where we work.' She keyed the code. 'Just Paul, Ray and I have the code here.' She pressed her thumb against a smaller pad that emerged from the doorframe.

'Thumbprint recognition?' Abe Jackson asked.

'Yeah. It's all nonsense, of course. You should have heard Paul go on about biometrics.'

'How do you mean?' Kendal was looking at the reader. 'What would happen if I put my thumb here?'

'The door would slam and poisoned gas would flood the room,' Ray said, deadpan. 'Actually, the door would close, but the rest is just Hollywood. No, what he meant was that biometrics can be conned. For instance, a student in Germany just broke a secure system using a fingerprint he'd made out of superglue.'

'How did he get it off the thumb?'

'Ah that was the clever part. He used a releasing agent on the thumb, though if the owner of the thumb had been less fussy, he could have released it with a very sharp scalpel or just taken the whole thumb along, provided it was fresh. Now the clever part is the releasing agent. Most of the commercial ones dissolve the glue and the top layer of skin. This particular one is now an industrial secret in its own right and the kid has a job waiting for him with one of the top chemical companies.'

'When he gets out of jail,' Lyndsey said sardonically, 'but even iris recognition can be fooled. A lot of US companies are using RF ID. Basically, tiny implants like you put in your pet dog. Much more reliable, but still not foolproof.'

'Sounds like an infringement of human rights,' Kendal said.

Lyndsey shrugged. 'Some clubs and health spas in California use them. They're almost a fashion accessory, 'cept of course you can't see them. It's the new must have for the moneyed classes. Through here is where Ray and I work.'

Mac wandered into the office and glanced around. Two desks and two benches packed with computer equipment and electronic gizmos he could only guess the purpose of.

One desk was almost scrupulously tidy, one stationery tray and a pen pot on the right-hand corner. The second a clutter of files and folders and photographs. He was faintly surprised to find an image of Ray and what was obviously a group of friends in one. Then thrown completely as he recognised Lyndsey in another.

Ray laughed. 'We use that desk for brainstorming,' he said. 'The other when one or other of us has some serious work to do.' He shrugged. 'I know it sounds a bit weird but it works for us.'

'And what would you be brainstorming?' Abe asked. His frown told Mac that he did not approve of such frivolity.

Ray picked up another of the pictures. This depicted the two young members of the team and Paul, an arm around each shoulder. They all smiled out at the camera, all looked happy. Lyndsey's hair was let out of its tight restraints and blossomed in rich curls around her head.

'We both worked on the games development for part of the week,' he said. 'The rest of the time we were involved in whatever project Paul had on the go. This last month or so, we were refining an electronic surveillance system we'd designed for a client last year. It wasn't difficult work, but there was a lot of complexity. Paul believed we were fresher, more creative, if we could switch hats from time to time.'

Lyndsey had come over, she touched the picture with some-thing close to tenderness and laid a hand on Ray's arm. 'Who the hell shot him?' she asked, her voice suddenly thick with tears. 'He was a good man, he was an alive sort of man, not like so many people. You know what, Inspector. You look out there and you see all the people just sleepwalking through life, just spending their days griping and moaning and you tell me what's fair. Why couldn't the bastard have shot one of them instead of Paul?'

There was no good response to that one. Mac was silent for a moment, then he asked if they ever saw Paul outside of working hours and got the same response as he had been given by Amelia. Paul met people for a drink sometimes. They liked him, as a person and as a boss, and Mac got the odd feeling that Paul knew where the line was drawn between friendly employer and out-and-out friend and knew how and when not to overstep it.

'You'll want to see the lab now,' Ray said. 'This is the airlock bit, so it might be a bit of a crush.'

He pressed something on the wall and a portion of it slid back to reveal a door. Another fingerprint lock and then a narrow lobby. Mac, Kendal, Ray and Abe Jackson crowded inside and Ray closed the first door before opening the second. They moved past him into the lab. Ray stood beside the doorway, frowning.

'There should be stuff laid out on that bench,' he said. 'It was here before Paul died. No one's been in here since.'

'Could it have been put away?' Kendal asked. He was circling the room examining the mass of silver-cased equipment and looking mystified.

'No, see he'd got everything in a specific order.' Ray crossed to the bench. Tiny labels had been affixed to the wooden surface. Numbers and letters written on them meant nothing to Mac, but were clearly meant to denote a sequence of some sort.

Ray looked truly disturbed. He opened cupboards, drawers, checked all available spaces. 'It's gone,' he said. 'Whatever he was working on. But how? Like I say, no one came in here.'

'And you don't know what he was doing?'

Ray shook his head emphatically. 'I told you, he'd work in here on his own most of the time. I mean, when it was an outside job. We all worked on our in-house projects in here but . . .'

'And if you had to guess,' Mac asked. 'Could you hazard anything?'

Ray shook his head again then said, 'Look, long shot, random guess just on what I saw, but I'd say it might have been some kind of jamming system, or some kind of advanced sonar.'

'Which?' Abe Jackson insisted.

Ray looked puzzled at his tone. 'I don't know,' he said. 'But if you're pushing me for an opinion, I'd have said both.'

TWENTY-SIX

On the way out of *Iconograph* Mac contrived to slip behind the rest of the group, pausing to examine one of the more unusual photographs. Lyndsey, just behind him and Ray, to whom he'd been chatting about the images, paused beside him.

'I have something more to ask,' Mac asked quietly.

'Sure. Anything we can do.' Ray glanced at the rest of the group who were now in the lobby. 'Shoot.'

'Does the phrase *The Power of One* mean anything to either of you?'

Ray laughed. 'Sure. It was a sort of in-joke. You know, Binary code, all ones and zeros. One way of thinking about it is like a switch, either off or on. Zero is off, one is on. Paul always joked that once you'd switched something on, anything was possible. You should never underestimate the power of one.'

'He meant it like individuals too,' Lyndsey added. 'Like, one person can make a difference. You do nothing, you're a zero.'

That made a kind of sense, Mac thought but didn't get him any further. 'What about *Payne 23*?'

Puzzled looks. 'No,' Ray said. 'Where did you see it? If I knew the context . . .'

'It's probably nothing,' Mac said. 'Just something scribbled in a margin. I found it kind of intriguing.' He smiled. 'Occupational hazard. Seeing significance in everything.'

Ray laughed. Lyndsey, Mac noted, had said nothing.

'Edward and Lydia, are they OK?' Ray asked as they moved on. 'Amelia said they'd gone away for a few days.' Mac was aware that Abe Jackson watched, eyes narrowed.

Mac nodded. 'They're staying with friends,' he said. 'We thought it might be best for them to get away. I think Mrs de Freitas was finding the media interest a little too much to handle.'

'Where have they gone?' Abe asked as they left. 'We should make sure they have adequate protection.'

'Oh, they do,' Mac told him. 'But they have asked their solicitor not to reveal their address for now. He's acting as go-between for any messages. I can give you his number?'

Abe frowned. 'I don't think that's appropriate,' he said. 'We need to know where they are.'

'They are not accused of any crime, Abe,' Mac said gently. 'I can't order them not to leave town. Now, how about you tell us what Paul was up to?'

For a moment Mac thought Abe was going to match his own intransigence, but he did not. He sighed. 'Paul was a revenger,' he said. 'Apparently one of the best in the business.'

The use of the word rang bells for Mac. Some obscure discussion he'd had with Tim on the history of magical illusion and the engineers who had . . . 'reverse engineering'. He said, 'You take an object; a . . . a piece of finished technology and you take it apart, find out how it's made.'

Abe nodded. 'Technology, or code or both.'

'Wasn't that what they did at Bletchley Park during the war?' Andy asked, surprising them all. 'They needed to know how the enigma coding thingys worked. Ian Fleming, you know, the James Bond man? Well he or someone managed to capture one and then the boffins at Bletchley had to figure out how it worked and how they could fool it.' He shrugged. 'I read a book,' he said. 'It was really exciting. Science, like, but really good.'

Mac was a little taken aback. Andy could be surprising. 'And what was Paul "revenging"?' he asked.

'I don't know,' Abe told him. 'I really don't.'

'And wouldn't tell us if you did,' Kendal surmised.

'Not if you didn't need to know,' Abe Jackson confirmed.

Tim ached. Not only that, he kept discovering bruises that he could not recall deserving. True, he had thrown himself from a moving car, hidden in undergrowth from armed men and run further and faster than he had since his school days, but he was still taken aback by what a toll this had taken on his body.

Rina fussed over him. Then got bored with fussing and left the task to the Peters sisters. By midday, Tim had tired of feeling sorry for himself – and being the focus of Bethany and Eliza's attention – and was recovered enough to want to see what Rina was doing.

'I've come to tell you it's lunchtime,' he said.

'Oh, good. How are you feeling now?'

'Do you really want to know? No, forget that. I'm aching all over and bruised to hell, but I'm still here and that's what matters.'

'It is indeed. You've called work?'

'Yes. I told Blake I'd had a bit of an accident on the way home. That my car was damaged and I'd hurt my hand. I don't like lying to them but . . .'

'Not a lie, Tim. Just a half-truth. And a magician with an injured hand is not likely to put on a good show.'

'I'll be fine tomorrow but he's told me to take the day anyway. I'll lose pay, of course. But then I've got my normal couple of days off to recover properly. I said I'd still go up and meet the engineer; we've still got the illusion to set up.'

'You'll need a car,' Rina said. 'You'll have to go up to DeBarr's garage and see if you can hire one and just hope yours has been dumped somewhere.'

He came over to examine the scatter of newspapers and printouts on Rina's desk. 'What are you looking at?'

'Well, I've isolated the newspaper and the edition that Mac's clipping came from and I've found this other advert. Look.'

'Funeral delayed,' Tim mused. 'I suppose there really isn't an Arthur Payne born in 1923?'

'Not that I can find. I've called all the local funeral directors and none have an Arthur Payne born on that date. One had a Ronald Payne, but I found his obit and I don't think there's any even remote connection. No, Paul put this in as a message to someone.'

'Where did Mac find the clipping?'

'In a book in Paul's flat. He didn't tell me what book and I didn't think to ask. I must be slipping in my old age.'

'Which advert came first?'

'The one delaying the funeral. Then this one, see. Arthur Payne. Born 1923. Funeral at Great Marham Church. Phone Paul for details. I called the *Echo*, no one really remembers taking the advert. I'd have thought the odd wording might have attracted attention.'

'Um, yes, if it had been *phoned* in,' Tim said. 'But for the last six months or so, you've been able to do it online and pay by card. I'd guess the advertising department just checks the copy to make sure it's not offensive and that's about it.'

Rina nodded. 'Tim, I'd forgotten that. You could be right and Mac will be able to confirm that Paul placed the advert.'

'Not really. Only that someone used his card.'

'True.' She frowned. Matthew could be heard, calling them both in to lunch. 'But most important, I think, is the fact that whatever delay there had been relating to the enigmatic Arthur Payne was now over. Whatever it was, Paul was ready to tell it or deliver it or . . .' She gestured irritably. 'Whatever it was. Tim, lunch, I think. We'll work better on full stomachs and I think we should give Mac a call, see if he can tell us any more.'

Edward couldn't settle. Bridie Duggan had made sure they wanted for nothing but he still felt like a prisoner. Effective house arrest, even with such attention to comfort, was still just that and after recent events he even felt wary about going into the garden.

The house was a bit of a strange one, he thought, with its weird mix of mock Tudor, UPVC double glazing and those columns by the front door that looked like someone had pinched them from the Parthenon. Inside, there seemed to be a bit of a powder-blue trend going on; all the downstairs carpets and those up both flights of stairs being in that particular shade. Bedrooms had been themed, apparently; the guest room he shared with Lydia dressed in someone's rather abstracted notion of art deco, though the glimpse he'd had of Joy's room was refreshingly just post-teenage. He was rather touched to see that this cool, calm young woman, still had a collection of bears and rag dolls arrayed on the old wooden trunk at the foot of her bed.

The Duggans' security system would have put some government buildings to shame, he thought. It was all controlled from a central room into which all the cameras – sixteen in all – sent their images.

'What happens if someone tried to cut the feed?' he had asked.

'They'll have a job doing that,' Fitch told him. 'Everything is channelled underground and then under the house.'

Edward didn't like to ask what had led to such paranoia. He had a vague idea that the nightclub businesses the Duggans ran had once been supplemented by less legitimate sources of income, but he didn't like to ask. It seemed rather rude, in the circumstances. He did, however, feel rather hemmed in. Used to the view of open skies and wide bay, this return to the urban felt suddenly claustrophobic and did nothing to soothe his frayed nerves.

The news from Rina and Tim had upset him terribly and roused feelings of guilt and anxiety that he couldn't shake. But what to do about them?

He'd spent the past hour talking to Lydia about going home, facing whatever it was they had to face and now, frankly, she was furious with him.

'People risked their lives to get us here,' she said. 'And no, I'm not exaggerating, am I? Bridie has the best security set-up here I've ever seen. Even Paul would have been proud to have designed something like it. A flea can't move without her knowing, never mind some homicidal maniacs in a red car. I'm not going anywhere. Not leaving this safe place. You want to ask Fitch to take you back, you go and ask him, but I'm staying here and I wouldn't blame him in the slightest if he told you to just go and catch the bloody train.'

'I'm just concerned for Rina and the others.'

'And what are you going to do to protect them if you go back? You'd just give her one more person to worry about and I think she's got her hands full already, don't you?'

'We should never have involved her.'

'Seems to me she involved herself and my god, I'm glad she did. I'm not the heroic type, Edward. I'm just the one that fills in the gaps, remember, does all the unglamorous jobs you and Paul weren't any good at. And I didn't mind. I was good at dotting the i's and crossing the t's and smoothing out the wrinkles in the deals you struck, but I'm not good at getting shot at. I never signed up for that when I took my marriage vows.'

A light knock on the door interrupted their quarrel. It was Joy.

'I just came to see if you needed anything,' she asked. 'Everything OK?'

Lydia sighed. 'Sorry,' she said. 'I suppose we were getting rather loud.'

Joy shrugged. 'Oh, you should hear Mum when she gets going. Makes you two sound like you were whispering. Look, Fitch just thought you'd like to know, he's managed to get some friend of his to run the registration through the police computer. He thought it might have been a stolen car but it wasn't. The registration number was for a car that didn't exist. It's a bit of a risk, doing that, especially with all the number plate recognition cameras around. It might have attracted just the kind of attention they wouldn't have wanted. They did seem very sure of themselves.'

'What does it all mean?' Edward asked.

Joy wrinkled her nose. 'I don't know,' she said. 'Fitch thought they were amateurish, because of the way they let us see them and all that, but now he thinks we were meant to think that. Kind of like a double bluff.'

'But to what purpose?' Lydia asked.

'If we knew that,' Joy said, 'we'd know what to do about it. Fitch says we've just got to wait for the next move.'

TWENTY-SEVEN

Richard Grey had considerable admiration for whoever had written this code, or rather, these layers of code. At first he had assumed that the machine code contained straightforward instructions for some new game-play the programmer had been creating. Every programmer has their own style; their own fingerprint as Richard Grey liked to call it and knowing who had written this particular piece of code, he was intrigued as to why Paul de Freitas had chosen to use machine code and not some much simpler computer language to develop what was, on the face of it, a relatively simple patch for an existing game.

All programming for games was created with back doors to allow the programmer to test out the elements of the game without the need for actually playing through entire levels. Regular players with a modicum of technical knowledge took delight in discovering these illicit ways in – hence the proliferation of forums and discussion sites for gamers where 'cheats' were exchanged and discussed. Far from being worried about this, many games designers would insert 'easter eggs', which were little surprises and prizes for those clever enough to figure things out. Often these would be an extra level of game-play or some new solution to a puzzle. Just occasionally, when too many tunnels had been dug through a particular game, or when a game was about to be re-released, programmers would patch the most well-known cheats and close some of the back doors and thus add to the challenge for old players as well as encouraging the newcomers. Richard knew of completists who bought every new edition of a favourite game, just to try and discover these little variations. Not as popular or as obvious – in fact, usually members only – these cheats also had their forums and their aficionados. Richard did not really number himself among them. In fact, he wasn't what you might call a player of games but he kept abreast of the latest trends because you never knew what would be important or when it might become so. Richard was at the top of his particular profession and he fully intended to remain there.

He had thought at first that Paul had just been working on such a patch. The game in question, *Eventides*, was a love-craftian RPG, first person, so far as Richard was aware and that was what had first alerted him to something being odd. He had gone away and phoned a friend, checking that he was correct in his first-person assumption.

Yes, his friend told him, though there had been rumours for a while of a hidden level played from the perspective of a woman called Lydia, a minor character in the original. 'It's some sort of an in-joke,' the friend told him. 'Paul de Freitas did the original story development as well as a lot of the game-play. *Eventide* was one of their first games, from when Paul didn't work for the company, he was just mucking about on the periphery.'

'And the in-joke?'

'Apparently, his sister-in-law is called Lydia. The story is, she was the one who put up the money to get *Iconograph* off the ground. The in-joke is that she looks like a secondary character, in the game and in real life, but she's the one calling the shots all the time.'

'And this hidden level, according to the rumours, does it have an underwater theme?'

The sudden silence on the end of the phone told Richard that it did.

'You know something,' his friend demanded. 'Christ, Rich, if you know something, you've got to let me in.'

'So you can print it in that dumb magazine of yours?' Richard laughed. 'Look,' he said more seriously, 'this is work. I can't tell you anything. But . . . do the rumours mention something about a kraken?'

Again the silence, followed by a burst of laughter and a string of expletives. Richard took that as confirmation and rang off. He sat staring at the phone, something at the edge of his consciousness telling him that though that might look like the answer, there was more to it than that. He went back to the sanctuary of his desk and ran the lines of code back across the computer screen.

He couldn't quite put his finger on it but . . .

Here and there were tiny fragments of unrelated code. At

first he'd thought they were just place markers. It was easy to lose the thread if you were interrupted programming or debugging. He had, long ago when he still did such things, used a similar system himself. But . . . no.

On the desk in front of him were three screens, the middle one running the lines of code. He switched the other to reflect the virtual machine, operating like a second computer from within his own system. Now he had two screens showing completely different pages. Slowly, he began to extract the random markers and place them on the second screen, compiling them in the order that they occurred.

'Find anything?'

He was so focussed on the task that he did not hear his boss. Richard jumped. 'Jeesus. Can you not creep up on a body.'

'So? What have you found?'

Richard Grey shook his head. 'That's just it,' he said. 'I don't know. It's just random fragments of code that don't belong.'

'And if you made an educated guess?'

'Then I'd be telling you to go and hunt a kraken,' Richard said. 'Look, I'm sorry, maybe I'm barking up the wrong tree entirely.'

His boss shrugged. 'Any connection between this file and the other? *Payne 23.*'

'Not that I can see. I sent that through to documents a couple of hours ago. It seems to be a list of names. I unravelled the binary to get a list of numbers and the numbers were a fairly simple alphanumeric substitution code. Clever, but not designed to be uncrackable. It took me two, three hours.'

'And can you get to the bottom of this new problem?'

Richard didn't want to commit himself but on the other hand he didn't want one of the most challenging puzzles that had come his way in months to be handed off to someone else. 'Oh, I'll get there,' he said. 'You can be sure of that.'

Hale was examining footage from motorway traffic cameras. It showed the four-by-four driven by Fitch and the red car following them. Hale would have given a great deal to have known the identity of the driver and his passenger.

'How did you lose them?' he asked quietly. His associate shuffled his feet, embarrassed.

'We know they went to the Martin woman's house. After that . . . we don't know when they left or when the driver picked them up or where from. Our all-points alert identified them up at the services and we've managed to backtrack to where they came on to the M5. The red car started to follow them from the services at Avonmouth.'

'And the plates are false, the windows tinted and the men wore baseball caps which means the cameras don't have a clear picture, even from the front. I got that already.' Hale took a deep breath. 'You let an elderly actress and a house full of ageing actors slip the de Freitas's out from under your noses and you don't know how.'

'At least we know where they've holed up.'

'And that helps? How? Bridie Duggan is well used to dealing with authority. She won't fold just because we might put the pressure on and she's got that place of hers tight as Fort Knox.'

'We get someone on the inside?'

'Oh, that's really going to happen. There's not one man or woman on her staff hasn't been with her for at least a decade and not one that doesn't owe her.'

'Which doesn't preclude . . .'

'Which adds to our problems. We don't have time for subtlety. Ian got himself killed because we pussyfooted about waiting for people to "cooperate". We don't have that luxury any more and,' he jabbed a finger towards the motorway footage still playing out on the overhead screen, 'we don't know who the hell *they* are.'

'Probably who killed Ian.'

'Oh, you think? Talk about stating the bloody obvious.' Hale turned around to face his unfortunate operative. 'Ian was a bloody good man. Tried, tested, loyal. Nothing I've seen so far convinces me you're worthy to lick his frigging boots. Got that?'

The associate left, wise enough at least to know when to keep his mouth shut. Hale fumed silently. Paul had promised to deliver and Hale had no reason to suppose he would renege on the deal. He had also told Hale that a record of what he'd found and the solution he'd created would be left somewhere, just in case.

'In case of what?' Hale had asked him.

'In case something happens to me. In case you decide I've been useful enough and I'm now surplus to requirements.'

'And who would that information be left for?' Hale had demanded, but Paul had just grinned at him in that infuriating way he had and had walked away, turning back to wave before getting into his car.

Some men, Hale reflected, live scared for themselves. Some live frightened of what might happen to others. Some, like Paul de Freitas, are almost untouchable in their assurance, their confidence, their simple inability to understand that they should feel intimidated. Hale had known a few men like that in his life. Most had been military men, others had been psychopaths. A few had been both, one occupation not of necessity excluding the other. A rare few, like Paul de Freitas, lived what looked like normal lives until you dug a little below the surface and you realised that they didn't really have a clue. Or rather, they didn't know how to see the social cues that said 'care now', 'respond now', 'kiss me now' or 'be afraid'. They knew those rules for living existed; learned by rote how to respond. They didn't have the inherent cruelty that came with some traits of abnormal psychology; oddly, for Paul, that was another cue that passed him by.

Life fascinated Paul de Freitas, but it didn't frighten him not even on behalf of others. He trusted Lydia and Edward to be able to look after themselves and Hale was absolutely certain that any message Paul had left would have been left for them.

Tim's Uncle Charles was a career warrior – Tim never thought of him as a soldier; far too prosaic for a man who'd led such an eventful life. As a boy, Tim's father had told him that Charles slept with a Kalashnikov under his pillow and a Luger tucked into his sock. Tim, completely ignoring the logistical improbability of sleeping on a pillow with a machine gun slipped beneath it, had focussed on the random fact that 'Uncle Charles sleeps in his socks'.

Later, he realised that the legend of Uncle Charles' unlikely bedfellows had become part of his subconscious to the extent that, in a rather drunken moment a few Christmas's ago, he had asked his Aunt Lucy if she minded.

She had replied that so long as Charles didn't mind her Beretta, she didn't see she had the right to object.

Uncle Charles, on leaving the army, had sidestepped into diplomatic protection and thence into more shadowy areas which seems to entail an awful lot of travel, so far as Tim could tell. Aunt Lucy certainly complained that he was never there. He's some kind of aide, was all Tim's father could say about the matter. He gathered that no one in the family asked, knowing they wouldn't get a satisfactory reply. So far as that was concerned, Tim wasn't about to challenge the status quo, but he did figure that if anyone he knew had access to the information he wanted, then Uncle Charles might be that man, and so he had asked.

Charles phoned just as the Martin household was about to sit down to dinner. Tim, half expecting the call, grabbed the phone as the others passed by, filing into the dining room.

Charles was typically to the point. 'The man's a phoney,' he said. 'Abe Jackson had a fine service record until six months ago. He was allowed to resign his commission rather than face a court martial, but there his connection with her majesty's forces and any other government body ended.'

'What did he do?'

'Now that's the question. I've managed to speak to his old commanding officer. Apparently, on his last operation, Abe Jackson lost four of his men to a roadside bomb. He's lost men before; we all have. Doesn't make it any easier. Seems he was annoyed, shall we say. He hunted down those that were responsible or, at least, those he believed to be responsible and he killed them. Or, at least, that's what his commanding officer understands to have happened. Nothing could be proved because none of his men would give evidence against him. All declared they were elsewhere at the time or didn't know where he was or . . . well, you get the picture. But his behaviour certainly became erratic and he was writing letters to the national press telling them that his men died because they lacked essential equipment. He was shipped back, hospitalised, finally persuaded it was in everyone's interest to quit with his pension intact.'

'What happened to him after that?'

'Well, his pension was paid into his bank account, but he's never touched a penny. Abe Jackson disappeared off the radar.

The truth is, Tim, no one was bothered. He'd gone, end of problem.'

Tim absorbed that. 'We'd better tell Mac,' he said.

'Your policeman friend? Oh, I've already sounded the alarm bells. He should know what's going on by now. I believe there's now a warrant out for Jackson's arrest.'

'On what grounds?'

'Oh, impersonating whatever it was he was impersonating, I suppose. They'll no doubt work the rest out as they go along.'

This was vague even by Uncle Charles' standards.

'Charles?'

His uncle sighed. 'They'll hold him on some aspect of anti-terrorist legislation I believe. Tim, I can't tell you more than that, but you lot down there seem to have stumbled into something larger than a murder or two. Oh, and that Hale fellow. He's not what he seems either, apparently, but I was gently warned not to go poking into business that doesn't concern me. Oh, and I was to pass that same message on.'

Tim laughed nervously. 'And that means?'

'I'm guessing it means that friend Hale is freelance. Cutbacks, you know. Sometimes work is farmed out, shall we say.'

'Right,' Tim said doubtfully. 'Charles, this sounds a little unreal.'

'Well it isn't,' his uncle said quietly. 'Remember that, Tim. This isn't an illusion; you can't control any of this with sleight of hand. It's serious and dangerous and my advice to you would be to let it go.'

Superintendent Aims was not a happy man. He felt he had twice been taken for a fool and DI Kendal had somehow been a party to it all. Kendal listened to him rant for a while, stopped listening after he had established that the problem was that neither the mysterious Hale nor Abe Jackson were what they seemed and set his mind instead to analysing what Jackson might have been after, what he, Kendal, and Mac might have told him that they might regret and what to do about it next.

Next was to call Mac.

'World's going to hell,' Kendal pronounced.

'You've only just noticed? Well, I take it that we're not going to get the extra help we were promised. On the plus side, neither are we now constrained by military intelligence.'

'Were we ever?'

'Not so you'd notice. Seriously though, Dave, what the hell is going on?'

'If you find out, best let Aims know before he has a heart attack. Mac, it's late in the day, I'm for getting home and trying to get to grips with all of this tomorrow.'

'You'll not find me arguing.'

Mac lowered the receiver, his mind playing with the facts.

'Penny for them?' Miriam said, setting a mug of coffee down on the table between the two sofas.

'That was Kendal. It seems Abe Jackson is a phoney, or at least, he's not what he claims to be.'

'Aren't those two the same things?' She settled beside him, leaning with her back against the arm of the sofa and her feet in his lap, her own mug cradled between her hands.

'Not exactly. I mean, Abe Jackson isn't working for the government . . . not now. But he's an ex-soldier, he's moved in those circles, so it isn't exactly an out-and-out lie, but . . .'

'He isn't now. OK. So who is he working for?'

'That,' Mac considered, 'is probably the main question. The other being what was Paul doing that everyone seems to want a part of? Jackson, Hale . . . I mean we can presume they aren't working on the same side.'

'Can we? And Hale isn't kosher either.' She frowned. 'It has to be something about security. National, international, local. No, bigger than local. Something anti-terrorist?'

'Paul was a games designer.'

'And before that, he designed high-end security systems. And, if we can believe Jackson about anything, we know he was reverse engineering something.'

'Which may or may not have something to do with sonar or radar which maybe implies something underwater?'

The phone rang again. 'That'll be Rina, or Tim,' Miriam predicted. 'I can tell by the tone of the ring.' She got up and handed him the phone, bent to kiss his cheek. 'Don't be long,' she said.

Mac watched as she disappeared into the bedroom and then answered the phone. Miriam was right, it was Rina, Tim having reported back on his Uncle Charles' message.

'Rum deal,' Rina said. 'Mac, I know Miriam is there tonight, so I won't keep you, but Tim wanted me to pass on Charles'

warning. He's concerned, Mac. Charles thinks this is something very big and very dangerous and he thought that before
Tim told him about being driven off the road. He's all for
coming down to sort things out, but Tim's managed to persuade
him otherwise.'

'Should I be glad about that?'

'Oh yes,' Rina said with feeling. 'I've met him twice and
he's a lovely man, but, well, you know how once I told you
there were three types of people? Those who lead, follow or
get out of the way?'

'Yees,' Mac said cautiously.

'Well, neither Charles nor I could ever be classed as
followers, but at least I give people the opportunity to get out
of the way. Charles most certainly does not.'

TWENTY-EIGHT

I t was getting dark outside and Lydia was sick of the television. She heard Joy go past in the hall, recognising the girl's light footsteps and, desperate for someone to talk to, followed her into the kitchen.

Joy turned and smiled. 'Hi.'

'Is it OK if I get a cup of tea?'

'You know it is. Anything you like. I was just about to get something anyway.'

Lydia pulled out a chair and sat down at the kitchen table. It was the one thing at odds with the chrome and black, sleek and shiny kitchen. It, and the four chairs tucked beneath it, were old and rather tatty. The red Formica table was the same sort Lydia recalled from cafes of her childhood. The chairs had been re-covered, but had fifties greasy spoon written all over them.

Joy noticed her examination.

'It was from Granddad's place,' she said. She pulled out a chair and plonked herself down. 'My grandparents owned a little chemist shop. They've retired but it's still going. Dad got a couple and their son in to run it like it had always been. In Granddad and Grandma's day, they had this bit of a space at the front of the pharmacy, with seats so people could sit down while they waited for their medicines. Grandma started making tea for people and selling cakes and biscuits and it got to be a place people came to gossip or just to be with someone. You know? The old people really liked it and Dad grew up coming home from school and helping out at the shop.

'He grew up poor, so did Mum. So did everyone round where they used to live but the little chemist's was a place people came to for a cheap cuppa and a bit of company and, when Gramps retired, Mum had the table and chairs brought here.' Joy laughed. 'She's just as sentimental as Dad was, you know?'

She got up to make the tea.

'You must miss your dad,' Lydia said.

Joy nodded. 'Dad was a Jack the Lad, always in trouble in his teens. Dad was a thief, no getting away from that. He was other things too, but as time went on he got into more legitimate stuff and now, I guess, we're almost respectable. Even Gran says she can own him again. But he was a great father and I've been really lucky. Mum is . . . well, Mum. I'd never get her to decorate any house of mine, but they both brought me up like I was their princess and my brothers were princes. We miss Dad a lot. Hell of a lot, but we've got one another and that's . . .' She broke off, smiling a little mistily. 'Were you close to your brother-in-law?'

Lydia laughed. 'Once, I thought we were very close. We dated for about six months. We were both about your age, I guess. I liked him a lot and for a while I thought he really liked me. Loved me, even. Then I realised he wasn't capable of that.'

'How come?'

Lydia shrugged. 'Paul could seem perfect. He was kind, considerate, gentle, but it was all like he had learnt how to be those things by watching other people. He didn't feel it, if you know what I mean. We eventually had this long talk and he admitted that he liked me, but he couldn't seem to go further than that. He didn't know how. It was like . . . Paul was the most fantastic solver of puzzles and player of games. That was how he lived his life; kind of second-hand through other people and through his puzzles and his games. He was fine if he could treat life like a puzzle or like a really complicated game. Could identify the rules and kind of react according to the rules, but he couldn't improvise. You know how much we improvise in our daily lives.'

Joy laughed. 'I never really thought about it, but I suppose, talking for myself, maybe ninety-nine per cent. I was never much good at rules. So . . . how can I put this. You fell out with one brother and in with the other?'

Lydia groaned. 'Oh, that sounds *soo* bad. No. I broke up with Paul and didn't see either of them again until after University. Then Edward and I bumped into one another and we got talking and one thing led to another and . . . Paul was best man at our wedding.'

'And Edward understands how to improvise,' Joy said with a cheeky smile.

'Oh, yes. You may not think he's the improvising type, but I've never regretted getting married. Never regretted helping him to set up the business. Or of bringing Paul on board. It worked well. I just wish he had confided in us.'

'Maybe he thought that wasn't in the rules?' Joy suggested.

Lydia nodded. 'Maybe so,' she agreed.

Abe Jackson had lived by his instincts and his training for more years than he cared to remember. It was instinct that warned him, training that helped him to make his escape.

Abe would say that every place had its own soundscape. Every location could be identified not only by the way it looked but the way it sounded and the way it felt. He could stand outside of a house and know if someone was inside. Could sense the subtle changes generated when even the most skilled of searchers had examined a room. Could hear the smallest changes in the soundscape once he'd grown familiar with any location. Abe never claimed supernatural abilities; he just figured his skills were based on sharpened instincts, careful observation and the desire to stay alive.

New recruits would smirk and inwardly snigger at Abe Jackson's claims. Those that remained with him for any time would soon correct the doubters. Abe *knew* these things and, perhaps by some strange osmosis, those he trained also acquired such capacities. They watched, they listened, maybe they laughed at first, but then they learnt to copy, to identify, eventually to trust.

Abe was not there when they came for him. Tonight he had watched some detective thing on television, guessing from the second scene who the killer was; still vague at the end as to why he had done the deed. He had wandered down to a local pub for a late dinner, eaten alone, then come back to the hotel at closing time. He paused, more from habit than expectation of trouble, at the corner of the street before turning down towards the hotel. And he had known that something was wrong.

He crossed the road so that he could look down towards the hotel without turning the corner. At this time of night, he had noted that the stretch in front of the hotel tended to be almost empty. Guests would wander back for the night. Taxis occasionally pull up in front of the three steps. For three cars to be parked in the street; that was different. Parked, but not empty.

For a couple to sit for a few minutes before one or both getting out, now that was a normal enough thing, but for three cars to be occupied, one by a pair of men, one by a woman, one by three people; that was unusual. Abe stood in the shadow of a doorway and he watched. Two figures loitered just inside the lobby and another chatted idly to the evening receptionist.

Overkill, he thought. He must have more of a reputation than he thought.

Abe turned and walked back the way he had come, grateful for the training that had long ago taught him the value of planning an escape, even from the most benign locations. His car was parked two streets away and his emergency pack already in the boot. Abe Jackson glanced around, then waited for five full minutes to check there was no one near his car, then he got inside and drove away.

At the hotel, Superintendent Aims and his team waited.

TWENTY-NINE

She needed the laptop to get the rest of the narrative. Paul had promised he would give her the key for safe keeping. He had told her what book he would leave it in, told her too that if anything happened to him he was leaving that particular volume to his sister-in-law, Lydia. She had tried not to mind, but despite her probing and teasing he had never promised her anything. Never given her anything that was personal either.

Taking the book from Paul's flat had not provided her with the information that she needed but she had it now, delivered almost incidentally. Now, if she had the laptop, she could find the file, know something more of the story.

She had parked about a half-mile from the de Freitas's house, noting as she drove by that a police car was parked outside with two officers inside. When she crossed the lawn at the rear of the house, it was possible to see that the car had gone. Creeping around the side of the house, she saw that one man had been left on patrol. Was he there all night or just to take a look around?

She hid among the trees and he wandered, checking doors and shining a light through the windows, watched him as he made his way back to the front. Dawn was showing itself in a lightening of the sky and a faint pink glow on the horizon. She was due in for the early shift. Time was not on her side.

The policeman's voice carried clearly on the still air.

'A bloody hour. You must be kidding. Can't someone else come and fetch me?'

She heard the faint cracked voice on the other end of the phone but could not make out the words. From the one-sided conversation she gathered that his partner had been diverted to a domestic, leaving him stranded at the house on the hill. She was faintly surprised seeing that the de Freitas's were absent, that he was even there, but she supposed that the police were used to checking on properties they knew were empty. Inconvenient for her, though.

Satisfied that he was unlikely to inspect the rear again, she crept back to the kitchen door. A spare key was kept beneath a plant pot full of herbs, there for the housekeeper in case she arrived when the owners weren't there. Frantham, she thought, was still one of those places where people rarely thought to lock their doors, at least, outside of the tourist season. Praying that no one had slid the bolt inside, she slid the key in the lock and turned it slowly, flinching at the sound of the sneck sliding back.

She held her breath, waited to be heard. Nothing. Just the dawn chorus starting in the line of trees that edged the de Freitas's land and the faint sound of an early car passing on the road.

She opened the door just far enough and slipped inside.

Paul's room. Top of the stairs, second door on the right, facing out over the garden. The hall was the danger point. The police officer might turn and see her through the glass panel in the door. She could see him as she emerged from the short corridor between the kitchen and the hall. He had his back to the door, was clearly bored, shuffling from foot to foot. Knowing that she'd lose her nerve if she hesitated, she scurried across the hall and took shelter on the stairs, glanced back at the front door and breathed relief that the officer had not moved. Then ran swiftly up to Paul de Freitas's room, dived inside and closed the door quietly behind her. The room was dimly lit, not enough of the dawn light yet permeating to allow her to see as clearly as she needed. Nervously, she took her keys from her pocket and gripped the tiny penlight she had attached, thankful that at least she knew where to look. She opened the wardrobe door, withdrew the deck shoes sitting on the wardrobe floor, and pulled out the insole from the left and then the right.

There.

Hidden beneath was a news clipping announcing the funeral of Arthur Payne. Born 1923 and a phone number that, despite what the advert said, was not that of Paul de Freitas. She replaced the shoes, stuffed keys and torch and clipping back into her jacket pocket and shut the wardrobe doors, relieved that she now had the note Paul was supposed to have left inside the book. Irritated too that he should, at his age, see fit to play such childish games.

She fancied she could hear his laughter and his voice. 'Half in the book, half in my laptop case, maybe. I haven't decided yet. I'll put the full version in my shoe. The light-blue ones I don't wear.' Then more seriously, 'If anything happens, this is who you call, you understand that, don't you. I made a promise and I have to deliver on it. If I can't . . . if for any reason I can't . . .'

She closed her eyes to stop the tears from falling, told herself she was nothing but a fool, then silently, she got to her feet and crept back down the stairs and out of the house.

Half an hour later she was at work, signing in at reception.

'Hi, Lyndsey, you're early, even for you.'

She shrugged. 'I was awake, I thought I'd make an early start.'

She passed out of the reception area and made her way to her office, the adrenaline that had carried her through now draining, leaving her trembling. Once safe in her office, she took out her mobile and dialled the number quoted in the advert, hoping as it had no other code, that this was a local call.

'Do you have it?'

'Not yet, but I know how to get it now. The police have the computer . . .'

'Not now, they don't.'

'But they'll have copies of the drive. Look, I know what to look for, but only Paul had the complete key.'

There was no reply from the man on the phone.

'Did you hear me?'

There was only silence. She dropped her phone back into her bag and stood uncertain in the middle of the room. What now? She had expected something more. Something definite.

Dial the number, Paul had said. They'll know what to do. Well, Lyndsey thought bitterly, if they did, whoever they were, they didn't seem about to let her know.

THIRTY

Mac walked to work. It took ten minutes if he hurried and fifteen if, as usual, he dawdled, pausing often to look out to sea and enjoy the leisurely start to his day.

Life in Frantham was very different from his life before, still in a seaside town but in a much busier area and with a much larger team. When he had first arrived, he had been bored and unsettled, thought himself unable to adjust to the quiet and the intimacy of the small community. Life since then had, in reality, been anything but quiet and Mac had found himself challenged by events and, as he walked in today, he was very aware that this case and what had started out as a murder inquiry, had become unbelievably complex.

Once out of Frantham Old Town the path took him on to the wooden walkway leading around the cliff and above the ocean and as the new town of Frantham came into view, Mac saw a familiar figure leaning against the railing. Hale.

The temptation to turn back was momentarily overwhelming, but then Hale looked in his direction and the impulse had to be put aside.

'You lied to me,' Mac said conversationally taking his place on the rail beside Hale. He glanced further down the walkway but they seemed to be alone.

'No friends,' Hale said. 'No associates. Just the two of us.'

'But you still lied to me. Who the hell are you?'

'I lied about my employers,' Hale said. 'Not my employment. How are Mr and Mrs de Freitas?'

'Well, and safe.'

'Perhaps. You've had dealings with a certain Abe Jackson.'

'What of it?' Mac asked.

'You know he had the de Freitas's followed when they left here?'

'What makes you think it was him?'

'Because it wasn't me,' Hale said flatly.

Mac considered. 'What do you think Abe Jackson wants?'

he asked. 'He seemed to think that Paul was working for the government?' He let the question hang but no response. 'He mentioned something about reverse engineering certain technology?'

'I wouldn't know.'

'Like hell you wouldn't.' He straightened up and began to walk on. Hale fell into step beside him.

'I work for the government,' Hale said. 'But not in their direct employ, that much is true. Inspector . . . Mac, Paul was doing some very specialised research. He promised to get the results of that research direct to me. He and one of my men, Ian Manning, they were doing final testing on the work when they were attacked aboard Paul's boat. I'm led to think that it was Abe Jackson's doing. He is very capable of such an operation. Very capable. And now, it seems, you've lost track of him.'

'It seems to me,' Mac suggested, 'that if you'd been so sure of that, you'd have taken action against him yourself. No, I don't buy it.'

Hale said nothing for a moment. They crossed from the walkway and on to the promenade.

'So,' Mac continued, 'if Paul and your man weren't killed by Abe Jackson, and you didn't do it yourself, then there must be a third party involved. And I ask myself, what could be so important that so many people want it? What was Paul doing that was not only worth killing for, but was worth killing *him* for? And that leads me to a further question. Or a further observation. There is no question that Paul was killed by accident; he was executed, kneeling on the deck, shot through the back of the head. Which, as I've said, makes me wonder. Did whoever it was on board that boat kill him because he'd already handed over whatever it was they wanted, handed it over and therefore rendered himself useless? Or did they kill him because they knew he was ready to hand it on and they wanted to prevent that?'

'And do you have an answer to any of that?'

'Not yet,' Mac admitted. 'Not yet, but I promise you we will get there. I have an objection to people being shot, in Frantham particularly. There's been far too much of it going on.'

'You are beginning to sound like your friend, Rina,' Hale told him.

'That's no bad thing,' Mac said, wondering, slightly anxiously, what Hale might know about Rina Martin. 'Incidentally, while we're asking questions, did your people take Paul's laptop?'

'Why would you think that?'

'Because I know Abe Jackson didn't and if it wasn't you, then it must have been our fabled third party. And my second question. I visited Paul's lab, his inner sanctum as his assistants called it. Whatever he was working on was gone.'

Hale flinched. A tiny movement, soon hidden, but Mac noted it.

'You don't have it, do you? You're as in the dark as we are?'

Hale had recovered himself. 'I doubt that, Mac,' he said. 'I doubt that very much.'

THIRTY-ONE

Tim was at the Palisades Hotel for the first time since his eventful night. He had rented a car and Rina had accompanied him. Red-haired Andy, Mac's probationary constable, had followed them over, ostensibly as protection, though, as he freely admitted, Rina would probably be a greater force than he. He had told the owners, Blake and Lilly, that he was investigating Tim's accident, as the other driver had left the scene.

Tim had come to meet the engineer who had come to help plan the Pepper's Ghost illusion and Andy, having spent some time talking to the hotel owners and interviewing staff, joined them in the main ballroom.

Blake and Lilly were watching as Tim and the engineer paced the stage, discussing something technical that involved much hand waving.

'So, what's going on?' Andy wanted to know.

'I think they're figuring out how to fix the glass,' Rina said.

'Were the staff able to tell you anything?' Blake asked. 'I really hope it wasn't a guest from here. I don't see how it could have been. Tim was almost the last to leave that night.'

'Almost the last?'

'The night porter was late arriving so Callie stayed on for an hour.'

'Did he say he'd be late?'

'Oh yes, it was all arranged,' Blake assured him. 'Callie left about a half-hour after Tim.'

'Well, no one saw a thing,' Andy told them. He turned his attention back to the stage. 'So, what's this all about, then?'

'Creating ghosts,' Rina told him. 'Tim is working on revamping a very old illusion. It's going to look amazing.' She beckoned Andy to the side of the stage. 'Look, there's a little orchestra pit, lower than the stage and a partition which blocks the view of the audience. The actor or magician stands there, in the pit, with a light there and a mirror on this side, furthest away from the stage, set at an angle. The light is set to illuminate the actor. His reflection in the mirror is then projected on to the glass sheet hung above the stage. If it's done right, the audience won't be able to see the glass, all they'll see is a shadowy image, ghostly and transparent, floating above the stage. Very spooky and very impressive.'

'That'll work?' Andy sounded unconvinced.

'Oh yes. Tim says this is the perfect stage for it. Have you talked to this Callie, yet? She may well have seen something.'

'Not yet,' Andy said. 'She's not due on duty until,' he glanced at his watch, 'about now, actually.'

Rina nodded. 'I'll come with you,' she said.

'Oh,' Andy wasn't sure that was the way it was supposed to be. 'I suppose so, Mrs Martin, but I think that should be my job, really.'

'Nonsense,' Rina told him. She glanced back at the stage, making sure that Tim was still gainfully employed and not likely to wander off without her. 'Now, where will she be?'

They found Callie in a small office off the reception area. She was glad to hear that Tim was all right but felt she could add little.

'Tim left, the car park was empty apart from my old banger. I'd have noticed if there was anyone else around.'

Rina looked out through the main entrance. Callie was right. The car park and the exit on to the road were in full view.

'There was one thing, though. I didn't think about it until now.'

Rina turned. 'What was that?' she asked, earning herself a slightly resentful look from Andy who felt that should have been his question.

'Well, probably nothing, but just a few minutes after Tim left, this big black car . . . at least I think it was black, could have been blue or green I suppose. You can't really tell that late at night, can you?'

'So, this car?' Andy prompted.

'Speeding, it was. I saw it go by on the road. Heading towards Frantham. I mean, I thought, oh I'm glad he's not going my way. I turn right, you see, outside the gate, not left like Tim does.' She paused for breath. 'I remember thinking about Tim, that the car would be going the same way.' She turned quizzical eyes on Andy and then on Rina. 'Was it the car that caused Tim's accident, do you think? Oh, my lord,

I should have called the police, should have told someone about a dangerous driver, but I never thought, and with Frantham police station being closed they'd have had to come all the way out from . . .'

'Thank you, Callie,' Rina interrupted her flow. 'I doubt the police would have been able to get anyone out here fast enough to have made a difference, so don't you worry about it.' Tim appeared in the lobby, saw Callie, and ducked back into the dining room. Rina hid her smile. 'We'd better be off, then,' she said. 'And don't you worry.'

'You realise,' Andy said as they made their way back to where Tim was waiting, 'that by the time she gets home tonight she'll know the make and model of the car and have a full description of the driver and be telling all and sundry that the police should have done something about it anyway. Psychic, she expects us to be.'

Rina patted his arm. 'I know,' she said. 'Just lucky then that we talked to her now when her memory had only been partly refreshed.'

'I suppose,' Andy agreed. 'Do you think she even saw the car?'

'Oh, I think the car was real enough, probably the fact that it was speeding, but I doubt she thought any more about it. I doubt very much she anticipated consequences for Tim or that she should report it,' she shrugged. 'I don't suppose she gets much in the way of excitement. Are you ready, Tim?'

'I am, we've done all we can today.'

'Then we'll get on,' Rina said. 'Andy, I want to take a look at the place where Tim went off the road, so we'll be stopping for a moment.'

'Right you are, Mrs Martin, but I don't think you'll find anything. CSI took photos and that. Of the tyre tracks and that. But there weren't much else.'

'Nevertheless,' Rina said firmly, 'I'd like to take a look. I'd like Tim to show me exactly what happened.'

'Fine, by me,' Tim told her, 'so long as there's no running to be done. I've done my share of running for the year.'

Rina stood thoughtful and silent beside the little copse in which Tim had taken shelter. She knew it, of course, but now, seeing it with fresh eyes as a place of refuge, she was struck by how small it was; how little cover, how few places to hide.

She tried not to think what might have happened if they had found Tim, and done whatever they planned to do. The thought of Tim dead, or beaten or in any way hurt, sliced in to her belly, reminded her so horribly of that agony she had felt when her beloved Fred had been taken from her. It was not that she loved Tim in anything like the same way as she had adored her husband. Not the same *way*, no, but with something of the same intensity. Tim was her friend, her ally, maybe her surrogate son. Rina would not have been able to allocate a single relationship to him, but the thought of life without Tim was an unbearable notion.

She bent to examine the tyre tracks, more to hide the fact that tears pricked at her eyes than because she thought she could tell anything by looking at them. She straightened up. 'Show me where you hid.'

Tim led them into the copse. It looked different in daylight and, like Rina, he was struck by how little cover there actually was. He vividly recalled the tightness in his chest, the dry mouth and the all-consuming fear that he would be discovered. The leaves and grasses he had thrown himself down upon still showed signs of bruising. 'Here,' he said. 'I got as far under the bushes as I could and lay down flat. I was dressed in black, but scared to hell they might see my face, so I kept as low as I could. I thought when they turned the car headlights this way they were sure to spot me. I'd have completely lost it if they'd come all the way into the copse.'

'So, why didn't they?' Rina wondered. 'Tim, when they came looking for you, what path did they take?'

Tim pointed. 'Through there, other side of that tree. I guess it looks like an easier route and you can get through right into the field. I think they assumed I must have run.'

Rina nodded slowly. She backtracked to the road and looked back to where Tim had lain hidden. He was right; the trees opened out and gave a view across fields and sea. The lighter glimpse of moon and ocean may well have drawn them to look that way rather than the thicket and tangle across the route that Tim had chosen.

But it still didn't feel right. Had they just intended to frighten Tim, force him to back off? But to back off from what? Unless someone, the men in that speeding car, knew that she and Tim had protected the de Freitas's and that Tim had smuggled them from the house, then there was nothing to say that Tim had either interest or involvement in this confusing affair.

And if they'd seen Tim take the de Freitas's out, why hadn't they intercepted him then, or tackled Lydia and Edward when they'd been alone at the farmhouse?

No, only one set of people that Rina could think of had witnessed Tim's direct involvement and that had been those up at the de Freitas's house when she and Tim had gone to collect their belongings.

The men who had shot at them.

In which case, those men knew exactly who she and Tim were and where they could be found.

'I think we should go now,' Rina said, a theory beginning to form in her head.

Tim started the car and allowed the silence to grow for a few minutes.

'So,' he said, 'what is the analytical machine that is Rina's brain telling her?'

'That they meant to scare you that night, to scare you badly enough to force you to act . . . or not to act. Truly, Tim, I've not worked that one out yet, but it occurs to me that the men who ran you off the road and the men up at Edward and Lydia's house are one and the same. It makes me wonder, also, if they really were such bad shots as they seemed to be.'

'How do you mean?' Tim asked.

'I mean, Tim, that despite your valiant attempts at defensive driving, your car is still a large target and the rear screen one that even I could hit with very little difficulty. A good shot could have shot out a tyre. A good shot could have killed you or me. I doubt the headrest would have been much of a disruption to a speeding bullet. Tim, that gun-man fired at the gatepost, he wanted us scared but not injured. Not dead.'

'Considerate of them. And those two in the car?'

'Maybe they thought we'd not taken enough notice the first time.'

'And if they'd caught me?'

'Then I'd probably be visiting in hospital. Tim, if they wanted you dead, wanted either of us dead, I get the feeling that is exactly what we'd be.'

'Rina, you're not making me feel any better.'

'I think, Tim, that our gun-toting friends view us as a minor inconvenience, but one that might be frightened into being useful.'

'Useful? How?'

She sighed. 'I've got to admit, that bit escapes me at present, but I'm thinking that they may be wondering what, if anything, the de Freitas's told us. Lydia and Edward are out of play, out of reach. We, on the other hand, are not. So, maybe they're wondering, what have we been told? Nothing or everything? Did Paul confide in any or all of us? That message on Lydia's phone frightened them enough to run away, but they didn't do what most normal people do, they didn't go to the police, presumably because Paul had somehow instilled in them some fear of authority. Given them some reason for not trusting the usual sources of protection.'

'Rina, we're back to there being a police informant or something.'

'Which may or may not have been Abe Jackson or the mysterious Hale. You know what, Tim, I think this is a case of no one being at all sure what anyone else has or knows or is going to do. I'm inclined to bet that we have three quite distinct entities here. Hale's lot, whoever Abe Jackson is working for and this other tribe.'

'How do we know they're not working together?'

'Because, so far, none of us except Paul and that poor man with him has wound up dead. While our three groups try to second guess whatever it is they are trying to guess, no one dare take anyone or anything out of the game. Not properly, not completely. I think that Paul de Freitas may have been more savvy than any of us have given him credit for. More stupid too.'

'How can he be both, Rina?'

'I think whatever he had that these people want, he hid it in different places, maybe allowed several people to have just part of the picture.'

'Like an insurance policy? Like posting a letter to your lawyer "to be opened in the case of my death"?'

'Something like that, but as Mac's already spoken to his solicitor I suppose we must assume he didn't do that. Pity, I've always rather liked it as a dramatic device. Stupid, because he has now made any number of people into potential targets. Right now, I'm hoping that enough people want the secret badly enough that they want to keep every potential secret keeper alive and, mostly, intact. But I don't imagine that will last long as a safeguard. I don't imagine it will be long before one or other of those involved decides that if they can't have whatever it is Paul was hiding, then no one is going to.'

The tall man had watched their foray into the copse and the woman stand thoughtful, gazing in his direction. For a moment he thought she had seen him, though he'd been careful to stand close in cover, not allow any part of his silhouette to be seen against the skyline.

'What are they doing?' The voice on the mobile phone was quiet but no less demanding for that.

'Just looking at the wood. I think he's showing her where he hid.'

'Are they alone?'

'No, that young police constable is with them. Nevins or whatever his name is. They're leaving now. What should I do?'

'Let them go. We've surveillance in place.'

The tall man closed his mobile phone and slipped it back into his pocket, waited until Rina and company had gone and then returned to his car, parked on the grass verge in the shallow scrape of a parking spot walkers used to access the cliff path from the road.

Tim Brandon had surprised them that night and that was a bad thing. Surprised them and showed also that their local knowledge was sadly lacking. He hated to have so little time to prepare, to recce an area of operation. All the maps in the world were no substitute to seeing the terrain first-hand. They had been surprised too by Tim Brandon himself, had made the mistake of seeing him as a soft target, likely to be scared out of his wits and so easily controlled.

Two errors compounded into one almighty fuck-up; he was wise enough to know he would not be forgiven for a second.

THIRTY-TWO

Abe Jackson watched Mac leave the police station and walk along the promenade. He turned off on to Newell Street and, Abe assumed, Peverill Lodge.

He was certain enough of his assumption not to bother following; besides, Newell Street was less crowded than the promenade and Mac was not such an easy tail that Abe could be complacent. He watched as Sergeant Baker and Andy Nevins also took their leave. Baker walked home every night. Andy usually drove, but Abe knew that tonight he was planning to meet friends and have a night out. One of them was driving and Andy's car left parked safely behind the police station.

Kendal had been there earlier, but had left close on an hour before as had the two officers he had borrowed to collate the sackfuls of evidence – or potential evidence – Mac had brought from Paul's flat.

Abe had been surprised by the way the whole operation had been kept so low-key. Voices from the top advising caution, no doubt. Managing the media. Not that they'd be able to keep the lid on for long, Abe thought, as the story they'd put out about a tragic accident on board *The Greek Girl* wouldn't cut it for long. The media reports had, so far, given the impression that Paul had been alone on the boat, but too many people had seen the second body being brought off. Even given Abe's own dealings with official dissembling, he was astonished that the pretence had held for this long.

Abe waited, watching the world go by and the boats sail into the marina. Families, late at the beach, were enjoying the evening sun and then he turned back along the promenade and made his way to the rear of the police station. There were three cars parked in the tiny space. Mac's own, Andy's little Fiat and the official, area car. Abe had already familiarised himself with the terrain. The small yard was at the head of a cul-de-sac. A few houses backed on to the little road, but unless you had a reason to be there, it was not somewhere anyone would need or want to be. Once inside the yard, he could not be seen from the road, nor was he overlooked from any of the nearby properties. Abe slipped between the cars. He had already selected his point of entry earlier in the day, checked out the ageing alarm system while he had been there legitimately, with Mac, and he decided now not to wait for dark. He might be able to make himself invisible in the yard, but start shining a torch around and there was a fair bet someone would notice an unusual light. There were no street lights in the dead end of a road and Abe was pretty sure that, much past seven o'clock, there would be little ambient illumination in the cramped little yard even at this time of year.

Mac's car was parked close beside the wall. Abe clambered on to the bonnet and took a careful look around. The wall was still high enough to conceal him from the road. The small window at the back of the police station had a simple latch. Abe had noticed when he had first visited the police station that the little room beyond was just used for storage, but that the door had no lock and, from there, he was out in the main reception area. He had brought with him a glass cutter and a roll of tape bought at a local DIY warehouse. He donned thin latex gloves and, carefully, he cut a half-circle above the latch leaving an inch or so of glass still attached. He taped across the cut, so it would not fall, then cut the rest. A light tap and it freed itself from the rest of the pane, kept from falling by the tape. Abe fished a tough, zip-lock bag from his pocket and slipped glass cutter, glass and tape inside, then reached in and released the latch.

This window, he knew, was not alarmed and he knew too that once out of the storeroom, he'd have thirty seconds to reach the panel and unset the alarm. The same to get out again once it had been reset.

The latch was stiff; Abe figured it had been years since anyone opened it. His worry was that the window would have been sealed by equal years of over-zealous decorating, held fast by sedimentary gloss paint.

He need not have worried. Re-decorating had clearly not been on anyone's list of 'must dos' for a long time. Abe opened the window and jumped lightly down from the sill, closing the window behind him. Out of the store room, into the front of house, the panel for the alarm was behind the desk. It had a lock but the key, as Abe had also noted on his visit, hung on the wall beside it. He opened the panel and unset the sensors, watching as the light blinked out and hoping there was nothing more sophisticated that he was unaware of, and decided, judging by the rest of the set-up, that thought was just paranoia on his part.

Mac's office door was open and the case file in the cabinet, together with the bags of assorted detritus he had collected from the flat.

Abe flicked through the crime scene photographs, looking not so much at the bodies as at the background, examining what was there and what was not.

Updated reports told him that Mac and Kendal were little further on than they had been when his subterfuge had been discovered and he'd lost access. He read with interest an account of Tim's misadventures, which Mac had copied into the file in the belief that this might be related to the death of Paul de Freitas.

'No doubt about that,' Abe said softly. Question was, who? Not Hale, he thought. Hale was more subtle, more patient than that. There were additional notes, too, about the visit to *Iconograph*. Abe had noticed that day that Mac had hung back, chatting to Lyndsey and Ray, but had been unable to get close enough to hear what had been said. Mac had noted in the file that he had asked them about *The Power of One* and the phrase *Payne 23*. He had recorded Ray's comments and noted that Lyndsey seemed oddly silent on the subject.

They still had no name for the second man on Paul's boat. Nothing more than the first name of Ian.

'Manning,' Abe said. 'His name, Mac, was Ian Manning.' He found one of Mac's business cards in a desk drawer, wrote the name on the back, and lay it in a prominent position on Mac's desk. Then rummaged through the collection of evidence bags not yet submitted for forensic examination. Had it been Abe's call, the lot would have gone, and he suspected Mac would have liked to do the same, but Abe knew the deal. Each test cost money and ninety-nine per cent of what Mac had collected, and was currently collating with help from Kendal and his assistants, would prove irrelevant. Abe glanced through the selection of bank statements and web printouts, takeaway brochures and shopping lists and decided, as Mac had already done, that there was nothing here. The one exception being the *Payne 23* clipping that he had already seen . . . and the pack of pills, which he had not.

Abe turned the blister pack between his fingers, knowing who they had belonged to and what they meant and that they had nothing to do with any relationship of Paul de Freitas with anyone.

Lyndsey Barnes, assistant to Paul de Freitas, had met Ian Manning, minder to the same, and they had fallen for one another. Simple as that. Ian had no proper base down south; Lyndsey shared a flat with a couple of girlfriends, so Paul had allowed them to meet up in his. Result, one happy couple, but also one young woman drawn further into her boss's affairs than would usually have been the case and what Paul might have told her, outside of working hours, was something Abe would give a great deal to know. Abe and others too.

He dropped the pills back on the desk, straightened everything up, and packed it back in to the filing drawer.

Abe would never have allowed this relationship to develop. If Ian had shown interest in Lyndsey on Abe's watch, he'd have taken him off the watch, given him a good dressing-down and an ultimatum. Keep away from the girl until the work was done. Anything otherwise was messy, sloppy, unpredictable and by the time Ian had realised that for himself, it had been too late. He'd tried to tell Lyndsey that it was over, but been unable to do so because he hadn't believed it himself. Abe didn't want to think that Ian's distraction was what had got him killed but he knew it hadn't helped. The girl had become an unwilling chink in his usual armour and Ian had died, Paul de Freitas with him.

Abe had lost a good friend and when the opportunity to run interference had arisen, Abe had grasped it with both hands. That the brief he had been given had gone rapidly astray and Abe found himself ordered out had done nothing to dissuade him. His masters may not want him in the game now but, too bad. They'd invited him to the party and, just because the host had thrown a strop, Abe saw no reason to leave just yet.

'You were a good man, Ian,' Abe said softly, glancing down at the name he had written on Mac's business card. 'But always a fool for a pretty face. Was she worth it, is what I want to know? Frankly, my old friend, I think not.'

'Can I come with you tomorrow?' Tim said. 'Or would that be too unofficial?'

'To Manchester? I don't see why not. I'm using my own car and to be honest, I'd appreciate the company and the extra pair of eyes.'

'Good. Thanks. You'll be all right, Rina?'

'Oh, course I will. We're all being careful and you can't stay chained to the house. Give my best to Joy,' she added with a sly smile. 'Tell her she's more than welcome to come and stay for a while once things have settled down. You know, I do find all of this a little ironic.'

'Oh, what particularly?' Mac asked.

'That you and Bridie Duggan should both end up on the same side. Considering her background and history and all that.'

Mac laughed. 'I like Bridie,' he said. 'For that matter, I liked James, though I doubt it would do to say so in front of Superintendent Aims.'

'His nose still out of joint, is it?'

'Oh yes. Very much so. Dave Kendal says he's practically apoplectic and looking very hard for someone to blame. You can't be too hard on him though. I knew Hale wasn't what he said he was, but I still don't know exactly what he is and for all I do know, he may well be working for the government or the MOD or something just as unlikely.'

'And your money would be on?' Rina asked.

'Well, given the warning passed on via Tim's Uncle Charles, I'm guessing something at least semi-official. Unless, of course, they just want to give him enough rope and see if he saves them the trouble of hiring a hangman.' He frowned. 'For what it's worth, I think you're probably right, Rina, about there being three distinct parties involved. I'd pretty much reached the same conclusion. I told Hale as much and he argued, but he didn't tell me I was wrong.'

'And still no sign of Abe Jackson? What did you make of him, Mac?'

'Well, again for what it's worth, I thought he was an honest-seeming man and I felt, had the circumstances been different

we could have got along comfortably enough.' He shrugged.
'But what do I know, I liked Jimmy Duggan and he was a
career criminal, so I'm not so sure you should trust my judgement when it comes to character assessment.'

He got up and stretched wearily. 'Best be off, early start if
we're driving up there. Seven thirty, Tim?'

Tim winced, he was not by nature an early-morning person.
'So long as you don't want conversation for the first hour,'
he said.

Rina waved Mac off and then returned to her little front
room. Tim was thoughtful. 'Not so long ago you'd have been
suggesting he stay in the spare room,' Tim said. 'A lot has
changed, Rina.'

'Mostly for the better,' Rina agreed, 'though I could do with
a little boring routine for a while. It's all been a little too
exciting lately. I could do with living in slightly less interesting times.'

Lyndsey had wandered down to a local cafe-bar she and Ian
had liked and sat in the window looking out at the quiet street.
She missed him so much and the worst of it was, she couldn't
tell anyone about him. Few people knew they had been
involved. Two people, to be exact. Paul and Ray. It was impossible to keep anything from Ray; she worked far too closely
with him and he with Paul for that kind of thing to stay secret
for long, but her flatmates didn't know. They guessed she'd
had a boyfriend and teased her a bit, but she'd even lied about
his name and, to be truthful, wasn't close enough to either to
confide. She'd been the third girl, moving into an already
long-term agreement, taking the smallest room and, to be fair,
the smallest share of the rent. Sisters, Jennifer and Suze, were
pleasant enough and as work took up so much of her time
anyway, it had been fine. Until she met Ian.

The flat share had been a cheap option when she'd first
moved down to work at *Iconograph*, something of a stopgap
until she decided whether or not she wanted to stay in Dorset
and it had allowed her to save, put a fair bit of her salary
aside for the deposit on the house she felt she should be
working for, and that her *family* had always told her she should
be working for.

'Why?' Ian had asked. 'Is that what you really want?'

'No, I want to chuck it all in, bugger off round the world for a year, meet a nice guy and go to Las Vegas to be married by a Korean Elvis.'

'Then why don't you? Why don't we?' He had reached across the table and taken her hand almost shyly. 'You've already met the nice guy and I'd be happy with a Korean Elvis too.'

She had laughed, not sure whether or not it was a real proposal. Not sure either of them was ready for her to accept if it was. She had clasped his hand, happy, content to let things be, see where it led.

A week later he'd been telling her it would be better if they split up for a while, though she could see in his eyes he meant not a word of it.

A week after that he was dead and she understood why he thought they'd be better apart. Understood that he was scared, not of the relationship, not of the commitment, but of something less abstract.

'What if I'd said yes?' Lyndsey whispered at her own reflection in the window glass. 'If I'd said yes, would you have gone away with me? Then, right then? Would you still be alive?'

She fumbled in her bag for a tissue, pulled out the small cellophane-wrapped pack and with it the newspaper clipping. For a minute or so, she sat with the clipping on the table, staring at it. She had tried the number twice now, but with little response and was starting to think that she'd have to give it up and let it go . . . whatever it was. But she had made a promise to Paul. A promise Ian knew nothing about and, more than that, whatever this was all about was, she was certain, what had killed both her lover and her boss.

She searched her bag again, this time for her mobile phone, and dialled the number on the scrap of paper.

'Look,' Lyndsey said into the empty space that opened up at the other end. 'I've got something you want. You have to talk to me. Talk to me now or I give it to the police, you understand me?'

No voice, no human sound, just three or four clicks as though something had been pressed or some mechanism engaged. Then the silence closed and her phone went dead.

Angrily, Lyndsey stared at it, then threw it back into her

bag in disgust, together with the pack of tissues and the scrap of paper. Ian was gone and her last ephemeral contact with him, with whatever he had been involved in, seemed to be fading too.

Abe Jackson's problem was that he was used to being part of a team and current events had found him rather out on a limb. He had resources he could call upon. Old colleagues or people who owed him favours or had reason to be nervous of offending him, but he didn't want to waste resources he may have need of later.

Of the three categories of potential help, old friends were the most reliable, working down the food chain from that to those too afraid of him to say no. There was, Abe knew from bitter experience, always the chance that, once the habit of fear had become established, there may well be others more frightening or more immediately threatening than Abe himself.

He had set a couple of former colleagues the task of watching Lyndsey. It helped that they'd also known Ian, but was not perfect, neither being able to commit the time and energy to the task that Abe would have liked. They were family men now, and regular civilians.

The value of even such sporadic watchers had proved its worth though. He had left the police station and found two missed calls on his phone. Lyndsey had gone out, he was told and all had seemed quiet but then . . . 'Company,' Abe's associate said. 'One in the building, two outside. You want a hand?'

'Hopefully not. I'm on my way.'

The drive was no more than twenty minutes but the fear that Lyndsey might return before then made it seem so much longer. He parked at the end of her street and joined his friend, staked out on the ground floor of an empty flat Abe had rented almost opposite the building in which Lyndsey lived.

'Anything?'

'She's still out. Green car, three down on the left, parked behind the Mondeo.'

Abe nodded. 'And the other man?'

'I saw the ground-floor tenant go in half an hour ago. Everything looked normal. I'm guessing our boy is waiting on the first-floor landing. There's a dogleg in the staircase. That's where I'd be.'

Abe nodded agreement. 'You know where she went?'

He shook his head. 'Left ten minutes before I relieved Niall, went down towards the centre of town, so he said.'

'We need more bodies. It just can't be done with two part-timers.'

His friend took no offence, knowing the truth of that. 'I'd say it felt like old times,' he said wryly, 'but even old times were better prepared and equipped than this. So, what now?'

Abe considered. 'Sit tight,' he said. 'I'll drive past the flat, see if I can pick her up on the way back. Did she look like she was going for a night out?'

'Jeans and a blue shirt, nothing out the ordinary. Shoulder bag, no jacket.'

Abe nodded, 'I'll drive out, circle round, park up again at the end of the road. Bell me if they move.'

He left by the back door and through the entry between houses, turned without glancing down the road and returned to his car. Driving past the watchers, he glanced into his rear-view mirror. Two men, thirties, clean shaven and short haired. One wore a short-sleeved shirt, the other a dark T-shirt. Abe didn't recognise them but he knew the type. Not so long ago he had been one of them. Maybe, he thought, he still was. One of the dispossessed, trying hard to construct a new role after twenty-odd years of having it defined for him.

He drove on down the block, but there was no sight of Lyndsey. He turned left at the end of the road, preparing to swing round and back almost to where he parked before. He dare not make another circuit. He would be noticed; *he* would have noticed and he had no reason to believe they would be any different.

His mobile buzzed. 'You just missed her.'

Abe swore. 'Where is she?'

'Fifty yards, maybe, from the car. They must have seen her. What do you want me to do?'

'Nothing. Stay put and don't expose yourself. I may need you later.'

He rang off before his friend could argue, accelerated round the last corner and into Lyndsey's street. He could see her now, walking with her head down, shoulders slightly hunched, utterly unaware. The two men were out of the car. He undid his seat belt, knowing it would restrict what he had planned.

Lyndsey paused, preparing to cross the road, hesitating as she saw his car, and waited, perched on the edge of the kerb, for him to go by. Abe put his foot down, passing the two men in the car, aware of their reaction as his vehicle was recognised as one which had passed before. He screeched to a halt next to the young woman, reached across and opened the passenger-side door.

'Get in!'

She stared stupidly at him. 'What?'

'I'm a friend of Ian's. Get in.'

Startled, scared, she began to back away. Abe swore again. 'Fuck it, girl, look up the street. See those two, you do *not* want to be tangling with them. Now get your bloody arse inside!'

Bewildered, she stared at him, then looked up the street, and saw the men. 'Who . . .'

'In!' The watchers had begun to run, Abe knew it would take only seconds to close the distance.

Suddenly, Lyndsey knew it too. She chose, dived into the car, slamming the door even as Abe accelerated away, turning right this time and speeding down a side road, praying no one would step out from between the parked cars.

'Put your seatbelt on and hold tight.'

'Who the hell are you? Who the hell are *they*?'

'Ian and I served together. Like I said, he was a friend of mine. Now, keep your head down, and pray we can outrun them.'

She stared at him, eyes scared and wide, face pale. Something seemed to occur to her. 'Was it you I phoned or was it them? Was it them?'

'Girl, I don't have a clue what you're on about.' He glanced in the rear-view, and swerved the wrong way into a one-way street. Halfway down he pulled into a parking spot between two other cars, cut the engine and slid down in the seat. 'Keep down!'

'Why . . . why have we stopped?' She moved a hand towards the door handle and Abe hit the button on the driver's-side door, engaging the child lock.

'Don't even think about it.' He watched in the rear-view mirror for their pursuers' car to go by, then started the engine again and pulled out cautiously. He drove down the remainder of the one-way street and out on to another densely residential road, blessing the fact that traffic was almost non-existent and there would be no one to remember a car emerging the wrong way from a one-way street.

He turned right again at the end of the road, heading for the centre of town.

'Where are we going? Where are you taking me?' Her voice shook, her hands clutched spasmodically at the strap on her bag.

'Somewhere safe. We'll work it out from there. Look, Ian thought a lot about you. I promised him, if anything happened, I'd do my best to look out for you. That's what I'm trying to do. I'm sorry I had to scare the pants off you to do it, but believe me, you'd be a damn sight more scared by now if I'd not been there.'

'Should I believe you? How did you know? Who were they and I mean, who the hell are you?'

He was watching the traffic in his mirrors, anxious and wary. So far, they seemed clear, but Abe would be much happier once more distance had been put between them. 'First, you've no reason to believe me; not much choice, either. Second, I've had a friend keeping an eye on you. He tipped me off, as it was, but it was all a bit too little, too late. Third, my name's Abe Jackson. Ian probably called me Lincoln. His idea of a joke.'

She blinked, nodded, recognising the name. 'How do I know you're who you say you are?'

'Right now you don't. You want me to take you home? There's a third man holed up in your place. Sure he'd be happy to meet you.'

'No! I mean, no. I don't want that. I . . .' Her eyes widened again. 'What about Jen and Suze?'

'Jennifer, as I understand it, doesn't finish work until one. They'll be long gone by then and I'll call the local police, report a prowler, just to be sure. Suze stays over at her boyfriend's house on a Tuesday night. Any reason to expect she won't this week?'

'How do you know all that?' She had calmed down a bit but now the level of fear had risen again.

'I know because Ian told me. He said Tuesday was the only evening it was worth meeting at your place. The only evening you had it to yourself. I don't think he was a fan of Suze, though he seemed to think Jen was salvageable.'

'Salvageable?'

'Not a complete waste of space. He thought they were both airheads, though that's not quite the adjective he used.'

'He told you a lot about me,' she said quietly.

'He liked you. More than liked you. Lyndsey, you were the first woman I'd ever known him be serious about. I was one of his oldest friends, of course he talked about you. I told him he should break it off until the job was over. He said he was going to try, but to tell the truth, I don't think he was doing anything more than humouring me.'

'He did try,' she whispered. 'I didn't understand. Then . . .'

'Then it was too late. I know. What I don't know is what they want with you and that, girl, is what we are going to find out.'

Twice Abe glimpsed what he thought was their pursuers' car. Once at a crossroads and once three cars behind in a queue of traffic. Each time he told her to get down on to the floor and she crouched miserably in the footwell, fear exuding from every pore. Abe could smell it on her, acrid and familiar and he was disturbed and a little relieved to find that, in contrast, he was absolutely calm. He had gone beyond the adrenaline rush, the tension, the – almost – stage fright that he associated with the preparation for combat. Beyond that and into a kind of steady state mode of clear thought and something close to enjoyment. He knew himself, knew his enemy, knew what to do and that was all there was.

He was, though, profoundly glad to be out of the town and on to darkening country roads.

'You can get up now.'

'Are you sure?' She was scared enough for her voice to shake and she was pale with shock.

'I'm sure.' They'd had the advantage of surprise this time, and squeaked clear. Abe knew they would not be so lucky another time. His phone rang and she jumped. 'It's all right, just my friend checking in.'

They spoke briefly, Abe assuring him that they were all right, learning that the third man had left Lyndsey's building.

'Clear yourself out of the flat, don't either of you go anywhere near the place again. I'll be in touch.'

He rang off. 'You have a mobile with you?'

'Yes.'

'Take the SIM card out, chuck the rest out of the window.' He smiled at her. 'Open it first.'

'Throw my phone away?'

'Yes. Look, girl, modern phones carry a GPS tracker. If they have your number, you only have to make a call and they can track you.'

She shook her head. 'I know that's possible, but that's high-tech stuff. They won't have . . .'

'Yes, love, they will. They do.'

'Then I won't make any calls.'

He sighed. 'You might say that, might even believe it but truly, you have that temptation, you'll give into it sooner or later. Besides, some phones can be traced even if they're not turned on. I don't want to take that risk.'

'And what about your phone?'

'Pay as you go, not registered, and I change it every few days.'

He watched from the corner of his eye as she took the phone from her bag. This was crunch time, the final act of trust and letting go. She stared at it for several moments and then opened up the back and removed the SIM. 'I suppose that makes it harder to trace if someone finds it. Not having a SIM card, I mean.'

'Not foolproof, but it helps.'

She wound the window down and tossed the phone without a second look. 'Happy now?' She sounded angry, bitter, her voice thick with tears.

'Not happy, no. I won't be happy until we've sorted this.' He tried to inject a more sympathetic tone in to his voice, understanding that she needed this but aware that it was not quite his forte. 'Look, we hide out tonight and we talk, try to sort out what's going on. Tomorrow, well, we're going to need some help and it's a question of who we can trust and how far and, I know this isn't easy for you but . . .'

'Isn't easy!' Her voice cracked, almost squeaked with outrage.

Maybe, he thought, his attempts at sympathy had misfired. Maybe he was even worse at it than he'd thought.

'Isn't easy. You grab me off the street, you make me throw away my phone. You claim to be a friend of Ian's, you . . .'

'Saved your life,' he said harshly. 'Girl, don't forget I just saved your life.'

THIRTY-THREE

Morning brought developments even before Mac collected Tim for their trip to Manchester.

Kendal phoned, telling him to switch on the morning news. He caught the local bulletin halfway through and realised that the story had now fully broken. Paul de Freitas had been shot aboard his boat, T Greek Girl, and he had not been alone. Another man had been killed and the rumour was that he too had been shot.

'Police have not yet issued a full statement about the killings.' The reporter was clearly relishing his moment. 'Was this a double murder? A murder suicide? At the moment all we can do is speculate . . .'

'Speculate away,' Mac muttered under his breath. 'That's what the rest of us are doing.' He muted the television and picked up the phone again and spoke to Dave Kendal.

'Formal statement?'

'Will be going out mid-morning. Yours truly has the job of dealing with the press conference. That's being timed to co-incide with the lunchtime news. Expect Frantham to be awash by then. A double murder is national news.'

'And the official line is?'

'That there are issues of national security here, hence the low-key investigation. We ask our brethren in the media to accept that we can't issue full details yet and then sit back and let them invent what they like. You never know, one or the other of them might get it right before we do.'

'I imagine Aims is not pleased.'

'Aims is surprisingly sanguine. Handling the media is some-thing he does know how to do, by and large. He's joining me for the press call, making the main statement and I think the plan is to look grave and impressive while I do my damnedest to answer questions I don't actually know the answers to.'

'Some people have all the fun. I'll warn Baker and Andy we're about to be famous yet again.'

'Oh, Andy enjoys the fuss, you know he does. You're still going up to Manchester?'

'Any reason I shouldn't? I can stay if I'm more use here.'

'No, I think you're best keeping to your plans. The de Freitas's will need reassurance once they see the news and you never know, the added pressure might jog some memories loose.'

'Do we know how the media got hold of the full story?'

'Oh, Mac, you know as well as I do, dozens of people saw the second body brought ashore. Speculation must have been rampant among the local journos. I imagine one or other of them decided to let the cat out of the bag, just to see how big a cat it was. I've no doubt we'll see some sort of exclusive in the local dailies.'

Mac considered he was probably right. He made a couple of calls, priming Sergeant Baker and Andy Nevins, then drove round to Rina's to collect Tim. She had heard the news on the radio.

'Inevitable,' she said. 'But it will put the pressure on, Mac, and not just on the investigation. I suspect things will really start to move now.'

THIRTY-FOUR

D id you get some sleep?' Abe was frying bacon over the camping stove that Tim had left at the farmhouse. 'Must have done,' Lyndsey said. 'I remember looking at my watch at half one and the next thing I knew it was morning.'

'There's tea over there and the kettle boiled just a few minutes ago. There's milk in the cool box.'

She frowned. 'You're prepared. How do you know this place anyway?'

Abe flipped the bacon. 'You want eggs?'

'Um, yes. Thanks.'

'We have a certain lady called Rina Martin to thank for our accommodation, though she doesn't know it. She hid Lydia and Edward de Freitas here before a friend of hers came to collect them and take them to a place of safety. I'm sort of hoping she might do the same for you.'

'I don't understand.'

'Let's just say I keep my eyes open. Rina knows about this place because of a kidnapping Mac – that's DI McGregor – was investigating. Long story, but let's just say I'm taking advantage of their local knowledge.'

She poured water from the kettle on tea bags and poked them impatiently with a tea spoon. 'So,' she said. 'What now?'

'We ask for help.'

'From this Rina whatshername?'

'Martin. Yes.'

'Why? What is she, some sort of superhero?'

Abe sighed. He removed the bacon from the pan and broke eggs into the bacon fat, lowering the heat when they began to spit. 'She is someone who seems able to get things done,' he said. 'And the de Freitas's trusted her; she didn't let them down. With the possible exception of Inspector McGregor, she's the only person outside of some of my ex-colleagues that I'd take a chance on.'

'The exception of the Inspector? Why?'

'Because he might well feel obliged to involve others and that is something I'd very much like to avoid. Pass the plates, will you? Just there. And there's a loaf of bread somewhere, behind the cool box, I think. Good.'

'And what can this woman do that you can't?'

Abe raised an eyebrow. From being scared stupid by him last night, she seemed suddenly to have turned him into a potential saviour. 'Protect you, I hope. Sit down. Let's eat.' He sliced bread, passed her the butter and set to with appetite. After a moment's hesitation she poked at her food and then, as though realising how hungry she was, she began to eat too, falling silent.

Abe watched her, seeing a little of what Ian had seen. She was pretty, certainly. Loose dark curls softened what might have been a rather too angular face. Bright blue eyes, clouded with deep anxiety the night before, now clearer after sleep and a break from the tension.

She was clever, Ian had told him. Intelligent and smart too and the two did not always go together. Resilient, Abe decided. She was still scared, yes, but with some food inside of her and a cup of strong tea, life would not look quite so bad.

Abe was a great believer in the settling effects of bacon, eggs and tea.

'Rina, there's a man on the phone wants to talk to you. Say's his name's Abe something or other and you know all about him.'

Matthew could be a little vague on detail, Rina thought. She put down her dishcloth and made her way through to the hall. Of course she knew about Abe Jackson, but what on earth was he doing calling her?

'Mr Jackson. What can I do for you?'

'Mrs Martin. You can meet me.'

'And why should I do that?'

'Because there's someone in need of your help and, as I understand it, you're rather good at that sort of thing.'

Rina pursed her lips, amused and also somewhat disturbed. 'What sort of someone?'

'Her name is Lyndsey Barnes. She was one of Paul de Freitas's closest associates. Mac may have mentioned her to you?'

'He may have done. Mr Jackson, why should I get involved?'

'Because,' he said, 'you are now intrigued and because, that is what you do.'

Rina came to a decision. He was right, of course. 'When and where? No, *I'll* tell *you*. Noon, at the marina in Frantham Old Town. I take it you can find your way?'

Abe Jackson rang off and Rina assumed that the meeting had been arranged.

'Rina, you can't.'

She frowned, she hadn't noticed the Montmorencys loitering at the other end of the hall.

'Eavesdropping, Matthew? Stephen? That's not very polite.'

'Looking after you,' Stephen countered. 'Tim isn't here to do it and neither is Mac.'

'Therefore,' his brother continued, 'it falls to us to take their place.'

'And what makes you think I need looking after?'

The brothers exchanged a look and then Matthew laughed, replying for both of them. 'Because we all do, Rina dear. That's just the way it is. Now, get yourself ready. Stephen will stay here and take care of the ladies and I will come with you.'

Rina looked askance at them. 'Well, you know how it hurts his knees if he has to walk too far,' Matthew added, as if that had been her question.

She nodded, finally, agreeing there was a degree of sense in that. 'All right, thank you, both of you. And Stephen, we'll check in with you every half-hour. If you don't get a call, contact DI Kendal immediately. He'll know what to do.'

Mac and Tim had taken a break at services halfway to their destination. Somehow, he was only mildly surprised to see Hale, walking towards him across the car park.

'Who's that?' Tim asked.

'That,' Mac said, 'is William Hale.'

'Ah. Right. Is that a good thing or a bad thing?'

Hale paused a few feet away.

'Are you following me?' Mac asked.

'I didn't follow you, no.'

Mac let it pass.

'I want to talk to the de Freitas's. That is where you're going.'

Mac saw no reason to deny it. 'Sorry, can't be done.'

'Believe me, Mac. I have their interests at heart.'

'I find it hard to believe you have any interests except your own.'

'Harsh, Mac. And what do you think those might be?'

'Are you going to tell me? From what little I've seen of you, you like to talk even if you don't give any straight answers.'

Tim was studying something across the car park, close to the restaurant entrance. Mac followed his gaze. Two of Hale's men; the two he had met that day in Paul's apartment – them or their clones – stood waiting by the automatic doors.

Mac sighed. 'If you want to talk, you can buy us both coffee. It's too hot to stand out here.'

Hale stood aside, gesturing elaborately that they should precede him. Mac began to walk, Tim beside him. He wondered if Tim felt as he did, that though Hale had approached them empty-handed and the suggestion to go inside was his own, he could not help but feel as though he had a gun at his back.

Hale found them a table close by the window and his men went to get coffee. 'Biscuits too,' Hale said. 'Or cake. Something sweet anyway.'

Today they were casually dressed. Jeans and chinos and short-sleeved shirts, though Hale still wore a tailored jacket, despite the temperatures. Inside the restaurant, the air conditioning whirred and Mac could feel the chill on his back and arm. He wondered if Hale had planned it that way. The two men joined them at the table and Mac wondered how they might look to the casual observer in a situation full of families and holiday makers. Five men, clearly serious, obviously not in recreational mood and, despite the casual dress, still in albeit invisible uniform.

'So,' Mac said, picking up directly from what had been said outside. 'And your interest is?'

'Security,' Hale said.

'National security?'

'Well, as it turns out, yes. But my initial concern was a matter of industrial espionage. I work for a company that produces surveillance systems. Not your domestic, common or garden CCTV cameras, you understand, but systems designed to detect objects or structures or other systems that governments or individuals wish to hide. Our own government included.'

Sonar, Mac thought. Some kind of radar. That was Ray's speculation concerning Paul's latest work. 'Go on.'

'The company I work for designs systems for the Ministry of Defence. Some time ago, we were set a challenge. There's a new breed of submarine designed and built and recently commissioned. You know, I'm sure, all about stealth aeroplanes; this is a submarine with similar capabilities. It's signature, I'm told, is similar to that of a small dolphin; not bad when you consider this thing is longer than a football pitch and carries up to thirty-eight Tomahawk missiles.

'The other half of its capacity is that of detection. I'm told that its sonar is so well designed that it could, theoretically, sit in the English Channel and hear a ship leave New York.' He spread his hands in a 'would you believe it' gesture. 'Impressive stuff.'

'And . . .' Mac prompted.

'And our challenge was to design a system that could intercept this behemoth; our challenge was to detect the undetectable. If we could do it there was a chance that others could too . . .'

'And did you?' Tim asked. 'Though I suppose you must have done seeing as Paul was trying to figure out how it was made.' He frowned. 'No, I've got that wrong, haven't I? You made it, someone stole it . . .' He shook his head. 'Either way you look at it I'm turning Paul de Freitas into the bad guy and I'm not sure I'm happy with that.'

'You are almost there,' Hale told him. 'Let's just say that the people I work for came close to succeeding and that other people got wind of their success.'

'The idea was stolen,' Mac said.

'The first thing we knew was when the rumours started. A device for sale that looked remarkably like ours, but, we were happy to find, theirs was no better than ours; it was merely different.'

'So you got yourself one of these pirated devices and that's what Paul was examining.'

Hale nodded. 'I'd worked with Paul before he joined his brother in *Iconograph*. Paul had always done work on the games but he'd also had his own company as you may already know.'

Mac nodded. 'It went bust.'

'He was persuaded it would be more profitable if it did. Paul was a fantastic designer, just a little too high profile to be fully useful. As part of *Iconograph*, he could keep his profile but at the same time be utterly discreet.'

'And did Edward know about this?'

'Edward chose not to. Paul was good for his business.'

'And so, you got the pirated device to Paul. He reverse engineered the technology and . . .'

Hale drew a deep breath. 'He made it work. Ironed out the kinks, designed a new chip set. And then the problems really started.'

'In what way?' Mac sipped his coffee, and shoved it aside. It tasted, he thought, like soap. 'Paul, I have it on good authority, was a fundamentally honest man . . .'

'A statement I would like to agree with. Now. Though I had decided, previously, that Paul was nothing but a crook willing to sell out to the highest bidder. In fact, we had evidence that he'd done precisely that.'

'So you had him killed.'

'No, that wasn't me. Ian was his minder, not his executioner. Mac, we were still gathering evidence against Paul de Freitas when he was killed but as it turned out the evidence pointed in a very different direction. What we think happened is this: the third party who designed the pirated device got wind of his success. They wanted what he had, threatened him in some way. Paul pretended to give them what they wanted but it must have become clear pretty quickly that he had cheated them. We have to assume they then had him killed.'

'A little counterproductive, I'd have thought.'

'I think they believed they could get what they wanted without him. So far, none of us have been successful in that regard.'

Mac considered. 'What was *Payne 23*? Was that a signal for you to contact him? Or for them?'

Hale shook his head. 'You're slipping, Mac. You should have checked your facts. The number on the advert wasn't Paul's. It goes to some kind of automated system which then diverts the call to . . . to wherever.'

'You don't know or you aren't saying?'

Hale shrugged, spread his hands expansively. 'I need to talk to Edward and Lydia de Freitas.'

'So, why don't you talk to the local police?' Tim said. 'I'm sure they could arrange it, seeing as how you're almost a government agent or something.' He grinned suddenly. 'You know, my Uncle Charles reckons you're some kind of free-lancer. Work for whoever pays best . . .'

Hale frowned. He was, Mac noted, still in control, but Tim had definitely struck a nerve.

'I will ask them if they wish to speak with you,' he said. 'But I will not push them to do so, nor will I facilitate it. The best I can offer is for you to provide me with a contact number and the rest is up to them.' He stood, prepared to leave. 'Goodbye, Mr Hale. Thank you for the coffee.'

Tim followed him from the restaurant, resisting the temptation to look back at Hale and his followers.

'That was weird,' he said as they got back into Mac's car. 'You think they've bugged us or anything?'

Mac shook his head. 'Who knows. What did you make of all that?'

'A mix of truth and misdirection,' Tim hypothesised. 'You know how it is? The best lies are those based on a kernel of truth, but I'm intrigued. How does Abe Jackson fit into all of this? Hale didn't mention him once.'

'No,' Mac agreed. 'He did not.'

'And it all fits in with the notion of there being separate groups, all after the same thing.'

'Which Paul hid . . . somewhere.'

'Mac, do you think we're looking for the complete tracking device thing, or just some part of it. The bit Paul got to work?'

'That I don't know. Ray and Lyndsey said that whatever he was doing was now missing from the lab. I saw the layout on the bench. Spread out, it covered, I don't know, six feet by two. Put together, we'd be looking at, I suppose, something that would fit into a large holdall or sports bag. Theoretically, I suppose, either one of them could have walked out of *Iconograph* with a bag and no one would have looked twice. Security was tight around that central lab, but I don't think it was an issue in the rest of the building. Not from what I've seen of the place at least.'

'Which leads me to another question. Would the MOD farm out such a project to an outside company, knowing that security was, well, a bit average?'

'Maybe they didn't know,' Mac said. He glanced into his rear-view mirror. 'Hale and co. don't seem to be following us,' he said. 'The way I see it is this. Whoever Hale works for was working for the MOD. They didn't let on that the competition was maybe ahead of the game. Instead, they got hold of the pirate device, gave it to someone who, on the face of it, seems utterly unlikely, i.e. Paul de Freitas, a man who works with his brother in a company creating computer games. We know he did outside design work. Perfectly legitimate work. Tim, it's low-key, unlikely, safe.'

'So Hale wants to recover this device, recover whatever it was Paul improved and not let on to the powers that be that anything went missing in the first place.'

Mac shrugged. 'Something like that, I guess. Problem is, he's not the only one chasing the prize.'

THIRTY-FIVE

R ina may not have met Abe Jackson but she had no
trouble in recognising him and he obviously knew her.
The man with the tanned face and wind-reddened cheeks
walked purposefully across the marina terrace, a young woman
with dark curls keeping close behind.

Abe moved with confidence, glancing from side to side,
but with no sense of anxiety. In contrast, Rina could see that
Lyndsey was scared. She clutched at her shoulder bag, held
her lightweight jacket closed across her chest with a hand so
tight-fisted the knuckles were white. Her face, pale beneath
the scatter of freckles, was tight and tense.

'Sit down, my dear,' Rina said to her. 'Mr Jackson would
like to be where you are, Matthew, if you don't mind.'

'Of course, Rina.' Matthew moved from his chair and Abe
took his place. Matthew had been sitting with his back to
the clubhouse wall, his position enabling him to see the
entire terrace and the little walkway leading from the harbour.
Re-seated, Matthew had his back to the water and to the
crowded terrace.

She noted the twitch of amusement as Abe sat down. He
accepted without comment when Rina ordered her favourite
Pimms for them all.

'Not a place I would have chosen,' he said. 'No vehicle
access, no way out if we run into trouble.'

'I already have that covered, Mr Jackson,' Rina told him.
'But you'll understand that I like to be on my home ground.
I know the regulars here and I can spot the tourists and I'd
like to think that I'd notice anyone like you, anyone that didn't
belong.'

'Fair point. And your fall-back position?'

Rina laughed, delighted that he'd decided to accept her into
his game. Lyndsey looked up sharply, startled. Mirth was
clearly not something she could handle just now.

She flinched when the waiter brought the drinks, hugged
her bag more closely and shook her head when Rina pushed

the drink towards her. Abe sipped at his, interested to know
what it tasted like but unconvinced that it was for him.

'My fall-back position,' Rina said. 'You see the line of little
boats tied up just below this terrace. You see the red boat with
the outboard engine, third from the left as we are looking at
it? Well that belongs to a friend of mine. The keys are in my
pocket and I suggest, should you need to use this fall-back,
then you round the headland, look for a tiny beach at the base
of the cliff. There's a small cave there and at high tide, which
is between now and about three this afternoon, you can drift
the boat right into the cave. I know, because my friend tried
it out a few weeks ago. You might get a little bit wet, but
there's a rather rickety set of steps that will take you back up
on to the cliff path. You'll come out close to the De Barr
Hotel, not a bad place to hide out, but if you want something
more private, then I suggest you turn to your right and follow
the path. The next house along happens to be empty. It was
a children's home until quite recently. For the last few months
it's been closed for renovations, but they are now complete
and the builders gone.

'Now, what did you want from me?'

Abe was laughing. 'And how do we get out of there? What
about my car? Don't tell me, you have a tame driver as well
as a tame boat owner.'

He sobered, glanced around at the crowd on the terrace.
Rina raised her glass and sipped elegantly. 'All locals,' she
said, 'apart from the family having lunch over there, but I
suggest you start talking, Mr Jackson. I may have organised
an escape route just in case, but I really don't want to have
to use it. I have enough of a reputation for eccentricity without
having to create a diversion while you borrow a boat.'

'This friend of yours. Does he know you've volunteered
his pride and joy?'

Rina shrugged. 'Oh, he'll get over it. He shouldn't leave
his keys in the ignition if he doesn't want them used. But to
business, Mr Jackson.'

Abe nodded. He glanced anxiously at Lyndsey. 'Ian and
Lyndsey were having a . . . relationship,' he said. 'Ian was
my friend and he was also the second man on Paul's boat.
Towards the end, he was getting worried that things were
getting out of hand. That Paul's life might be in imminent

danger. I promised to keep an eye on Lyndsey, should anything happen to him.'

He went on to tell Rina and Matthew about the men at Lyndsey's flat, how he had hidden out with her at the farmhouse. How he now needed to get her somewhere safe but didn't know who he could trust.

Rina considered. 'Did Ian say why he felt the danger was so great? Did he give any clue as to why anyone would want to kill Paul? As I understand it, he was doing some work for the security services.'

'And quite a number of people seem to have wanted it. Lyndsey thinks he tried to keep what he was doing safe by spreading the information around. Just a week before he died, Paul went out with Lyns and Ian and the other guy they work with. Ray. He was in a good mood, isn't that right, Lyndsey?'

The girl nodded. 'Yeah. He was joking around, talking about some new level he was developing for an old game he and Edward made years ago. It was going to be re-released soon, but he said he was playing around with a new concept. A kind of real world element. He wanted there to be hidden stuff out there in the real world and he said he was going to start by hiding bits of the puzzle for us to find.' She shook her head. 'We thought nothing about it. I mean, he treated everything he did like a game and he was always pissing about. We'd get to work sometimes and he'd have reprogrammed our computers so we had to test a level on a new game before we could even log on. I never even thought about it.'

'So, what changed?' Rina asked.

'Ian and I met up a few days later and he said he thought there was more to it than that. He said Paul was worried about threats. Someone had been threatening his brother and Lydia and it was because of what he was working on. Ian thought Paul's game wasn't a game and he made me promise if anything happened I'd try and get my puzzle to the right people and I've been trying to do that. But it's all screwed up, isn't it? Paul's dead. Ian's dead. I was nearly dead.'

She sounded furious, bitter and angry.

'How?' Rina asked. 'How did you try?'

She dug in her bag, took out the news clipping, and handed it to Rina.

'I've seen this,' Rina said. 'And the other one, posted a couple of weeks later.'

'I was to phone that number,' Lyndsey said. 'Tell them I had what they wanted. I tried a couple of times and no one would talk to me. I tried again last night. I'd decided that would be the last time. There seemed like there was no one there but just this clicking on the other end, like someone had picked up but then all I could hear was background noises. I told them I had part of what they wanted, then I rang off. I didn't know what else to do. After a bit I decided to go home and then . . . well Abe told you the rest.'

'This number,' Rina said. 'We'd all assumed it was Paul's?'

She shook her head. 'No, I don't know who it is.'

Rina frowned. Big mistake, she thought. Neither she nor Mac, so far as she was aware, had even thought to check and that was a fairly fundamental mistake. She let her gaze drift across the crowded terrace. The family had left now and the table was occupied by two men ordering drinks and poring over the lunchtime menu. Two other newcomers, a man and a woman, perched on the harbour wall. They were dressed in shorts and T-shirts, the man with a short-sleeved denim shirt over his.

'Do you know them?'

'No,' Rina said. 'The man and woman don't look right. The other two, I'm less concerned with.'

'Why?'

'Because I just saw them holding hands under the table.'

Abe chuckled again. 'Could be a bluff. Rina, I know you got the de Freitas's away from here. Can you do the same for Lyndsey?'

Rina returned her focus to the girl. 'What were you supposed to give these people?' she said.

Lyndsey shook her head. 'That's just it,' she said. 'I don't really know. It was something on Paul's laptop, like I said, a new level for *Eventide*. He just gave me clues so I could find the key to get into it. That's all know.'

'So, nothing physical. It's all in your head?'

She nodded.

Rina sat back. 'Abe, you know our fall-back position?' The two newcomers at the table were now on their starter course and their body language suggested they were totally oblivious

to anything other than their food and one another. The couple
sitting on the wall, however, though sitting close were obviously not together. She watched them carefully, noting the
way the woman's gaze flicked back and forth across the
terrace, focussing momentarily on Rina and then shifting
elsewhere. Under the pretext of fishing her bag out from
under the table, Rina shifted position so she could see what
was drawing the woman's attention. Two men stood chatting
close by the path that led back into Frantham Old Town. She
glanced at their shoes; definitely not sailors. She took her
mobile phone from her bag, fiddled with it and then laid it
on the table with an exasperated sigh.

'Abe?'

'I see them. Lyndsey, are you ready?'

'What?'

'Keep close. Get ready to run.'

She looked fearfully at Rina.

'It will be all right,' Rina told her hopefully. 'Matthew. I
think it's time we called home, don't you?'

'Right you are, Rina.' Matthew scraped back his chair and
scooped up the mobile phone that had been sitting on the
table. He peered at it, and wandered over towards the wall as
though unable to get a signal.

A waiter approached their table, asking if they wanted
anything more and Rina asked for menus. 'The food here is
really rather good,' she told Abe.

He smiled at her. 'I'll remember that for later reference.'
He looked up sharply, momentarily confused as Matthew's
voice, raised in anger, cut across the terraced space.

'I think that might be your cue,' Rina said.

Matthew had thrown himself into the role. His search for
a phone signal had taken him close to the harbour wall. He'd
been so relaxed, pausing to exchange a word or two with
acquaintances, to grumble about the lack of signal, a common
complaint this close to the lee of the headland. Finally he
settled on a position close to the harbour wall, but at a reason-
able distance from the couple. They glanced his way but then,
as he began the process of fumbling through his phone book,
turned their attention elsewhere.

No one had been prepared for Matthew's next move. He
swung around to face the couple, his body rigid with shock

and his expression a picture of outrage. 'Just what did you say?'

The couple exchanged a glance, looked around as though to check that Matthew's ire really was directed at them.

'I asked you, what did you say? If you think that language like that is appropriate in a place where families are having lunch . . .' Matthew gestured dramatically at the spectacularly family-free terrace. 'That kind of language may be appropriate wherever it is you come from, but it isn't here.'

The man moved off the wall, puzzled and confused now, not sure if this was a set-up or the man confronting him was simply mad. He held out his hands in a gesture of placation.

Matthew howled and backed away. 'He tried to strike me. Look at him!'

Matthew did not need to make such a request. No one was looking anywhere else.

Abe took Lyndsey's arm and led her quietly to the terrace steps. Rina hurried to Matthew's side.

'What did he do? You should be ashamed of yourself. Can't you see he's an old man? We're not used to the likes of you round here.'

The man stepped forward. 'Now look here . . .'

Rina took an answering step back. From the corner of her eyes she could see the two men at the other end of the terrace begin to move. She shifted position, partially blocking their view of Abe and Lyndsey.

Matthew was now in full spate, claiming that the young man threatened to strike him and that he wasn't so old he couldn't give as good as he got. Others came over to remonstrate. Waiters hurried to the scene and, much to Rina's satisfaction, inadvertently slowed the progress of the two others.

The sound of a boat engine fired up and revving hard drew the attention of the woman still standing by the harbour wall. She shouted something at her companion who swung around and, to Rina's horror, produced a gun.

She saw it only for a moment and then the man was running, the woman with him. Rina could hear from the shouts and screams that she was not the only one who had glimpsed the weapon.

She took her friend's arm. 'You've not lost your touch, Matthew,' she said happily as they watched the boat power away. 'Now, we've just got to stick to our little story.'

Matthew nodded. 'I enjoyed that,' he said. 'In fact, I don't think I've had so much fun in years.' He frowned and glanced at his watch. 'I think we've got a bit of a problem though.'

'Oh?'

'Well, it's more than half an hour since we checked in with home. Stephen will have phoned DI Kendal.'

Stephen's call had been patched through to DI Kendal, who had just left the press conference. He groaned inwardly, summoned back-up and headed for the marina. He arrived just as the chaos was subsiding, too late to make arrests. Rina and Matthew were on the terrace, sympathising with the manager while around them staff and members of the public were straightening furniture and buzzing with excitement. Uniformed officers, summoned by the staff when trouble had started, were already on the scene. Kendal made himself known to them.

'What the hell went on here?'

'Someone stole a boat, there are rumours that someone shot at them. One man fell in to the bay and a woman had a fit of hysterics.'

'Someone had a gun?'

'So we're being told. Whoever it was, they'd scarpered by the time we got here. We're getting statements, but people had already gone when we arrived and there's only been the two of us.'

Kendal indicated the officers who'd followed him there, told them to get up to speed and help out. Then he crossed to the woman who seemed to be the hub of it all. 'Mrs Martin,' Kendal said. 'Just what was going on here?'

The manager turned to him, and Kendal found himself the focus for renewed outrage. He endured several minutes of the tirade, gathered that the manager could not believe the behaviour he had just witnessed and seemed to think that at least two of those responsible were police officers of some sort. 'Something official, anyway,' he finished. 'And, one of them was armed. I saw it. I saw. The Gun.'

Kendal began to remind him that armed officers were not the norm in Frantham Old Town. Then, noticing that Rina and Matthew were slowly moving away, he handed the job of placation over to the uniformed officers who had come with him.

'Witness statements,' he said. 'Names, addresses. Mrs Martin and your friend. With me. Now.'

Rina sighed. 'I think we're in a bit of trouble, Matthew. Inspector Kendal, can we at least phone home. Everyone will be worried.'

'We're entitled to a phone call,' Matthew insisted. 'We know our rights.'

Kendal sighed. 'In the car,' he said. 'Now. You call home and I am going to be calling Mac.'

THIRTY-SIX

B ridie Duggan had welcomed Mac and Tim with her usual effusiveness, embarrassed both Tim and Joy by making it obvious she knew Tim's motivation for the visit and then, after making sure they all knew that lunch was nearly ready, left Mac to talk to Lydia and Edward.

'You're comfortable enough here?' Mac asked.

'Oh yes. Being killed by kindness, but we're fine,' Edward told him. 'We saw the news this morning. Bridie says we should be prepared, in case someone finds out we're here. She says the media have ways of discovering these things.'

'She could be right,' Mac said. 'But I imagine that will be less of a problem here than it would have been back in Frantham. Edward, did Paul say anything out of the ordinary in the weeks before he died? Did he do anything odd, something you didn't think about at the time but which seems memorable now?'

Edward shook his head. 'He seemed his usual self, not happy, not unhappy. Just Paul.'

Mac thought for a moment. 'Did he mention having a girl-friend? Was he seeing anyone?'

Lydia laughed. 'God, no. Paul rarely dated. I think . . . I think I was his last serious attempt. Why?'

'We found a half-empty pack of contraceptive pills in his bathroom cabinet.'

Lydia looked away and Mac recalled her reaction when he had asked if they were hers.

'What? No, that can't be right. If he'd met someone, he would have said.' Edward was clearly bemused. 'Lydia, did he . . .'

'No, he never mentioned anyone. Anyway, he was never there, was he? He lived aboard the boat more than he lived in the flat. Dammit, he stayed with us more than he lived at the flat. I can't see how he'd have found the time to see anyone, let alone get involved enough for them to be having sex on a regular basis.' She sounded as put-out as she had the day Mac told them Paul was not alone on his boat. Maybe, Mac thought, it still hurt that she and Paul had been unable to form the kind of relationship she had once wanted.

'Why did he want you to have that book. The A.A. Milne?'

Lydia smiled. A real, gentle smile, soft with memory. Edward reached out and took her hand. 'Oh, silly reasons. You know, we all knew one another when we were kids.'

'I hadn't realised that.'

'Yeah. Our parents were friends. We moved away and lost touch for a while, met up again in our teens. But the book belonged to Edward and Paul's father. He had nicknames for us all. Paul was Tigger, Edward was Eeyore and I was the wise owl. I wore round glasses and always had my head in a book. I always loved the book. I'm not so sure I'd want it now.'

Mac sighed, wondering where to go with this next.

'He was a generous man in his own way,' Edward said quietly. 'Not ostentatious, but surprising. He'd remember things. You know, you'd mention that you liked something and he'd store that away, suddenly produce a picture or a book or a CD. Just small things, but he'd remember. Like that music box.'

'Music box?'

'Oh, it's nothing relevant,' Lydia said. 'I saw this music box in a charity shop. It was like one I'd had when I was a little girl. We laughed about it, I'd thought it was so grown-up, so special, with the little dancer inside and the velvet lining and all that. I almost went in and bought it, then thought I was just being silly and didn't. When I got home, I sort of regretted being too grown-up and mature to have indulged. Anyway, a couple of weeks later, there's a fancy parcel sitting on my dressing table and inside was the music box. He'd put this card inside with an owl on it. He told me it was to keep my treasures in.' She smiled sadly, tears shining in her eyes. Edward clasped her hand tighter and pulled her down to sit beside him on the sofa.

'When was this?' Mac asked quietly.

'Oh, a couple of weeks before . . . before he died.'

'And it's still back at the house?'

She nodded. 'Yes. Why? You don't think . . .'

'Truly, I don't know. Lydia, where would I find this music box?'

'On the windowsill in our bedroom. Why?'

Mac pursed his lips. 'It may well be absolutely irrelevant,' he admitted, 'but I'd like to see it.'

Abe was worried. He felt too exposed up here, too out on a limb. He hurried Lyndsey along the cliff path, hoping that this Hill House place Rina had mentioned was close by.

He was angry with himself as much as anything. He should never have agreed to meeting in a place that took him so far away from his car. True, Rina had made it possible for them to escape, but it had been such a close-run thing and Abe was in no way certain they had not been pursued. In one detail only, he had deviated from Rina's plan. Once they had found the little cove she had talked about, he had got Lyndsey close in to shore then turned the boat back out to sea, with the engine running. He had then waded ashore. In the heat of the August day his clothes were already drying, the denim of his jeans tightening on his legs.

'Did they follow us?'

'I've seen nothing. Keep moving. It can't be far.'

She stumbled along beside him and he knew that her nerve was fast failing her. The worry was that she would panic now. Do something completely stupid just to put an end to the stress and fear. He needed to get her somewhere she might at least be able to maintain the illusion of safety. Hope she could sleep through the worst of the anxiety. He'd seen this level of collapse before. He had no doubt that, given the opportunity, she would escape into unconsciousness.

The path turned and he breathed a sigh of relief. 'That must be the place.'

Checking for other walkers, any users of the coastal route who might spot them leaving the path, he led her through a small gap in the hedge and half dragged her across the wide lawn. Rina had mentioned a conservatory that ran the full length of the rear of the building. She was right about the doors, small panes of glass that gave easy access to a simple bolt. He hustled Lyndsey inside, glanced back to make certain they were alone and unobserved, then sat her down in one of the random collection of easy chairs while he examined the inner doors. Moments later, he was taking her inside and settling her down on one of the old but comfortable sofas in the sitting room.

'I'm going to try and find a blanket. You're shocked and wet and cold. Take off your jeans and I'll hang them somewhere to dry and then I want you to get some sleep, OK?'

She nodded, her hands moving ineffectually to unfasten her belt. Abe left her to it and went to check the rest of the house. He discovered a blanket on one of the beds and coffee, left by the builders, in the kitchen. Power was still connected and he found the fuse box, and switched it back on. By the time he had returned to the sitting room, she was lying down and almost asleep. She still hadn't managed to remove her sodden shoes and wet jeans.

Abe sighed. He helped her out of the wettest clothes, and covered her with the blanket, tucking it firmly around her. Got a cushion to slip beneath her head.

'Get some rest,' he told her. 'I'll dry these out.'

He stood in the doorway, watching her, hoping she'd be all right, worried that this was all too much for a young woman who spent her life with the technical and the virtual and for whom reality had now impinged so unpleasantly. He took the wet clothes and found a sunny spot in the conservatory and hung the jeans over the back of a chair. His own clothes were still damp on his body, but he'd endured worse and he ignored the discomfort, and went through to the kitchen to make use of the builders' coffee.

THIRTY-SEVEN

Because of the number of people in her house and the sense that this was a bit of an occasion, Bridie Duggan had laid out lunch in the dining room. Mac had never had a great liking for glass tables and this was a monster of one, supported on elaborately curving chrome legs. An equally monstrous sideboard took up the space along one wall and Mac examined it with interest, realising that, in direct contrast to the very modern table, this was a genuine antique. Heavily carved and almost touching the ceiling, he could not help but wonder how on earth she had got it into the room.

Bridie saw him looking. She came over, stroking the polished surface affectionately. 'Flame mahogany veneer,' she said. 'But it's old, so it's gone this lovely gold and just look at the detail on that carving. The auctioneer said it was made around 1820 and we got it for a song because no one has room for this sort of thing any more. That vandal at the auction house talked about breaking it up and selling the top separate. We couldn't have that, not with something so lovely, so we left a bid and we got lucky.'

'It's certainly impressive,' Mac said. He figured that was probably the safest word to use. 'How did you get it in here?'

'Oh, the top comes off, but it still had to come in through the patio doors.' She smiled happily. 'Jimmy loved auctions,' she said. 'We've a house full of stuff we bought together.'

It was certainly an eclectic collection, Mac thought, but he was saved from further comment by the arrival of Tim and Joy, closely followed by Fitch and the de Freitas's. It was very clear to Mac that Fitch had become far more than an employee since Jimmy Duggan's death and he wondered just how much. He found himself seated between Fitch and Lydia.

'Help yourselves,' Bridie said indicating the dishes of new potatoes, salad, glazed ham and chicken. Mac was absurdly reminded of the Famous Five books he'd read as a child. All that was needed now was hard-boiled eggs and lashings of ginger beer.

'That pair are getting on like a house on fire,' Fitch said, nodding towards Tim and Joy. 'It's getting serious.'

'Rina worries that she's a bit too young. I know that Tim worries about that too.'

Fitch shrugged. 'Joy's a grown woman, he's a good man. He'll not rush anything.' He paused. '*She* might though,' he added, grinning at the thought. 'Like her mother in that respect, is Joy. Sees what she wants and goes for it.'

Mac passed potatoes to Lydia.

'I'll be going back with you,' Fitch told him. 'Bridie thinks you need me more than she does. Joy's tagging along.'

Mac shook his head. 'I don't think she should. We still don't know what we're dealing with.'

'You try telling her that. Or her mother. It's all arranged and I don't really think you or I get a say in the matter.'

'How does this Hale keep finding you?' Bridie wanted to know. 'Is he psychic or what?'

'I hope not,' Mac said with feeling. 'That, I can definitely do without. I think our meeting on my way to work has a simple explanation. Anyone in the least bit familiar with my habits would be aware of where I'd be that time of the morning. As to the motorway, I think that has a simple explanation too but more complex ramifications.'

'Like what?' Bridie asked.

'Like it means he had access to the CCTV system, Mum,' Joy said. 'Which means either he is an official something or other or he has connections to someone that is or he has a bloody good hacker.'

'You mean he might be able to get someone to hack into the CCTV cameras?'

Mac nodded. 'Or, as Joy says, he is able to access them via official or other routes. It would be relatively easy to pick out a particular car. Number plate recognition systems could be set to trigger automatically and Hale or his contacts could track us all the way. Easy enough to intercept us at the services, though it would have been an educated guess as to which one we'd use or if we even stopped at all. Had the guess been mine, I'd have made the same call as Hale. Roughly halfway.'

He paused, thoughtfully. 'Bridie, I'm assuming you've had this place swept?'

'Oh sure, after that business with Pat and Jimmy, I've been

what you might call paranoid. I already lost a husband and a son. I don't take chances now, not with anything. I sent Fitch here on a course, couple of my other people too. This place is checked for bugs and so are the nightclubs.' She looked speculatively at Mac, jabbed her fork in his direction. 'You're thinking phone tap,' she said.

'I think we might as well make that assumption.'

'But can they do that? I thought you needed Home Office approval or somesuch.'

'Used to be that way,' Fitch growled. 'Bridie, pass the chicken over will you. Trouble is, all this anti-terrorist legislation means it's a good deal easier to get a tap and digital systems make it simpler still. Even local councils can intercept calls if they think they've got cause and there's evidence to say they've been using it even if they haven't.'

'We should assume Hale has the contacts to get it done,' Mac said. 'And I think we should be careful what we put out on our mobiles.'

'Maybe we should make use of that,' Tim said. 'Feed false information.'

'Good idea,' Bridie approved, 'but what happens when we actually want to make a proper call?'

'Ah,' Fitch said. 'There are ways round all of that.'

Just over an hour later, Mac and Tim left the Duggan house. Fitch and Joy were preparing to follow. One small refinement had been made to the original plan and two of Bridie Duggan's employees were to accompany them on the way back. The woman was slim and blonde and dressed in one of Lydia's trademark white shirts with a pair of faded jeans. The man was a little more heavily built than Edward, but Fitch was careful to pull the car right up to the entrance and open the rear doors wide before he got in. Any observer would simply catch a glimpse of a man and woman who looked like the de Freitas getting into the Range Rover and then subsequently heading south.

THIRTY-EIGHT

Tim's phone chimed, telling him that he had a text. His Uncle Charles.

'I didn't know he knew how to text,' Tim was impressed.

'What does he say?' Mac asked.

'Just that I should give him a call. You think we should use the mobile or a public phone?'

Mac thought about it. 'I think we should err on the side of caution,' he said. 'Find a phone box before we get on to the motorway and see what he wants.'

A quarter of a mile on, Mac saw a phone box outside of a row of small shops. He pulled into the cutaway at the side of the road and searched his pockets for change. Tim did the same. 'Can't remember the last time I did this,' he said. 'I hope I can remember how.'

Mac waited, watching the passing traffic as Tim fiddled with the phone, holding one hand to his ear to cut down the noise of the road. Five minutes later he was back in the car.

'That thing eats money. Any sign of Hale or his cronies?'

'No, nothing so far. So, what did Uncle Charles have to contribute? I don't imagine there was time for much of a conversation anyway.'

Tim laughed. 'He talks fast when he's excited,' he said. 'I just hope I've got it all right.'

He drew a deep breath. 'Right. Our man Hale. OK, he used to be army then MOD, pretty high-level and dealing not with diplomatic protection but kind of well, I guess witness protection is closest. Anyway, he was removed from post eight months or so ago. Charles says there was some sort of scandal, a conflict of interest. They thought at first that Hale was moonlighting for a private security firm, then found out he'd actually set the company up and was using his contacts to siphon off work that should have been done through official channels. Charles didn't go into detail, but apparently it was a big deal. However, that didn't stop Hale from having special status and the MOD from sometimes using his people when they needed something done that was a bit less than official. With me so far?'

'Pretty much.'

'Right. So that was all hunky-dory until a few months back his company was linked to an American security firm that was being investigated for taking kick-backs in Iraq. Hale did work out there during the first Gulf War and seems to have picked up where he left off in the second. But the most relevant thing to us is, he was in a position to have a lot of very confidential information not exactly passing through his hands, but certainly in reach and Charles reckons that Hale is a suspect in a number of really high-profile leaks. Don't know what was leaked or when, but it all kind of fits, doesn't it?'

'Well yes, I suppose it does,' Mac agreed. 'But his status now? All we've experienced suggests that he still has pretty high-level access.'

'Not officially, he doesn't. But Charles said his contacts gave him the impression that the powers that be are giving him the rope with which to hang himself. They know some of what he's doing, but I think they're hoping not only will he provide the proof, but he'll also tell them just how high up the chain this goes.'

'Andy was right,' Mac said. 'This is getting very James Bond.'

'Yeah, but we don't get to play with the cool gadgets. Anyway, Charles told me to be careful, not to underestimate Hale and so on and he'll dig a bit deeper as and when he can but he doesn't want to ring any alarm bells. Hale still has a lot of friends.'

Mac's phone rang and he realised to his annoyance that he'd forgotten to plug in the hands-free kit. 'Do the honours will you, Tim?'

The caller was DI Dave Kendal. 'Mac's driving,' Tim said. 'Can I act as go-between?' He listened, a slow grin spreading across his face. Mac, glancing sidelong at him, could see that he was trying hard not to laugh. He could hear the irritation and outrage in Dave Kendal's voice and somehow knew that the subject of his annoyance was Rina Martin. It was a thought confirmed by Tim's next comment. 'Does she need collecting, or will you give them a lift home? Thanks, I'll pass the message on.'

He rang off and then gave way to a fit of what could only be described as giggles.

'OK, what's she done?'

'Oh, not just Rina. Matthew too. Kendal is furious but he can't think of what to charge them with so he's given her a dressing-down and sent her home.'

'Tell,' Mac said wearily.

'Well, apparently she and Matthew went to meet Abe Jackson at the Marina. He had Lyndsey Barnes with him. Isn't she Paul's assistant?'

'She was, yes,' Mac confirmed. 'What the hell was she doing with Abe Jackson? For that matter, what was he doing wanting to talk to Rina? So what happened?'

'Rina *says* she was talking to Abe and Lyndsey, that some tourist couple started to argue and when Matthew went over and asked them to control their language they got very abusive. Abe took exception and a bit of a fracas ensued. She says, of course, that she then thought it her duty to get Matthew out of the way and doesn't know what happened next.'

'And what did happen next?'

'Kendal says that other witnesses claim Abe and Lyndsey got into a boat and left. The argumentative couple disappeared and then Kendal arrived, by which time the management had already called the police and a patrol car had already arrived. He took charge of Rina and Matthew and left uniform to take statements. He says she's not been very cooperative.'

'Of course not. God, Tim. That woman. Well, we'll sort out what went on when we get back. The big question now is what on earth Abe has to do with Lyndsey Barnes.'

'She has to have been in trouble,' Tim said. 'Why else would Rina have got involved?'

Mac looked sideways at him. In Rina's world, he thought, she was some blend of earth mother and superhero. He was uncomfortably aware that he too had been sucked all too willingly into that way of thinking.

'You're making the assumption that Abe is one of the good guys,' he said.

'Well, sure. If he was going to do Lyndsey any harm, he wouldn't have met up with Rina at the Marina and Rina must have given him the benefit of the doubt, or she wouldn't have made sure he could take the boat.'

'You're assuming she helped him?'

'Of course she helped him. Why, is another matter, but knowing Rina she had her reasons.'

The agreement was that Fitch should drive straight to Frantham, but Mac had planned a bit of a detour once they were off the motorway. He was worried about the possibility of Hale intercepting their mobile phone calls and it seemed wise to get an alternative. What he didn't want to do was to risk Hale getting to know that he'd purchased a new phone and Mac was wary enough of Hale's seeming connections for him to assume that was possible.

After the attacks on the London Underground, anti-terrorist legislation had tightened up in all sorts of unexpected ways and Mac knew it was now much harder to buy even a pre-paid mobile phone and not have to register it. True, he could have given a false address, but that seemed like an unnecessary complication. Instead, the plan was to get new SIM cards for their existing phones, use the new numbers for the calls they wanted to keep confidential and then revert to the old SIM for those calls they hoped Hale would intercept.

Mac made three stops at small shops he recalled sold SIMs. He bought chocolate and bread, milk and SIM cards, then extra credit from two local supermarkets. Briefly, he recalled, there had been a requirement for any store selling more than a set amount of credit to one customer to report the transaction. Mac realised he had no idea if this had ever been made official or if it had now been rescinded. Better, he thought, simply to spread his purchases around.

'I never even knew that,' Tim said when Mac explained his reasoning.

'It wasn't widely broadcast,' Mac said. 'And I doubt it's still an issue, but . . . well, you never know.' He laughed suddenly. 'I never thought I'd be so involved in smoke and mirrors. I feel like I'm playing a role here. Like I've been caught up in some game Paul de Freitas might have designed and I can't say I'm comfortable with it.'

'We do seem to be imbuing Hale with almost supernatural powers,' Tim agreed, 'but the fact is, two people have died and, I don't know, I feel like I came pretty close that night. Mac, I don't like to make a fuss, but I still feel shaky about it. I've been in tight spots before, but I honestly thought I might not make it out of that one.'

Mac nodded. 'I can understand that,' he said. 'And no, I don't think you're overreacting, if that's what you wanted to ask.'

'Thanks,' Tim said. 'And Mac, don't tell Rina how I feel.'

Mac chuckled softly. 'I don't need to,' he said quietly. 'Tim, she already knows.'

Mac halted the car in a lay-by a few miles out from Frantham, realising that it was almost time for Sergeant Baker to shut up shop for the day.

'Just checking in. Anything I should know?'

'Well, *Tonino's* has done a roaring trade all day,' Frank Baker said, referring to the little cafe on the promenade. 'I've said no comment, can't comment and plain, I really don't know more times than I can count and your Mrs Martin created some kind of furore at the Old Town marina. Other than that, not a lot. I finally put Andy on the "no comment" duty and he wound up talking cameras with the media lot, but give the boy his due, he kept them off my back. Got more patience than I have.'

'I heard about Rina,' Mac said. 'DI Kendal gave me the low-down. Anything else?'

'Well, yes, but I don't know what to make of it exactly and, Mac, I may have done wrong here but I figured I'd wait to see what you thought before we passed it on up the chain if you see what I mean.'

'No, I don't think I do.'

'Right, well I went into the office earlier today, saw one of your business cards sitting on the desk, like. Didn't think any more about it, then Andy spotted it and he said it looked funny and it did when he pointed it out. Laid out square on to the table edge as if someone put it there deliberate like. Not like something you'd have done. Then Andy noticed something written on it. Ian Manning, but it wasn't your writing. Far too neat. Andy recalled the man on the boat was Ian so we ran the name.'

Baker paused for effect and Mac prompted him. 'Anything?'

'Never been arrested, but he has a service record, left the army two years ago. He's in our system because he applied

for and got a doorman's licence, so we called the nightclub
he was working for. The owner reckons he was only there a
few months, but he was good at his job and they were sorry
to see him go.'

'Why did he go?'

'Offered a better job. More pay, apparently. The nightclub
owner thought he remembered Ian saying it was an old
colleague of his from his army days, set up some kind of
private security firm and he'd offered him a job.'

Hale, Mac thought. It had to be.

'So, who put the card on my desk?'

'That, I don't know. But someone got in and left it there.
It weren't there last night, Andy and I both agree on that.'

'Abe Jackson,' Mac said.

'You reckon?'

'I'd put money on it.'

THIRTY-NINE

I t had taken more time than he had liked for Richard Grey to finally unravel Paul de Freitas' hidden level but now he knew how to kill the kraken.

And he was fairly sure that he knew what the kraken was.

Still in game mode, his excitement at having mastered it outweighed any implication but as he scanned the list of names that had been revealed in the *Power of One* file and compared these to the intelligence reports on each one, it finally dawned on him that this elaborate level of the game had real world implications.

Dawned on him? No, he had anticipated that all along, but caught up in the challenge of playing the level and comprehending the puzzle Paul de Freitas had set, he had, for a time, lost sight of that fact.

It really was very clever, Richard thought. It was also very disturbing.

This hidden game inside a game, as he had discovered early on, differed from the rest of *Eventide* in that it was played from Lydia's point of view. Lydia had to collect a series of objects and pieces of information from other characters in the game. Together, these gave her the weapon she needed to kill the kraken in the final scene. At each stage of the game she had to fight, to play elaborate games against, or to solve puzzles in competition with, the other characters. All she had to help her was a musical box, the sort you'd give to a little kid with a dancing fairy and a little mirror in the lid. A compartment inside held 'treasures', but there was no way of knowing what they were until you pulled one out, or how useful it would be in that part of the game until you tried it.

Once out of the box, the treasures were kept in a bag Lydia carried and once she had them, she kept hold of them, even if she made a wrong play with one of them against the wrong character.

The treasures made no sense to Richard. They included a wise owl, and a pair of round-lensed spectacles. A snail with a red shell and a Christmas cracker. Frustrated, Richard decided that the so-called treasures might mean something to Lydia, but to anyone else they were just a nonsense. He'd had to resort to trial and error . . . a lot of error, before he'd finally solved enough of the clues and gathered enough of the kraken-killing objects to figure out what the game was all about.

Worst of all, there were no back doors, no facility for debugging. You just had to play the game.

Lyndsey, Ray, Lydia herself, Edward, Paul, someone called Ian and two others by the name of Mike and Phil. These were the opponents; the characters with the individual pieces of the puzzle and now Richard had the list of names and the intel about them, it all got very strange.

Mike Thompson had worked for Paul when he ran his own business. Phil Jameson was a mechanic who regularly helped him service his boat. Both had died within days of Paul de Freitas. One three days before, one on the day following.

Accidents, the police reports had said. A car crash and a fall from a ladder while clearing the gutters.

Both had suffered break-ins at home either just before or just after death but nothing obvious had been stolen.

Lyndsey and Ray were Paul's closest associates. Neither had turned up for work and they were definitely not at home.

Lydia and Edward de Freitas, Richard was told, had gone to ground. Ian and Paul were dead and in their cases there was no pretence at making it look accidental.

'So,' Richard mused. 'What do we have?'

He drew up a list of objects and clues that the characters had finally revealed. Lydia had her music box, of course, with all the 'treasures' inside. Lyndsey had a newspaper clipping on which a phone number had been written. Ray, something that looked like a missile launcher and Edward, for some reason, a rose bush, though it made more sense, he supposed, when he realised that the rose was named 'peace'.

The other two had, respectively, a locker key and an old car, make unknown – at least to Richard. It was weird-enough looking that he supposed a car buff might recognise it.

Checking that he had everything printed out, he shuffled his pages together and went in search of his boss, remembering only belatedly that he was away on some course or other.

Richard hesitated, then knocked on the door of the 'main man', Gil Sykes, who for the purposes of their little unit was 'big boss number one'.

'Can I have a word?'

Gil looked surprised, but gestured Richard to come in and sit down. 'Sure, what's wrong?'

Richard grinned. He couldn't help himself. He knew this was big with a capital B and felt justifiably proud of himself. Gil raised an elegantly plucked eyebrow and tucked an invisible strand of wayward bob back behind her ear.

'Nothing's wrong. I've solved it. I know how to find the kraken. How to kill it.'

He expected applause; instead she looked at him as if he'd gone mad.

'Kraken? Isn't that some kind of sea monster?'

'Well, yeah. But not this one. I mean that's what Paul de Freitas called it but I think it's a ship or maybe a submarine. I know it's stealth technology and I know the thing he was trying to hide was a device for tracking it. Finding it, even though it doesn't have a proper signature. You see . . .'

'Richard, what the hell are you talking about?'

For the first time he began to worry. 'Dave gave me this thing to solve? After Paul de Freitas and his minder were killed. They found two bits of code, see, hidden in the BIOS. I worked through the layers, realised one was a list of names and the other was another level of one of Paul's old games.'

'De Freitas . . . right?' A small glimmer of light seemed to dawn. 'There was something on the bulletin . . .' Gil closed her eyes for a moment as though accessing the information she had vaguely registered.

She opened her eyes and studied Richard. 'You'd better show me what you found,' she said, 'and bring me up to speed. Did Dave say who this was for?'

'Sure, he said it was a rush job. I've been on it twenty-four-seven. It's for Commander Hale?' The name had meant nothing to him, but he assumed it must to her. From the way her shoulders suddenly stiffened, Richard figured that it did. But he wasn't sure now that was a good thing.

'Have I done something wrong?'

Gil shook her head. 'Go back to your station, get everything ready for me. I just need to make a couple of calls. And Richard, don't worry. *You've* done nothing wrong.'

It was another two hours and close on seven o'clock when Abe got the call. They had what they needed to close the net on Hale. Abe was back on the payroll. Officially.

He sank down on one of the uncomfortable kitchen chairs at Hill House and felt relief flood through him right down to his toes. He'd been undercover before, but not like this. Not able to tell even those men he'd served with for so long that really, he'd not left in disgrace; not let the side down and he felt that the rumour-mill had told exactly that story.

Abe Jackson is out of control.

Abe Jackson finally flipped.

To make sure he knew the message was for real, they'd had his commanding officer make the call and Abe had never been so relieved or so glad in all his life to hear that particular voice.

'What now?' he asked.

'We close the trap. Abe where the devil are you?'

He told them, still anxious after all this time of trusting no one that he was walking into a noose of his own making. Hesitantly, he voiced his concerns, knowing they'd be understood. He'd sent men into deep cover operations, seen them when they'd returned, unable to accept that even their closest friends were still just that and not some agent sent to trick and deceive. He knew this was a normal anxiety, but analyse it all he liked, he found it hard to shake.

A slight sound made him look up. Lyndsey stood in the doorway, the blanket draped around her shoulders. She looked better. Wide awake and the tense pinched look gone from her face.

'Who was that?' she asked as he closed his phone.

'The cavalry, I hope,' he said. 'And I've told them to bring food.'

She smiled. The first proper smile he'd seen on her face. 'Good. I'm starved. Is that coffee?'

'Yeah, hope you can drink it black. The kettle works. You feeling better?'

She nodded. 'I'm feeling . . . OK. Yes, I'm feeling like I'm going to be all right.' She smiled again, a little awkwardly this time. 'Not sure how long that feeling will last, so make the most of it.'

'Hold that thought,' Abe told her. He filled the kettle and poked the jar to free up the hardened granules. 'This isn't over yet, but I do believe the end is now in sight.'

FORTY

Fitch and Joy had dropped Bridie's two employees at the De Barr hotel, leaving them with a corporate visa card and permission to take a few days' holiday and to hire a car, do as they pleased so long as they stayed put that night.

They then drove off to Peverill Lodge and Rina Martin to await Tim and Mac's arrival.

Tim and Mac had gone straight to the de Freitas's house. They arrived to find the place had been searched, hurriedly and messily and a back window shattered by whoever had been there.

The music box was still in the bedroom, knocked to the floor but otherwise ignored.

Tim was waiting for him in the Big Room.

'You found it then?'

'Yes.'

Tim turned back to take another look at the massive window. 'This is an amazing space; I bet the view is phenomenal in daylight.'

'Dizzying,' Mac said. 'You can't see the garden at all. It's very odd. Just sea and sky. Lydia said she felt as though she was shipboard.'

'So you'd not see anyone coming across the lawn until they were almost on you,' Tim mused.

'I suppose not. What are you thinking?'

He shrugged. 'I don't know yet.' The light was behind them, much brighter in the room than outside where the darkening sky promised a stormy end to an overheated day. He could see his reflection in the window, feet and legs below the knee cut off because of the sunken aspect to the room. His reflection strengthened, grew more solid by the minute as the clouds rolled in off the ocean, foreshortening the view so that there was the momentary illusion of the entire world coming to an end just beyond the window.

'We'd better go,' Mac said and Tim nodded, glancing back once from the top of the steps.

'I'd better call Rina to tell her we're on our way.'

'Do that.' Mac hesitated about where to put the music box, finally wrapping it up in a carrier bag with the chocolate he'd bought earlier and tucking it into the boot. What, he wondered, was the appropriate way to transport something that looked so banal but which had probably already cost lives? As he climbed into the driver's seat, Tim was talking to Rina and jotting down a number on a till receipt he'd found in the glove compartment. Mac waited, leaning back in his seat and closing his eyes. He daren't add up all the hours he'd been driving today, but figured if his car had been an HGV then he'd probably be well overdue for a rest.

'Abe Jackson has been trying to get hold of us. He couldn't get through and neither could Rina. New SIM cards,' he waved his phone. 'She was worried sick until Fitch got there and explained. I think we've got more white-flag waving to do.'

'I have chocolate in the boot,' Mac said. 'Never let it be said I'm not prepared. So, what now?'

'I'll call him, he'll tell us where to go.'

Mac had not been to the children's home since it had been closed for repair. He had driven past on quite a few occasions, noted the builders' lorries coming and going, but, situated at the end of a long and sweeping drive and therefore out of sight of the road, he'd not seen it during the rebuilding process.

At the top of the drive a man in the uniform of a military policeman signalled them to halt, then peered into the car and waved them on.

'Seems like they know us already?'

Mac nodded. 'What's a redcap doing here?'

'Isn't that what Abe Jackson was?'

A black van and two cars were parked just outside of the front door and Mac pulled up behind them. Other uniformed officers and some in civilian dress carried equipment into the house. All of the downstairs lights seemed to be on.

'Ookaay,' Tim said slowly. 'Now what?'

Abe Jackson came out to meet them. Lyndsey Barnes at his side. Abe looked confident and in control, in his element. 'Glad to see you,' he said. 'Come along in.'

They followed him into the kitchen. That too seemed to

have been invaded. A woman with a neat blonde bob and a very nervous-looking young man sat at the kitchen table, with a laptop in front of them and a pile of papers close by. The woman nodded in their direction but Abe made no attempt to introduce her. 'This is Richard,' he said. 'Richard cracked Paul's code. Now all we've got to do is gather the pieces together.'

He looked pleased. Mac just felt mystified, though he was now getting used to that state.

'Pieces?' Tim said.

'I'm one of them,' Lyndsey told him. 'But Richard solved my bit, so really they don't need me for that any more. Then there's Paul and Edward, Ray, Lydia, Ian and two other poor bastards that got killed for something they probably didn't even know they had.'

Mac fetched the music box from the car. Richard seized it, staring at it as though it was some holy relic. 'The one in the game. My god, do you know how much some people would pay for this?' He had the grace then to look embarrassed. 'I mean, people who play *Eventide*. I . . .' He gave up and handed it over to Gil who opened it.

'What am I looking for?'

'If it was something obvious,' Mac pointed out, 'then Lydia would have seen it.' He opened the lid and poked around inside. The card with the owl on it was still inside. Paul's message was scrawled across the back. 'For your treasures'.

'Get it examined,' Gil said, handing it over to one of the people Mac had seen unloading the van. 'What else is on the list? OK, I'll rephrase that. Who is left on the list still capable of telling us what their object means?'

'Ray,' Lyndsey said. 'We have to find Ray.'

'Not at work, not at his flat and his phone is switched off. Lyndsey, do you have any idea?' Mac gathered from the tone of Gil's voice that this question had been put before.

'I don't know. Maybe. I've been thinking and there was this friend he had from when he was a school kid. Ray was at boarding school and Toby was his best friend, but I don't know where he lived. It wasn't round here, Wiltshire some-where . . .' She cast an anxious look in Gil's direction. 'I'm really sorry.'

'There's bound to be something in his flat,' Gil said. 'Write down anything you can think of. We'll track him down.'

'What about Edward?' Mac asked.

'A rosebush,' Richard said rolling his eyes. 'I mean, a frigging rosebush.'

He remembered where he was and looked apologetically at Gil. 'It was called Peace, that's all I know.'

'There are rose beds at the de Freitas's house,' Mac said. 'Can Edward shed any light?'

'So far, no. We'll check out the house again.'

'You know,' Tim said. 'I think you're looking at it all wrong.'

Gil frowned. 'What do you mean?'

'I mean, Paul was a player as well as a designer, wasn't he? And games are all about misdirection. Look, this Hale, he told us that Paul ironed out the kinks in the design. He got the tracking thing to work. Now I don't know a lot about this sort of technology, but presumably it was computer controlled. Presumably it's like a programming thing as well as an engineering thing?'

'Maybe a new chip set,' Lyndsey speculated. 'Maybe a combination of those things.'

'Right.' Tim was feeling his way. 'Look, if I want a trick to work then I have to dress it right. The actual pay-off for the illusion might be pulling a card out of an envelope that's been sitting all the way across the room for the past half-hour, right? And the fact is, the card's been in my possession right until the very last minute, yes? But I have to misdirect, to add frills and fancy bits so that anyone watching, even if they've an idea of how it's done, they're going to be caught up in all the peripheral frills.'

'And your idea is that most of the objects are just peripheral frills.' Gil frowned, but nodded thoughtfully. 'So, how do we tell the difference?'

'Think about it,' Tim said. 'The only people Paul was really likely to trust with something this important are Lydia and Edward and Lyndsey and Ray and maybe not even Edward. No offence, but what Paul was into was way over Edward's head. It wasn't what he did.'

'You think Lydia would understand?' Gil asked.

Tim nodded thoughtfully. 'Lydia kind of puzzles me,' he said. 'She doesn't seem to *do* anything specific, but everyone agrees she's important. It's like she's the glue, the core element of the trick, the bit you don't see because you're so busy looking at the fancy stuff.'

'Which is why he wrote this from her perspective,' Richard nodded agreement. 'So all we need really is Lydia's thing, which we have in the music box and Lyndsey's which we've got and Ray, who's got the missile launcher.'

'The what?' Mac queried.

'That's what it looks like.' He struck his forehead dramatically. 'God, I'm so stupid! You're right. Spot on. The only things Lydia used to kill the kraken in the final scene were the missile launcher thing and Lyndsey's bit of paper and the music box. She stuck the missile launcher on the music box and she fired Lyndsey's paper rolled into a tube.'

Gil nodded. 'Right, so if that's true, that cuts down a little of the complications. But we still need Ray.'

She leaned back in her seat and surveyed them all. 'I suggest that those that can, get some rest. We reconvene tomorrow, eight a.m. Here. We need to draw Hale back out into the open, force a move.'

She got up and left the kitchen barking orders at people, asking questions of others. Mac felt he'd been summarily dismissed. 'Home?' he said.

'Home,' Tim agreed.

FORTY-ONE

I t was very late by the time Mac delivered Tim to Peverill Lodge but the Martin household was still up and in an odd, almost celebratory mood. Matthew was relishing his moment of glory and from what Mac could gather, had been telling and retelling the tale of how he and Rina facilitated Abe Jackson's escape so many times it had already taken upon the aspect of legend.

It was now up to Tim and Mac to provide an adequate sequel; Mac found himself unequal to the task, too tired to really care and with so many facts now buzzing around his head that he wasn't sure he could get them straight.

'Why don't you stay over tonight?' Rina asked. 'Unless Miriam's expecting you?'

Mac shook his head. 'At her sister's,' he said. 'But I think you've got a houseful as it is.'

'Fitch is taking the couch in my office and I've fixed up a camp bed in my room for Joy. I don't like the thought of you walking round the headland tonight or even down from the main road. Not after all that's happened.'

'In which case, I'll say yes. Gratefully.' He looked over to where Joy sat close beside Tim. 'You sure the camp bed will get used?'

'I think I'll insist on it tonight,' she said. 'But I think Joy will get her way soon enough. My question is,' she added mischievously, 'will Tim know what to do with her? He is a little naïve, you know.'

Mac almost choked on his tea. 'Rina, you should be ashamed.'

'So,' Fitch demanded. 'What's the next move?'

'Find Ray, figure out what he's hiding, put the word out to Hale that it's all in one place and to come and get it, I suppose.'

'Easy then,' Fitch agreed. He got up and stretched. 'Look, I think we should all get some rest now. It's been a long day and something tells me tomorrow might be no better.'

FORTY-TWO

Mac drove to Hill House the following morning, very conscious of every car he passed or that passed him but there was no sign of Hale or anything else untoward.

Abe Jackson was in the kitchen when he arrived. He seemed intent on providing breakfast for the entire crew. There was no sign of Gil, Richard or Lyndsey.

'Feel like a spare part,' Abe explained. 'Thought I'd do something useful.'

'Lyndsey?'

'Gone to fetch Ray. They tracked him down to a place in Wiltshire. Gil's gone with her. Richard is still asleep, so far as I know and everyone else is busy, busy, busy. One good thing though, they came well supplied.'

He flipped eggs expertly and then dished them on to large serving plates. 'Give me a minute. Or better still, grab that toast will you?'

Mac followed him through to the dining room with a stack of toast and a dish of butter. The place had been transformed. CCTV cameras covered every inch of the grounds and computer systems blinked at him from every available space. Abe cleared a gap amongst paperwork and set the dishes down beside crockery and serving plates. Mac added toast. A chorus of approval followed them from the room.

'They say an army marches on its belly,' Abe said. 'I'm assuming the geek squad does the same.'

He sighed, seeming at a loss now his hands were empty. 'No Tim?'

'No, he's spending a little time with Joy Duggan. He couldn't see what we might need him for this morning and I'm afraid intrigue and cloak-and-dagger is no contest compared to Joy.'

Abe laughed. 'Can't say I'd disagree. I'd happily be elsewhere now. It feels like I've done my bit and now I'm surplus.'

'I was under the impression there was to be a briefing,' Mac said, seating himself at the kitchen table, remembering what this place was like when the usual residents were there. Thinking of George and Ursula and the drama this house had already seen.

'Events rather took over,' Abe said. 'Lyndsey managed to talk to Ray early hours of this morning. Scared the life out of his friend's family when the police knocked at their door I expect, but better safe . . . She's got some clout, that Gil woman. Apparently Ray was planning on leaving this morning, didn't want to put his friends at risk and when Lyndsey disappeared, he'd feared the worst. He went to his friend Toby, not knowing where else to go, then got in to a panic in case the bad guys came after him there.'

'So. What now?'

'For me and thee, I don't know. Gil left all sorts of plans in train. She's got people in to fix up the de Freitas's house, seems to think that if Hale figures they're coming back he might approach them. Me, I don't know.'

Mac smiled. 'I've got a feeling that might be easier than you think,' he said. 'If Hale's people were watching the Duggan house yesterday, there's a good chance they think the de Freitas came down with Fitch. Bridie thought it might be good to throw a little confusion into the mix. Maybe she was right.'

He explained to Abe about the two employees of Bridie's who had driven down to Frantham and were currently in the De Barr hotel.

'She took a risk doing that. A risk with them, I mean.'

'A small one. True. What then? Lyndsey still has the phone number. Isn't that the simplest way to make contact?'

'She's already agreed to call them again. I did think she was going to fall apart on me that day we met Rina. She was in deep shock, like she'd been putting it off since Ian died and suddenly it all caught up with her. But she's rallied. Wants to bring Hale in. I think the thought he had Ian killed is a big motivator.'

'Like it is for you?'

'Like it is for me.'

The rest of the day was heavy with activity. There were phone calls made both in the clear, hoping Hale would intercept and other communications using the avoidance tactics they had devised. Mac spent a good deal of it with DI Kendal and Superintendent Aims. Aims, still suspicious after being taken for a ride, was not pleased by the latest revelations. He'd sent men out to arrest Abe Jackson and the man hadn't even had the courtesy to turn up. Now he was being told that Abe was not the one they wanted after all.

Mac was left with the distinct impression that Aims would have been happier if Hale had been the legitimate agent. With his tailored suits and public-school accent, he had been far closer to Aims' expectation of a spy than Abe Jackson could ever be.

It was also a day of activity up at the de Freitas's house. Glaziers were called in to fix the window and a team of cleaners to tidy up the mess. Local police investigated the break-in and forensic teams dusted for prints. Phone messages gave every impression that the burglary had been discovered by the house-keeper and the police were treating it as a common or garden crime.

Phone calls too, to the effect that the de Freitas had in fact already returned, and were staying at the hotel until their house was habitable.

Gil, returning at noon and learning about Bridie's bit of subterfuge, made full use of it and posted her people inside the hotel and on watch outside in case Hale should try to approach 'Lydia and Edward', but by late afternoon there had been no sign of anything untoward.

Tim had spent an hour with Gil just after she returned and in the afternoon the glaziers returned.

Lyndsey and Ray turned up with their escort at Hill House in the middle of the afternoon. Mac had been summoned.

Ray looked scared. His face almost as pale as his hair and Mac realised for the first time just how young Ray and Lyndsey were. It was something he had not really thought about before, but neither was much older than Joy Duggan. He felt a sudden surge of resentment against Paul de Freitas that he should have put such a weight of expectation and danger on such immature shoulders.

Then, he just got angry, not just with Paul, but with the whole regime that kept such secrets, developed such secrets. Stole them and traded them and had no regard for life. He fought down the irrationality of his feelings, pushed them

away knowing that this was the way of the world and there
was nothing he could do about it. Sometimes, it was very hard
to believe in Paul's concept of *The Power of One*.

Ray had a holdall with him. He set it down on the dining
room table and unzipped the bag, then stood back, dragging
his fingers nervously through his white-blond hair.

'I thought it was a game,' he said. 'Until Paul got killed. I
knew he'd written me into Lydia's game. I'd got the weapon,
the Kraken Hunter. When he was killed, I realised that it
wasn't just a game, it was like, real.'

'So you took this out of the lab?'

Ray nodded. 'Paul made me promise I'd keep the kraken
killer safe. He was drunk, so was I. We were playing the level
and having a laugh about it, then he got all serious and . . . I
thought it was the drink talking, but it wasn't, was it?'

He opened the bag and showed a jumble of parts, none of
which made sense to Mac. 'I hid it, then I ran to Toby's place.
I thought if I just kept moving maybe it would be all right.'

'Did you find what was hidden in the music box?' Mac
asked.

Gil signalled to someone and the box was brought over. It
had been stripped down to its constituent parts, even the little
dancer, naked without the tulle of her skirt.

Gil picked up the little doll. 'Look,' she said. 'It's very
nicely done.' She unscrewed the head, set it aside, slid the
body apart, showing a little compartment inside where the
torso had been hollowed out. 'The chip was in here,' she said.
'Paul made a lovely job of hiding it. Clever man.'

'And I had the code,' Lyndsey said. 'To get into the secret
level of the game. Richard found that bit, but he didn't get
the whole picture. There was a second level inside the first.
I thought I was making a patch for the game, but Paul put
my patch inside his new level. I'd never have made the
connection.'

'So, you have the whole thing?'

'It's going to be passed on to experts capable of testing it,'
Gil said. 'But if Hale was right and Paul succeeded in creating
something that will pick up the signature of the submarine,
then we need to know and we need to find ways of deflecting
it. But first things first. We have to take Hale out of the equa-
tion and we have to identify his contacts.'

'How serious is this?' Mac asked. 'How far do you think Hale's influence goes?'

Gil ignored his question. She screwed the head back on to the little dancer and handed it back to the technician. Mac figured she wasn't going to answer that one.

FORTY-THREE

I t was all in place. Hill House may never have been occupied for all the trace they left behind. Fitch had driven the couple pretending to be Lydia and Edward up to their house. They had made a great show of going inside, being upset, 'Lydia' in tears. Fitch had driven them away again.

A little later, Lyndsey had run from the cliff path, across the lawn, taken the key from under the herb pot and gone inside. She was carrying a holdall and from the way she moved it was obviously heavy.

Once inside, she walked through the house into the hallway, took out her mobile phone and dialled the number Paul had left her. She took a deep breath, knew she had to put on the performance of her life.

The same sense of opening up on the other end of the line, the clicks, the sense of space. 'I know you're there,' she almost screamed into the phone. 'I know you can hear me. Please, say something. Say something to me.' Stressed as she was, it cost her little effort to break down in tears.

'He's a madman. A crazy man. But I got away from him. He went to sleep and I ran. God, I thought that man never slept. He just kept on talking, kept on saying these insane things and Paul gave me this number. He said you'd know what to do. You've got to help me, got to come for me. Got to take this thing away and keep it safe. Paul said you would. He told me . . .'

'You have it all?'

Lyndsey whimpered, genuinely frightened. The voice seemed to come out of nowhere. She had given up on getting a direct reply. 'I've got it all. The chip. The code. The device. Got it all. Paul trusted me.'

'Stay there. We'll come to you. It will all be over soon.'

'You don't know . . .' But the connection had broken and the voice was gone. 'Where I am,' she finished softly. Obviously, they did.

Had they believed her?

She'd been told, speak to no one, look at no one, you've got to behave as if you're completely alone. It wasn't as hard as she'd thought it might be. She really, truly felt alone.

She went into the Big Room. Outside it was near dark, the sky deep blue and the line between cloud and sea now indistinguishable. She sat down in Edward's chair, the holdall at her feet. Unable to bear the enormity of the situation, she switched on the light beside the chair and leaned forward, head in her hands. She didn't need to fake the tears. They flowed freely. Scared beyond words, she wondered how long they would make her wait.

Silence.

Waiting.

Boredom. She had not expected waiting to be so tedious or for the utter terror to pass into something so banal. She seemed to slide past being scared and into some strange state close to lethargy. Lyndsey leaned back in Edward's chair and closed her eyes. That same desperate need for sleep that had overpowered her when Abe had taken her to Hill House, now set in again. She found that all she wanted was to give in, to seek the oblivion that had been so soothing, so relieving, so utterly peaceful.

And then the shattering of nerves, of silence, of everything. Lyndsey's world was filled with the noise of breaking glass. Of gunshots, of men shouting. Abe yelling at her to stay down. She was aware that he had dragged her from her seat and was now covering her body with his own, though she had no memory at all of him grabbing her and pulling her to the ground.

She curled up tight, making herself as small as she could, but Abe was telling her that it was over. That it would be OK now, that she was safe.

He let her up then, holding her arms and staring into her face, calling her name, then holding her tight while she sobbed.

'It worked love, it worked. God I was scared.' He was laughing, relief and sheer pleasure at a job well done.

'*You* were scared. I was . . .' She gave up trying to tell him what she'd been. Knew only that Tim's illusion had been good enough. He'd had so many doubts. She lifted her head to look at the devastation in the room. The massive expanse of glass that had once been the window was completely shattered and the second pane, angled inward in the middle of the room, also gone, just the anchor points that had held it from the ceiling remaining.

'Took a lot of nerve, that did,' Abe told her. 'Ian would have been proud.'

She tried to tell herself that she'd not really been in danger. She'd been placed behind a steel and Kevlar screen, the chair and the light putting her below the level of the barrier, like the orchestra pit at the Palisades which hid the actor playing ghost from the audience. The bright light placed behind her chair projected the image of her sitting in Edward's chair on to the glass that Tim had angled in the centre of the room.

Pepper's Ghost.

'Bloody hell, it worked.' Tim sounded so amazed that she had to laugh.

'You mean you had your doubts?'

'Well, yes, kind of. I mean all kinds of things could have gone wrong. Like if they'd used a scope, you'd have been kind of transparent.' He laughed slightly hysterically. 'Seems like he fired first and thought about it after.'

'You don't expect the thing you can see not to be there,' Abe said dryly. 'You're dealing with expectation, not reality. Even experts sometimes see the frills and not the heart of the trick.' He got up, pulled Lyndsey to her feet. The rest of the team was moving in now and Abe felt ready to leave them to it.

'Any chance of a bed at Rina's place tonight?' he asked. 'I've had enough of this lot. No offence to you,' he added, looking with something close to affection at Lyndsey. 'This just isn't my way, you know. Not a clean fight.'

EPILOGUE

R ina leaned against the railings and looked out to sea, Tim on one side of her and Mac on the other. They were standing on that part of the walkway that rounded the headland between Frantham Old Town and Frantham new.

'They arrested Hale last night, trying to leave the country,' Mac said. 'His is the tenth arrest, apparently. If you ask me there's going to be something of a witch-hunt going on. Gil told me that much out of courtesy, but she's implied that this is the last we'll hear of her and that we should just forget the whole thing.'

'As if,' Tim said. 'We did all right, didn't we?' He was still overwhelmed by the fact that his idea had worked. Disappointed but resigned that he'd never actually be credited for it.

'We did well,' Rina said quietly. 'And Lyndsey and Ray?'

'Ray will stay on at *Iconograph*. Lyndsey still says she wants to go but I think she may change her mind. Edward is offering a very attractive package, apparently. He wants to keep them both.'

'Do you think she'll give in?'

Mac nodded. 'I think she needs to feel wanted; persuaded. I think if Edward plays that right then she'll stay willingly, but I think there's a bit of her feels entitled to the extra attention. Ray, too.'

'I can't say I blame them for that,' Rina said. 'I've told Abe he should stay in touch. I'm interested to know what he decides to do with his life now. It can't be easy for him. No family, nothing outside of the army.'

'Rina,' Tim told her sternly. 'You can't adopt him. We really don't have the room.'

Mac laughed. 'I must be going,' he said. 'Miriam is coming over and I think I'm cooking.'

'Takeaway then,' Rina said.

'As it happens, Matthew has provided me with a recipe and a shopping list. I'm no longer a microwave man, Rina.' He leaned over and kissed her gently on the cheek, then bid them both goodbye and walked away.

Rina lifted a hand to touch her cheek. She could feel tears, unexpectedly pricking at her eyes.

Tim said nothing, he just took her arm and slipped it through his own.